THE DILAPIDATED DETECTIVES

Paul Weinberger

Thank you to everyone who has helped and encouraged me in the writing of this novel, particularly my wife Jo.

PART ONE: STILL VERTICAL

CHAPTER ONE

The house had originally been built in the early part of the nineteenth century, as the country retreat of a wealthy London merchant. Constructed in Bath stone, it was a splendid example of late Georgian architecture, albeit now weathered and partially hidden by ancient wisteria and climbing roses. It had survived in the same family for nearly five generations before eventually being requisitioned as a convalescent home for the wounded during the second world war.

Now it was the Fern Lea residential home. A residential home very much for the well-to-do.

It was a beautiful late spring morning and the warm sun had encouraged a number of residents to take a turn around the gardens. They chatted in twos and threes, propelled along by walking sticks, Zimmer frames and wheelchairs. It looked to be an enjoyable, if slightly mechanical, promenade.

One resident was entirely out of step with the rest. To begin with, he walked purposefully against the main flow of the promenade, seemingly lost in his own thoughts. But his appearance was unusual as well. If the dress code for Fern Lea could best be described as anything elasticated, he wore a shirt and tie and a well pressed pair of cavalry twill trousers. If the standard footwear was anything with Velcro fastenings, he wore a lovingly polished pair of brown brogues. Even his walking stick had an ornate, bone handle.

He walked on until he found an unoccupied bench and sat down. He was cross and he had been for some time. The trouble was, he hadn't fully worked out why. Or what to do about it. He attacked the daisies in the lawn with his walking stick.

Then he committed what was, for genteel Fern Lea, a revolutionary act. He swung his legs round and put his feet on the bench.

He stretched himself out full length and rested his head on the bench's arm. He closed his eyes for just a moment.

'Hello, you must be the new boy everyone's talking about.'

He came to with a start. He swung his legs back round quickly and sat up straight. He found himself confronted by a woman, probably in her late seventies, who wore a pretty summer dress with a floral print. She had a warm smile and an immediately sunny disposition. She clearly failed to fit the Fern Lea stereotype as well.

He was struggling with the slightly rhetorical nature of her question and only managed to grin, slightly inanely.

'May I?' she said, pointing to the bench. 'I'm Audrey, by the way.'

'Oh sorry, of course. I'm Claude.'

He budged up and she sat down. They managed a polite but awkward handshake.

'How are you settling in?' she asked.

'Honestly? I'm not sure I should answer that.'

'The rumour mill's been working overtime. Apparently you've had three run-ins with Mrs Woodbine in the first week. We think that's an all-comers record.'

'Ah yes, Mrs Woodbine. The Commandant,' he said. 'I think it's fair to say we haven't quite hit it off.'

Audrey smiled.

'Still, at least she hasn't found my escape tunnel yet,' he added.

Audrey laughed.

'Is it really that bad?' she asked.

A carer arrived from the direction of the house.

'Sorry Mr Simmons,' he said. 'Mrs Woodbine would like to see you in her office, please.'

Claude looked at Audrey and gave a resigned shrug. He got up from the bench.

'Impressive, Claude. Very impressive,' she called out as he set off.

Mrs Woodbine sat behind her desk, exuding confidence and tweed. In front of her was a bottle of whisky, one third empty. Claude stared at the bottle from his side of the desk.

'The rule is entirely for your benefit, Claude,' said Mrs Woodbine.

'Is it?' he asked.

'Alcohol in the bedrooms is extremely dangerous.

Particularly when anxiety is involved.'

'Anxiety? Who says I have anxiety?'

'I do,' she said firmly. 'Trust me, I'm trying to help you through it.'

'Mrs Woodbine, I've been having a night cap most evenings for the last twenty years. And here I am. How come you suddenly know better than I do?'

'Because I do!' she snapped, clearly not used to her authority being questioned. 'And that's my final word on the subject!'

She grabbed the bottle of whisky and placed it in the bottom drawer of her desk. She slammed the drawer shut.

Claude had been dismissed.

He wandered around aimlessly for a while, looking for something to help idle away the hours.

He re-traced his steps to the garden, hoping to find Audrey again. She'd gone and the bench was empty.

Eventually, he found himself in the TV lounge. He was trying hard not to succumb to daytime TV but the snooker was on. He sat down to watch, just for a frame or two. A long red was potted, leaving a tricky pink. Someone, somewhere in the room, pressed the remote control and abruptly changed the channel to Storage Hunters.

He returned to his room and lay on the bed, contemplating the insults of the day. After what seemed an age, the dinner gong sounded.

Meals at Fern Lea were always a buffet, for those that could serve themselves, and Claude surveyed the spread. He collected a plate and made for the lamb chops. Just as he reached the hot plate, Violet appeared from nowhere and barged him hard in the ribcage. It wasn't clear if this was malicious or whether she was just laser-guided towards the food. In any event, she bagged two lamb chops and left.

Claude tried again, only to be assailed by Arthur. His Zimmer frame banged hard into Claude's leg as he pushed forward. He grabbed a lamb chop and left.

'Watch out. The sharp elbows club is in session,' said Audrey, appearing next to him.

'Quite,' he said, rubbing his knee.

Audrey waved him forward to collect his lamb chop, bravely offering herself as a human shield against the marauding horde.

'How did it go earlier, by the way?' she asked.

'Oh, it was a triumph,' said Claude. 'I got a lecture about having alcohol in my bedroom. The last time that happened was sixty five years ago.'

Unfortunately, Audrey had already been sitting with another group of friends so Claude found himself a space and ate his dinner alone. Not wishing to risk personal injury over a pudding, he decided on an early night.

For some reason, he woke extremely early the next morning. He got up straight away and went through his normal routine: painstaking shave (wet, not electric), correct knot for the tie, perfect shine for the shoes. Breakfast didn't begin for another hour so he set off for a long walk around the garden.

There was no-one around except for a few staff

arriving to begin their shift. It was a lovely morning and he dawdled his way round, enjoying the peace and quiet. He stopped and practised his golf swing with his walking stick a couple of times, deadheading several dandelions in the process.

Eventually, his tour took him past the front of the house. Parked outside the front door was a black van with tinted windows. Claude stopped, intrigued. There was a buzzing sound and the front door opened. Out came two men dressed in dark grey suits, quickly pushing a stretcher on wheels which carried a zipped up body bag. They paused briefly when they saw Claude, seemingly startled to have bumped into someone so early in the morning. They looked at each other for a moment before loading the body into the back of the van. They drove off towards the front gate. Claude leant on his walking stick for a moment, thinking about what he'd just seen. Probably, it was nothing more than a retirement home trying to hide its grim reality from public view.

In any event, it was not quite the start to the day that he had been hoping for. He finished his circuit of the garden and headed inside to the dining room. At the buffet, he decided to keep his spirits up with a cooked breakfast. He picked up the tongs and was about to help himself to some bacon when Margaret appeared from nowhere. She shoulder charged him, knocking him sideways, before spearing four rashers of bacon with her fork. Seemingly oblivious to his presence she trod hard on his foot as she forced her way through to the scrambled egg. Claude was left staring at a solitary rasher of bacon.

After breakfast, he took refuge in the conservatory. He picked up the Daily Telegraph and read the sports pages before turning to the quick crossword. He'd managed to fill in a couple of answers when loud disco music suddenly started. The sort with a THUMP! THUMP! THUMP! bass line. He soldiered on and filled in another answer before a booming voice struck up.

'. . . . and left, left, left, kick! . . . . right, right, right, kick! . . . .'

His concentration ruined, Claude set off in search of the source of the disturbance and eventually found himself outside the activities room. Inside was a lycra clad instructor and about ten residents who were attempting a dance routine, with varying degrees of success. In the middle of the class was one person who was really rather good at it – Audrey. She smiled and waved at Claude, mid-kick. He changed his frown quickly to a benevolent smile.

He walked into the TV lounge. The BBC news had just started and he sat himself down. He was halfway through watching a report about climate change when someone, somewhere in the room, farted very loudly. He got up and left.

What with an unsuccessful game of chess (Arthur, his opponent, fell asleep halfway through) and an attempted game of Boules (abandoned for health and safety reasons), Claude eventually made it through to dinner.

He entered the dining room with a new strategy in mind: give up on the buffet, try the table service. He sat down with his plate in front of him and waited. After a short while Daphne, one of the carers, appeared. She addressed him with a tone which suggested she was aiming off for possible deafness and senility.

'Hello my lovely,' she said. 'Now, what can I get you today?'

'I'll have the sea bass, please. Thank you,' Claude replied, brightly.

Daphne took his plate and disappeared. She returned two minutes later and placed the food in front of him.

'Sorry lovely, the sea bass is all gone. I managed to get you some delicious vegan sausages, though. You'll enjoy those.'

Claude was left staring at his plate of vegan bangers and mash.

It had been two weeks since the difficult day of Claude's arrival at Fern Lea. His son and daughter-in-law had decided to wait that long before visiting again, to let the dust settle. Even so, they felt distinctly nervous as they pulled up at the front gate. Nervous, with a little bit of guilty conscience thrown in. David wound down his window and pressed the buzzer.

'Hello?' said the intercom voice.

'David and Alice Simmons. To see Claude Simmons?'

The gate clanked into life and rolled slowly backwards. The house was revealed in all its glory and they drove in along the meandering drive.

Mrs Woodbine met them, as arranged, in the large entrance hall and led them off to find Claude. She set off briskly towards the conservatory and David and Alice struggled slightly to keep up.

'By and large, he's settled in well,' she said, over her shoulder. 'He is suffering a bit from what we call transitional anxiety but that's perfectly normal.'

They went out through the conservatory's French doors and into the garden. In the distance, there was a solitary figure seated on a bench, reading the Daily Telegraph. Or possibly hiding behind it. Mrs Woodbine headed in that direction.

'Transitional anxiety? What does that mean?' asked David, having to jog the odd step to keep up.

'You know, difficulty adjusting to the new surroundings. In practice, it probably means he's going to tell you how dreadfully unhappy he is here.'

'And what should we do?' asked Alice, concerned.

'I suggest you do what I do – let it wash over you. We're taking very good care of him and he'll be through the transition period in no time.'

They arrived at the bench.

'Claude, your son and daughter-in-law are here,' Mrs Woodbine announced, before turning on her heel and heading briskly back to the house.

The three of them set off for a slow walk around

the gardens. David and Alice's nervousness had only increased after the pep talk they'd just received and an awkward silence set in.

'Mrs Woodbine seems nice,' said Alice, eventually.

'Oh, I wouldn't go that far,' said Claude, not playing along.

David's turn.

'You can see why Fern Lea is so popular. Such a beautiful house and such magnificent gardens. We had to push very hard to get you in here.'

'I'm very well aware,' said Claude, deliberately misunderstanding.

'No, no, I didn't mean . . . .'

'Relax David, I know what you meant.' Claude couldn't keep up the torture. 'Listen, I don't want to fall out with you two. But that doesn't change the fact that I've made a dreadful mistake in agreeing to come here. I feel like I've signed my own death warrant.'

'Please don't say that, dad.'

They came to another bench in front of a border overflowing with rhododendrons and azaleas. They sat down.

'Claude, this is all a massive wrench and clearly a shock to your system,' said Alice. 'But you've hardly been here any time at all and in a few more weeks everything will look completely different. Don't you think?'

'Ah, I see you've had the transitional anxiety lecture from Mrs Woodbine,' said Claude.

'Come on, dad.'

'Seriously, Mrs Woodbine is part of the problem.' His volume was steadily increasing. 'She starts every conversation with the assumption I'm senile. I'm not senile! Unfortunately, I've managed to check in here while I've still got my marbles!'

They all fell silent. Eventually, Alice weighed in. She was very fond of Claude and was trying to be kind. Unfortunately, it didn't quite come out that way.

'It's difficult to know what to suggest. It's not as if we can just jump in the car and drive you home. You agreed to putting the house on the market to pay for all of this. The house is under offer. The contents have been sold.'

This succeeded in bringing the discussion to an abrupt close.

They finished their tour of the gardens and walked slowly back to the car, filling in the silence with small talk. David and Alice drove off and all three exchanged a wave that was far too polite. Claude watched ruefully as the gate clanged firmly shut behind them.

After dinner that evening, he set off in search of Audrey, intent upon cheering himself up. He eventually found her seated in a corner of the lounge, chatting with Marjorie Watson, another resident.

'Good evening, ladies,' said Claude, politeness itself.

'Good evening, Claude,' Audrey replied.

Marjorie appeared to ignore the greeting, choosing instead to get up out of her armchair.

'Please have this seat,' she said tartly to Claude. 'I don't want to stand in the way of love's young dream.'

With that she wandered off, leaving Claude confused. Looking for enlightenment from Audrey, he sat himself down in the chair.

'What on earth was that about?'

Audrey laughed.

'Oh, don't take any notice of Marjorie. She has a compulsive urge to blurt out the first thing that comes into her head, completely unfiltered. I think it might well be a medical condition, a bit like Tourette's or something. She's actually very sweet, if you can get past the insults.'

Claude looked unconvinced.

'Anyway, who did I see you with earlier?' said Audrey, moving things along.

'My son and daughter-in-law,' said Claude.

'And how was that?'

'Oh, a complete and utter car crash.'

Audrey sat forward in her chair. 'Oh dear. I worry about you Claude. Do you think you might be trying to come to terms with the fact you feel your family has somehow . . . well, abandoned you here?'

Claude was taken aback by the directness of Audrey's question but was saved by the arrival of one of the carers.

'Sorry, here's your tablet Mrs Patterson,' he said.

He offered the tablet and a hot drink to Audrey.

'Thank you Stefan,' said Audrey, swallowing the tablet with a mouthful of the drink.

Claude wasn't off the hook.

'It's a fair question, isn't it?' Audrey persisted. 'I mean, I took the decision myself to come here after my husband died and I'm very glad I did. I like everything about it, not least being waited on hand and foot.' She gestured towards the departing Stefan to make her point. 'But you've ended up somewhere you absolutely hate. How did it happen?'

Claude took a moment. 'Well, David and Alice certainly aren't to blame. It's basically their inheritance we're using to pay for all this. Not exactly in their best interests, is it?'

Audrey persisted. 'So, what then?'

Claude wriggled. 'Must I keep talking about myself?'

'Yes, you must.'

He twiddled his walking stick. It was difficult, not least because he wasn't sure he fully understood himself what had happened. Or perhaps he hadn't properly come to terms with it yet. He tried to describe the train of events to Audrey, beginning with the sudden death of his wife. They had been happily married for forty five years and then she'd stepped out into the road one day without looking. Gone in an instant. Almost immediately afterwards he'd suffered a stroke, severe enough to mean that he'd had to spend a prolonged period of time in a nursing home. That was when the decision to move to Fern Lea was taken.

'I suppose I was at my lowest ebb,' he said, 'and to be honest, a retirement home looked attractive compared to a nursing home. But I'd actually recovered quite well by the time I got here and I knew as soon as I passed through the gate that I'd made a disastrous mistake.'

'That's very sad, Claude, but now at least I understand.'

Claude was delighted to have put his confession behind him. 'Let's change the record, Audrey,' he said. 'What about you?'

'I'm sorry but I'm going to have to remain an enigma for another day.' Audrey got up out of her chair, a little stiffly. 'Unlike you I'm living the dream here at Fern Lea. I've done a yoga and a dance class today and I'm exhausted. Tell you what though, since you're my new neighbour you could always walk me to my door.'

'I'd be delighted.'

Audrey took Claude's arm and they set off towards the bedroom corridor.

'Thank you. Shall we meet for breakfast tomorrow?' Audrey asked as they arrived at her door.

'I'll look forward to it, Audrey. Good night.'

'Good night.'

She went into her room and closed the door. Claude paused outside for a moment, collecting his thoughts.

Unfortunately for him, Marjorie Watson chose precisely that moment to come barrelling around the corner. She saw Claude and launched straight into a major misunderstanding.

'Hoping for a bit of hanky panky are we, Claude?'

'Marjorie, really.'

'I think you'll find your room is actually the one next door to Audrey's,' she said, clearly feeling that clinched the case for the prosecution. And with that she was gone, like a demented whirlwind.

Claude steadied himself with his walking stick, flustered for a moment. Then he turned and walked purposefully back to his room.

Inside, he headed straight for the wardrobe and pulled open the bottom drawer. He rooted around among the jumpers and the pyjamas and produced another bottle of whisky.

He poured a generous measure into a water glass from the table, picked up his iPad and headphones and flopped into the armchair next to his bed. He scrolled through his music library and found 'Kind of blue'. He pressed 'play'.

Nearly two hours later Claude was woken by a loud bang. He'd fallen asleep in his armchair and the alarm clock on his bedside table now read 00:12 am. The whisky glass was empty and the music had long since finished playing. He struggled to clear his head. He took off his headphones and listened intently. Had he imagined the noise?

Almost immediately there was a second loud bang, followed by a flurry of others - some loud, some soft and all at irregular intervals. They were coming from the wall adjoining Audrey's room: BANG, bang, bang . . . . bang, BANG . . . . bang, BANG . . . . bang, bang, bang.

After some considerable time, the banging

stopped. Claude hoisted himself out of the chair and walked to the wall, listening intently. He could hear nothing further.

He walked as fast as he could to his bedroom door and opened it. And in that instant he thought he heard the corridor fire door click shut. Didn't he?

Becoming more and more confused, he walked to Audrey's room. He put his ear to the door but again could hear nothing. He raised his walking stick to knock but thought better of it.

He headed back to his room and shut the door.

CHAPTER TWO

Claude's bedroom curtains were abruptly pulled back and the spring sunshine streamed in. Almost blinded by the sudden light, Claude could just about make out the spectre of Mrs Woodbine at the foot of his bed.

'Good Morning, Claude,' she said. 'I've brought you a cup of tea.'

She walked to Claude's bedside table and put down the cup and saucer. She remained standing there, menacingly.

Claude managed to half sit up in bed. 'This is a surprise,' he said, groggily. 'Am I in trouble or something?'

'No, of course not. But I do have some bad news, I'm afraid.' She paused, searching for the right words. 'Well, there's no easy way to put this but . . . we found Audrey Patterson dead this morning. It appears she died in her sleep. I know you two had become good friends so I wanted to tell you myself. I'm very sorry.'

'Oh Lord . . . . but . . . . last night . . . .' Claude struggled to form a coherent sentence.

'Listen, I know it's a lot to take in so please take

your time, Claude,' said Mrs Woodbine, slipping into professionally brusque mode. It was her standard defence against difficult questions and emotional outbursts. 'Come and see me in my office a little later if you'd like to chat a bit more. My door is always open.'

And with that she swept out of the room, efficiently collecting Claude's empty whisky glass as she went.

He was shocked and took some considerable time to ready himself for the day. He decided to skip breakfast and instead found himself a quiet bench in the garden. He sat down and did his level best to gather his thoughts.

As often happens when someone dies suddenly, he felt an irrational sense of guilt. He'd become very fond of Audrey in a short space of time and now he was certain she'd been murdered. Why hadn't he done something to intervene? What was he thinking of? For heaven's sake, just banging on his side of the wall would probably have achieved something. He attacked the daisies again with his walking stick, this time mercilessly.

He finally made a decision and got up. He turned back towards the house and unfortunately walked straight into Marjorie. A terse exchange ensued.

'Claude, I . . . .'

'If you've come to ridicule me Marjorie, I'm not in the mood.'

'But I . . . .'

'Given what's happened, it's not really a good

time.'

'No I . . . . '

'In any case, I have to go and see Mrs Woodbine. Excuse me.'

Now it was Marjorie who was flustered, although not for long.

'How bloody rude,' she said to herself, just loud enough for the departing Claude to hear.

Claude found himself in his usual seat in Mrs Woodbine's office. She had ratcheted up a gear into headmistress mode.

'If I had a pound for every time a resident has sat there and told me someone is trying to murder them, or kidnap them, or steal all their money then I would be a very rich woman indeed.'

Claude was trying hard to maintain his resolve. 'But I know what I heard.'

'Do you?' she said, immediately inviting him to doubt the evidence of his own ears. 'You've fallen asleep listening to loud music on your headphones and you wake up thinking you've heard strange noises. Then a door may have mysteriously closed but apparently there was no-one there. And all this lubricated with a glass or two of whisky. Yet again.'

Claude hung on doggedly. 'All I'm asking is that we just investigate things a bit further, for Audrey's sake. What's there to lose?'

'The doctor has already been, Claude. He examined Audrey's body this morning and found nothing out of the ordinary. The death certificate reads "Natural Causes" and the case is most definitely closed.

Now if you'll excuse me I have to have a difficult telephone conversation with Audrey's daughter about funeral arrangements.'

Claude had been dismissed again.

He pottered around the garden for a while, thinking about what had just happened. He felt quite strongly that Mrs Woodbine was doing her best to break his spirit. The interesting thing was, she was starting to have the opposite effect.

He made his way to the conservatory and sat himself down, hoping for a moment's peace and quiet. He picked up a newspaper and tried to bury himself in the sports pages but his respite was short lived. Marjorie arrived, unannounced, and plonked herself down in the armchair next to him, uninvited.

'Claude, can we bury the hatchet please?'

Claude lowered the newspaper wearily.

'Where? In the back of my head?'

'Heavens, and I thought I was the one with the acid tongue!'

Claude paused for a moment and thought about this. What he didn't need at the moment was yet another enemy, given all of his current battles.

'You're right Marjorie, I'm sorry.'

'I was actually trying to apologise earlier,' she said, glad of the chance to explain. 'All my life I have been opening my mouth and putting my foot straight in it. But given the events of yesterday I have truly excelled myself.'

'For what it's worth, I think Audrey was very fond

of you. I think she found your, umm, outspokenness rather funny.'

'Did she? Poor Audrey, she was very lovely. All those fitness classes didn't get her very far though, did they?'

Truer than you know, thought Claude.

'By the way, how did you get on with the old battle axe earlier?' she asked.

Claude smiled. 'Mrs Woodbine? Oh, it was a triumph. She already thought I was losing it. Now she thinks I'm completely demented.'

'About what?'

'Well . . . .'

'You and Audrey?'

'No, just about Audrey.'

'Well go on. What?'

Claude was cornered. He considered his options. If he didn't need another enemy, perhaps he needed an ally.

'Come on,' he said, getting up.

'Where are we going?' she said, struggling to catch up.

'To find somewhere quiet.'

They made their way into the garden and eventually found a bench in a secluded spot behind two ornamental birch trees. They sat down.

'For heaven's sake, Claude. What is it?' said Marjorie, impatiently.

Claude could think of no easy way to break the news.

'I think Audrey was murdered.'

Marjorie looked at Claude in wide-eyed astonishment. She blinked repeatedly. Her eyes began to glaze over and she appeared to blindly reach out to steady herself. And then she fainted.

'Oh lord,' said Claude, struggling to keep her upright on the bench. He produced a large white handkerchief from his pocket and attempted to fan her as best he could. He was about to go for help when she started to come round.

After a minute or so she seemed to have recovered and the light returned to her eyes. She suddenly remembered what Claude had said.

'Murder? Are you mad?' she blurted out, far too loudly.

'Shhhh!' said Claude.

'But how? What do you mean?'

Claude explained how he'd fallen asleep in his armchair the previous evening and been woken by banging noises coming from Audrey's bedroom.

'Banging? Like someone having nooky you mean?' said Marjorie. She was definitely back to her old self.

'No Marjorie, not like someone having nooky! It was a strange and irregular banging, something like . . . . ' Claude attempted to imitate the noise he had heard the night before by repeatedly banging his fist on the garden bench.

'Ooh!' said Marjorie, taken aback.

'If I'm any judge it was the sound of someone being suffocated with a pillow. Someone who was fit enough and strong enough to thrash around and fight for their life.'

'Goodness! Audrey – queen of the dance class!'

Claude and Marjorie met for breakfast the next morning. They sat together in a conspiratorial huddle. Marjorie looked around the room, surreptitiously sizing up the residents.

'I'm trying to work out who the murderer is,' she said.

'Oh, I don't think any of them are,' said Claude.

'What?'

'Forgive me being blunt, Marjorie, but suffocation requires a considerable amount of strength and a grim determination. I don't think anyone here is capable of that.'

A male carer walked past, pushing a resident in a wheelchair towards the cornflakes.

'What about a member of staff?' asked Marjorie.

'But I don't think that's very likely either. I mean, what would their motive be?'

'Well, they could just be one of those loonies you read about.'

Claude ignored this. He finished his scrambled eggs and put down his napkin.

'Shall we get some fresh air?'

He steered Marjorie towards the front garden and they ended up walking along the main drive towards the front gate.

'I think we should consider the fact that the murderer is an outsider,' said Claude. 'A family member. A friend. Someone looking for revenge.'

Marjorie was surprised by Claude's new found confidence. 'You seem to know a lot about all of this,' she said, eyeing him up with some suspicion.

'Well, I always loved murder mysteries on the telly, didn't you?' he said, not altogether convincingly.

'And you're presumably about to show me how our outsider got in through the main gate at midnight?' she asked.

'Oh, I doubt very much he came in through the main gate.'

Claude diverted Marjorie off the main drive towards some large shrubs to the left of the gate. They brushed past the shrubs and behind them found a perimeter wall, barely four feet high. Claude waggled his walking stick at the wall.

'More likely he just climbed over here.'

'Okay I'll give you that, clever clogs,' she said, begrudgingly, 'but what about the front door? How did he get through the security system there without giving himself away?'

'Ah yes, I've got a theory about that as well.'

Claude led Marjorie back towards the house. In keeping with the overall architectural grandeur, the front door had a substantial column on either side and was approached by a short flight of stone steps, half of which had been converted into a wheelchair ramp. They arrived and he pressed the intercom button.

'Hello?' said the voice of Mrs Mayer, the Fern Lea secretary.

'Oh hello, it's Claude Simmons. Can I come back in please?'

'You most certainly can.'

The door buzzed. Claude pushed it open and held it there.

'Right Marjorie, I want you to go in and pretend you're one of the night staff clocking off at midnight, please. I'm going to pretend to be the intruder. When you come back out of the door, just walk down the steps and head for the car park, as if it's simply your normal routine. Okay?'

'Okay.'

'And no cheating and looking back. Okay?'

'Okay.'

She went inside and while the door was automatically closing, Claude hid himself behind one of the columns.

After several seconds the door buzzed and Marjorie came out again. Getting into the role, she walked nonchalantly down the steps and sauntered off towards the car park. Unseen by her, Claude nipped out from behind the column and caught the door just as it was closing. He squeezed inside and it closed firmly behind him.

Hearing the door close, Marjorie stopped and turned around. There was no-one to be seen.

'Claude?' she said, slightly confused.

The door buzzed again and Claude came out, smiling broadly. He was starting to enjoy himself.

'See, it's easy. What do you think?'

'I think I'm going to have to up my game a bit,' said Marjorie.

Later that afternoon, she sat on her own on a sofa in the large entrance hall. Her mind was racing. Notwithstanding her bluntness and belligerence, she had actually led a quite sheltered, middle class life, screened off from a large part of the world. Crime was something she only ever saw on the news and always seemed to happen to other people, somewhere else. Until she met Claude. Suddenly, she had been thrust into the middle of his ad hoc murder investigation. And now she was about to commit an act that Mrs Woodbine would almost certainly regard as high treason.

A corridor led off the main hall to what was the admin area of Fern Lea. The first office inside the corridor was visible from the hall and Marjorie had her gaze fixed upon it. Eventually, Mrs Mayer emerged from the office. She was carrying a sheet of paper and disappeared off further down the corridor. Marjorie waited a moment. She looked around the hall to see if anyone was coming. She stood up. Mrs Mayer reappeared and went back into her office. Marjorie sat back down. After several minutes, Mrs Mayer exited again, this time with a large sheath of papers. She walked across the hall and off to another part of the house.

Marjorie stood up and scurried across the hall into the office. She quickly examined the contents of Mrs Mayer's desk. She opened the two desk drawers and peered inside. She turned her attention to the shelves on the wall. There was a whole row of what appeared to be DVD cases, each with dates handwritten on their spines. She took one down and opened it.

Mrs Mayer walked back into the room.

'Ah Mrs Mayer, I was just looking for you,' said Marjorie, holding a DVD in her hand.

Five minutes later, she found herself sat in front of a stony-faced Mrs Woodbine. Neither of them spoke and the only noise in the office came from the drumming of Mrs Woodbine's fingers on the desk.

Eventually, the door opened and Claude, who had been tracked down by one of the carers, was ushered in. He looked at Marjorie and Mrs Woodbine, bemused.

'What's happened?' he asked.

'Sit down please, Claude,' said Mrs Woodbine. 'This is a very serious matter and I want you to know I hold you fully responsible.'

'Sorry? Responsible for what?' he asked.

'For the attempted theft of the CCTV footage from Mrs Mayer's office, of course.'

'But . . . .' stammered Claude.

Marjorie interrupted him. 'In Claude's defence, he didn't . . . .'

Mrs Woodbine interrupted Marjorie. 'I don't want to hear any more thank you, Mrs Watson. It is Claude and Claude alone who has filled your head with all this nonsense about Audrey and murder.' She was extremely cross. 'I do not want the other residents upset by this. Let's have an end to it!'

They trooped out of the office, slightly shell-shocked, and made their way to the garden. They found a bench and sat down.

'Stupid bloody woman,' said Marjorie.

'Who? You or Mrs Woodbine?' asked Claude, pointedly.

Marjorie looked at him. Given the circumstances, even she realised an apology was necessary.

'Fair point. Sorry, Claude.'

They sat in silence for some while.

'Do I get a chance to redeem myself?' asked Marjorie, eventually.

In truth, Claude was more cross with Mrs Woodbine than he was with Marjorie. Given the dressing down he'd just been given for something he hadn't even done, he was starting to feel that Mrs Woodbine's attacks were becoming personal. Vindictive, even. But her tactics continued to have the reverse effect. Each further accusation only strengthened his resolve and he was more determined than ever to uncover the truth about Audrey. That's why he needed Marjorie. If he was going to war with Mrs Woodbine, he continued to need her as an ally. A compulsive, impetuous, erratic ally, but an ally nonetheless.

'We need the address of Audrey's daughter,' he said. 'Do you think you could find that without causing an international incident?'

'I could!' said Marjorie, delighted to have been given a reprieve. She thought about it a bit more.

'Why do we need it?'

'Because we're planning a breakout.'

CHAPTER THREE

There was a knock at Claude's door. He opened it and found Marjorie standing outside, clutching a piece of paper.

'Marjorie, what a pleasant surprise. Come in.'

'Thank you.'

It was the first time she'd seen Claude's room and she looked around at the bare walls. There were no paintings, no photos, no ornaments. Nothing but an iPad and an alarm clock.

'Claude, your room has "I'm not stopping" written all over it,' she observed. 'I'm surprised you've even bothered to take your coat off.'

'Thank you, Marjorie. Now, is this one of your usual drive-by character assassinations or is there actually a point to your visit?' Claude smiled benignly, in an attempt to avoid further escalation.

'Ah yes,' said Marjorie, remembering herself. 'I just wanted to tell you that I've put the CCTV incident behind me. You're going to be proud of me.'

'Am I?' he asked, suspiciously.

'First of all, here's the address for Audrey's daughter that you wanted. I got it from Mrs Mayer.' She handed over the piece of paper she'd been holding.

Claude looked at it, surprised. 'Mrs Mayer? You mean the person who's already dropped you in it once with Mrs Woodbine?'

'Don't worry, I sent in my friend Violet to get it for me. She said she needed it to send a condolence card.'

'So Violet knows our plans now?'

'I very much doubt it. She's almost certainly forgotten the whole incident by now.'

Claude frowned. If he understood Marjorie correctly, she was admitting to using her friend's dementia for her own devious ends. He was trying to work out whether to be horrified or impressed by this when she set off for the door again.

'Anyway, we need to get a move on,' she said. 'I've organised our getaway car as well. Come on.'

Claude grabbed his walking stick and struggled after her.

'Just try and look natural,' she said, as though they were committing a bank robbery rather than walking up the main drive at Fern Lea. They reached the gate and Marjorie stopped. 'Wait for it,' she said theatrically, checking her watch. She stood stock still and stared at the gate. Claude looked baffled.

A taxi turned into the driveway and stopped. The driver spoke into the intercom and the gate rolled open.

As the taxi drove past them, Marjorie grabbed Claude's arm and started to march him briskly out through the gate. 'I learnt this bit from you, Claude. Quickly now!'

They found themselves outside as the gate rolled shut again.

'There!' said Marjorie, triumphantly.

'What do you mean "there"?' asked Claude. 'The taxi's inside and we're out here. And the driver's probably giving the game away as we speak.'

'Don't worry. I ordered it in a fictitious name so there's no-one to pick up. He'll be back in a minute.'

Sure enough, the taxi reappeared, without a passenger. The gate rolled open and it drove back out.

'Taxi!' Marjorie called out.

The taxi stopped and they both got in.

'Most impressive, Marjorie,' Claude conceded, as they set off.

'Glad to be of use at last. I'm a bit confused, though. Why are we going to see Audrey's daughter rather than going straight to the police?'

This was a good question. 'To be honest, I fear the same reaction from the police as we got from Mrs Woodbine. And I fear the same lecture about old people fretting about murder, robbery or whatever. I'm starting to think that no-one in authority even hears what you say when you're over seventy.'

'Quite. That being said, I'm not entirely sure Audrey's daughter is going to be that overjoyed to hear from us.'

Indeed she wasn't.

'You'd better come through, I suppose,' said Catherine Owen, having reluctantly allowed Claude and Marjorie in through the front door. She led them into the lounge and they all sat down.

Mrs Owen was clearly not in the best of health which probably didn't help her mood. She was painfully thin and walked with a pronounced stoop. Her frailty was further underlined by a persistent and hacking cough.

'I'm a bit confused. Are you here on behalf of Fern Lea?' she said.

'Well not exactly. We . . . . umm . . . .' Mrs Owen's appearance had taken the wind out of Claude's sails.

'Why are you here then? There's no date for the funeral yet if that's what you're after.'

Claude continued to dither. Buoyed up by her earlier successes, Marjorie wrenched the baton from him.

'The truth is, Mrs Owen, we believe your mother may have been murdered.'

This produced a volley of coughing from Mrs Owen.

'Murdered?' she said, eventually regaining her poise. 'If this is some sort of old person's joke then it's in very poor taste.'

'No, not all,' protested Marjorie, completely forgetting her own extreme reaction when she'd heard the same piece of news. She tried another tack and explained about the strange noises Claude had heard coming from Audrey's room on the night of her death. Unfortunately, she hadn't entirely thought this through either.

'That conjures up a lovely image of my mother's final moments. Thank you so much,' said Mrs Owen.

Marjorie blundered on regardless. She listed all

of the classes that Audrey had taken at Fern Lea – dance, pilates, yoga – as if this were somehow proof that she couldn't possibly have died in her sleep.

'Let me just stop you there,' said Mrs Owen, bluntly. 'Firstly, my mother's GP examined her body and found nothing suspicious whatsoever. Secondly, she had a serious heart arrhythmia which you obviously didn't know about. It meant she shouldn't really have been doing the fitness classes but she chose to ignore the advice.'

'Ah,' said Claude.

'Now, if there's nothing else,' said Mrs Owen, struggling up from her chair.

Claude and Marjorie were unceremoniously ushered out and the front door was closed firmly behind them. They walked dejectedly back down the garden path.

'What is it they say on American TV?' Marjorie asked, rhetorically. 'Oh yes, I think we just got our arse handed to us.'

'Nicely put, Marjorie,' said Claude.

Not only had visiting Mrs Owen been a mistake but they realised they had also made a strategic error in not asking the taxi to wait. They walked in silence in the direction of the main road. After a while they came to a bus stop and sat down on the bench provided. It was starting to get dark.

'I hope you're not starting to doubt yourself,' said Marjorie.

Claude thought about this for a second. 'No, I'm not. But I am starting to wonder if it's a lost cause.

You know what they say: it's not what you believe, it's what you can prove.'

They were interrupted by the noise of a police siren. They looked back up the road to see a police car speeding along with its blue lights flashing brightly in the dusk.

'Ooh, somebody's in trouble,' said Marjorie.

The police car screeched to a halt in front of the bus stop and a uniformed policeman got out. 'Mr Simmons, Mrs Watson?' he asked.

'Yes?' chorused the astonished Claude and Marjorie.

'Would you mind accompanying us to the station, please?'

Half an hour later they were sat in front of the reception desk at the local police station, under the watchful gaze of the Duty Sergeant. They were forced to share the reception area with a group of drunken football supporters who had been brought in on a charge of public nuisance which they were doing their level best to live up to.

Eventually, a plain clothes officer arrived at the desk and spoke to the Duty Sergeant.

'Are these my two, Ted?' he asked, pointing to Claude and Marjorie.

'Yes, sir. And would you mind taking them back up with you, please?' At that moment, the football crowd broke into another inappropriate song. 'I'm afraid we're a bit busy down here with the X-Factor auditions.'

The plain clothes officer rolled his eyes. 'Mr Simmons, Mrs Watson, I'm Inspector Ben Follett,' he said, approaching Claude and Marjorie. 'Would you mind coming with me, please?'

Marjorie jumped up immediately. She was starting to enjoy herself. Claude, on the other hand, looked unusually nervous. They walked along a corridor, up a flight of stairs and into a busy, open-plan office. The Inspector led them to a desk in the corner which was occupied by a young, fresh-faced officer. 'Let's sit here, next to Constable Deacon. He can take a note for us, can't you Constable?'

'Yes sir,' said Constable Deacon, sitting up straight.

The Inspector rounded up some chairs and they all sat down.

'I take it you know why you're here?' he asked. Before they had a chance to reply, he launched into a description of what he described as the trail of chaos they'd left behind them. Apparently, Fern Lea had been in a state of red alert since their disappearance. For a while they'd been top of the missing persons list.

'Ooh, you make us sound like Bonnie and Clyde,' said Marjorie.

Inspector Follett ignored her. 'Then you arrived at the home of Mrs Catherine Owen who has now filed a formal complaint of harassment against you both.' He had had to deal with her irate phone call personally and he wasn't at all pleased about it. 'It turns out from my conversation with her that Mrs Owen is suffering from stage four cancer. Did you know that when you turned up to tell her that her mother had been murdered?'

Even Marjorie was rattled by this. Claude mustered a response. 'Of course we didn't know and we're very sorry.' Actually, Claude was surprisingly defiant. 'I take full responsibility, but just because we've blundered into a mistake doesn't change the facts.'

'Which are?'

'Which are that Audrey Patterson was murdered. Mrs Owen thinks she died of a heart problem. I believe she was suffocated.'

Inspector Follett clearly had no sympathy with Claude's argument. He pointed out, in a slightly insensitive way, that the police were inundated with old people making allegations about murder and robbery.

'I had no idea,' said Claude, raising an eyebrow in the direction of Marjorie.

'But there's something different about you, isn't there?' the Inspector went on. 'Something persistent, not to say dogged? I have to ask, do you make a habit of these sorts of accusations Mr Simmons?'

'Well . . . .' Claude was in the process of summoning up a defence to this charge but was rudely interrupted by Constable Deacon.

'Bloody hell!'

'Constable, please,' said the Inspector, crossly.

'Sorry sir.' The Constable was staring at his computer where he had clearly been googling. 'But it says here: Claude Simmons . . . .'

He looked up. 'Detective Chief Superintendent Claude Simmons!'

There was a stunned silence, eventually punctured by the Inspector.

'Bloody hell! Psycho Simmons. The man with the best clear up rate in the Metropolitan Police. I knew I could hear a distant bell ringing.'

Unsurprisingly, Marjorie looked shocked.

'I'm sorry Marjorie, I'll explain more later,' said Claude. 'But I didn't want everyone to get tangled up in my previous life – it's all so long ago it almost feels like a different me. Plus I hated the "Psycho" thing. It makes me sound like the villain, doesn't it?'

Marjorie, as ever, was quick to recover. 'I'm already starting to like it, Claude. It takes years off you,' she said.

She was also quick to spot an opportunity to pull rank. She looked the Inspector straight in the eye and asked him how he felt about opening a murder investigation, given that the Chief Superintendent thought they should have one.

While the Inspector was working out how to deal with this, the Chief Constable walked past the doorway. He was in full uniform with his briefcase in one hand and his cap under his arm. He looked like he was on his way home but he glanced into the office and stopped immediately. He walked in.

'Claude? Claude Simmons? I haven't seen you in, well, I don't know how many years. How are you, sir?'

'Still vertical, thank you,' said Claude, taken by

surprise for the second time inside a minute. He looked the Chief Constable's uniform up and down. 'But it's you we should calling "sir". How are you, Peter?'

They shook hands warmly.

The Chief Constable had been a part of Claude's Serious Crime Squad in the Met for about six years and he was the first to admit that he'd learned pretty much everything he knew during that time. He turned to Inspector Follett, smiling.

'Claude was the scourge of the serial killer. The grislier it got, the better he was at it.'

'I'm sure, sir,' said the Inspector, somewhat wearily.

'But what brings you here, Claude? Did I hear mention of a murder enquiry?'

Claude and Marjorie had got used to no-one listening to them but the Chief Constable sat down and listened to every word of their story. When he finally got up to leave, he was pursued along the corridor by an anxious Inspector Follett. The Chief Constable was a big man with a purposeful stride and the Inspector was forced to chase after him.

'I just want to check that we're all happy with the decision, sir?' said the Inspector.

'Well I certainly am,' said the Chief Constable.

'Based on the opinion of someone who's . . . . ?'

'Old? Decrepit? Apart from the walking stick I thought he was in excellent shape. Same old Claude, really.'

'What about the lack of evidence and the fact that

the crime scene is now completely compromised?' the Inspector persisted.

'But I think Claude is right, we don't need to worry about any of that for the moment. Let's just get the post mortem done quickly and see what the pathologist finds. He might find nothing.'

They pushed through a pair of double doors and found themselves in the car park where the Chief Constable's car was waiting. He was becoming irritated with the Inspector's prevarication and decided to force his hand.

'Is it that you're worried about telling the deceased woman's daughter about the post mortem? Mrs Owen is it? I'm happy to do it for you if you'd like.'

'Oh no, that's fine. I'll do it, sir.'

The Chief Constable climbed into the back of the car.

'And let's keep this quiet until we know what we've got, even from the manager of the home. We don't want the old folks terrified needlessly about a murderer in their midst, do we?'

Not long afterwards, Claude and Marjorie were chauffeured back to Fern Lea in a squad car, as befitted the upturn in their fortunes.

' "The grislier it got, the better he was at it." You really are a dark horse,' said Marjorie.

Claude gazed out of the car window. He felt he owed Marjorie and everyone else an explanation as to why he hadn't revealed his police background after Audrey's death. The trouble was, the explanation wasn't very satisfying and involved him revealing just how self-absorbed he'd become. He'd had a stellar career in the Met where he'd risen to an extremely high rank. Now, due to a series of unfortunate events, he'd found himself at Fern Lea where the last thing anyone thought of him as was the scourge of the serial killer. Instead, he'd become just another resident plodding along, deciding on any given day whether to watch Countdown or join the basket weaving class. In truth, he'd been just plain embarrassed about it. Ashamed, even. He hadn't told anyone because he couldn't stand for anyone to see how far he'd fallen.

He played the story over in his mind. Clearly, it was far too confessional for Marjorie and the last thing he needed was her telling him to butch up. So he decided to concentrate on another aspect of the story. One that was still true but that was a little more sensationalist, tailored for Marjorie's consumption.

'You can understand why I've kept my past quiet,' he said. 'I mean, so many people, Chief Constable Selby included, have a view of my career that I barely recognise. They all seem to have me down as Atilla the Hun or something. Just because I had a knack for catching serial killers didn't make me some sort of hard-nut policeman. And then there's the ridiculous business with my nickname. Criminal psychology was always my thing. That's where "Psycho" comes from. Not from the fact that I was a rampaging lunatic.'

Marjorie looked at him. 'Perhaps you're right,' she said. 'But you can never fully tell when someone else gives you a nickname, can you?' She grinned.

They drove on in silence for a while. The police car slowed down as it approached Fern Lea.

'Can we agree one final thing, please?' asked Claude. 'We say nothing to anyone about Audrey and the post mortem. Not a word.'

'On that subject, Claude, my lips are sealed.'

CHAPTER FOUR

'**M**orning Psycho!' said Margaret breezily as she shuffled past Claude in the corridor the next morning. Claude stopped in his tracks, taken aback.

Another resident, Arthur, pottered along in the other direction with the aid of his Zimmer frame. 'Morning Psycho!' he said, smiling broadly.

Claude set off for the dining room and found Marjorie, having breakfast. He sat down.

'Marjorie, I thought we agreed on complete secrecy,' he hissed.

'About the post mortem? I haven't said a word to anyone.'

Doris walked past carrying a bowl of cornflakes. 'Good morning Psycho!' she called out.

Claude held out his arm in the direction of the departing Doris, as much as to say, 'what about that then?'

'Oh, I just told everyone that to throw them off the scent. It's worked rather well hasn't it? Besides, your profile needed a bit of a boost Claude. You're much too modest about yourself.'

'You're too kind, Marjorie,' said Claude, still cross.

'But look at the difference it's made to all the inmates. I've never seen everyone so full of beans.'

Harry was wheeled past on his way to the toaster. 'Good morning Chief Superintendent!' he said.

'That's a bit better,' said Claude, mellowing. 'Good morning!'

'And if you want final proof that I did the right thing, Mrs Woodbine hates the Psycho thing,' said Marjorie. 'Here she comes now.'

Mrs Woodbine approached Claude and Marjorie's table at a brisk pace. 'Claude, can I see you in my office please?' she said officiously before turning on her heel and departing.

Claude started to get up from his chair. Marjorie picked up a copy of a newspaper from the table and offered it to him.

'Do you want to put this down the back of your trousers?' she asked, trying hard not to laugh.

Claude ignored her and set off to face the music. He walked past Marjorie's friend Violet who looked up from her bowl of Cheerios. 'Morning Wilko!' she said with a smile.

In Mrs Woodbine's office, Claude took up his normal place in the naughty chair. She went straight on the attack.

'I rang your son and daughter-in-law to let them know about yesterday's events and, as you might expect, they're both very concerned.'

'Ah,' said Claude.

'They went away to think about it and they've just rung back to say it's probably best if you go back and live with them temporarily, at least until things are a bit more settled. I really think that's the best decision for everybody concerned.'

Claude took a moment to process this information. 'David and Alice are wonderful, aren't they? I'm so lucky to have them.'

'Good that's settled. I'll draw up the paperwork.'

'Oh no, I don't want to go,' Claude said, to the consternation of Mrs Woodbine.

'What? But you couldn't wait to leave last week.'

'You were right all along Mrs Woodbine. That was just, what do you call it? .... oh yes, transitional anxiety. I definitely think I'm through that now and I'm starting to enjoy myself.'

Sylvia plodded slowly past the doorway, leaning heavily on her walking stick as she went. 'Morning Psycho!' she said, brightly.

Claude made a mental note not to let himself become so self-obsessed again. Nobody had been even vaguely interested in the fact that he'd failed to reveal his past identity. Instead, they'd all instantly latched on to Marjorie's lurid version of the story. Overnight, he had acquired a flourishing fan club.

He smiled at Sylvia and turned back to Mrs Woodbine.

'Besides, how can I disappoint my adoring public?' he asked.

Two days later, it was pouring with rain and Mrs

Woodbine was trying to close one of the windows high up in the entrance hall. She was employing a long wooden pole and didn't look as if she was fully in control of it.

Mrs Mayer arrived, looking a little flustered. 'Umm, Mrs Woodbine, there's an urgent message for you.'

'From who?' said Mrs Woodbine, continuing to wrestle with the window pole.

'From, umm, the police.'

Mrs Woodbine visibly flinched. Wisely, she put down the pole before she did some damage with it. 'The police? What on earth do they want with us?'

'They wouldn't say I'm afraid. But they want to see you at the police station as soon as possible.'

'Me? On my own?'

'Umm, well . . . . '

'Spit it out woman.'

'Actually, they'd like to see Mrs Watson and Mr Simmons as well.'

'What?'

Mrs Woodbine's incredulity continued well into the car journey to the police station. She was driving her Ford Fiesta and Claude and Marjorie were sat in the back. It was still pouring with rain and the windscreen wipers were working overtime.

'But why would the police want to see all three of us?' she said. 'I mean, I do hope that Audrey's daughter hasn't decided to press charges against you two. That's just the sort of publicity we don't need at Fern Lea.'

Marjorie could not let that pass. 'So to be clear, you think Claude and I might be going to prison and all you're worried about is Fern Lea's reputation?'

'That's exactly right.'

The three of them were collected from the front desk by Constable Deacon and taken to a room that doubled as a makeshift video conferencing facility. There was a large TV screen with a small camera hanging from the top that pointed back towards a row of chairs. Everybody sat down. They all felt tense, except Mrs Woodbine. She was starting to develop an impending sense of doom.

After an interminable wait, Inspector Follett arrived. He had his notebook in his hand and launched straight in.

'Thank you all for coming. As some of you already know, Chief Constable Selby himself ordered a post mortem on the body of . . . .'

He checked his notebook. '. . . Audrey Patterson.'

There was a sharp intake of breath from Mrs Woodbine. She looked in horror at Inspector Follett and then at Claude and Marjorie.

'I'm hoping that Professor Ross is now available to take us through the findings,' the Inspector continued. 'Constable, if you will . . . .'

Constable Deacon pointed the remote control at the screen and it flickered into life. A group of circulating white dots appeared briefly on the screen before giving way to a live picture of a pathology lab. A man in his fifties stared back at them, evidently being filmed by his laptop. He was dressed in medical scrubs covered by a large apron.

'Hello Inspector!'

'Hello Professor!'

They greeted each other with that universal relief that comes from an IT connection being successfully made.

'Good morning everyone,' the Professor continued. 'I'll get straight on with it if that's okay.'

He briefly studied his notes.

'Now, Audrey Patterson was found dead at the Fern Lea residential home on the morning of May 3rd. Her medical notes showed she had a heart arrhythmia for which she took the drug Amiodarone. However, heart malfunction was certainly not the cause of death.'

Claude and Marjorie exchanged a glance.

'All other organs were healthy and toxicology was normal, leaving one obvious fact staring us in the face at the autopsy.'

Mrs Woodbine fidgeted nervously in her seat. She felt the Professor was staring straight at her.

'To large areas of the front of her body, Mrs Patterson had suffered significant bruising consistent with one single event . . .' He paused momentarily, adding to the drama. '. . . the physical act of suffocation.'

That was enough for Mrs Woodbine. She broke out in a loud and uncontrollable coughing fit. Marjorie leant over and clapped her on the back, slightly too hard.

'Pull yourself together, woman,' she said, in a

stage whisper. 'The pathologist is starting to size you up as his next customer.'

Mrs Woodbine eventually managed to regain her equilibrium and the Professor continued.

'Crucially, she had considerable bruising around her nose and mouth, almost certainly caused by the application of extreme pressure, probably with a pillow. She had bruising to her hands and feet as she flailed around in self-defence, probably striking the wall and the bed frame. And I'm afraid the attacker eventually subdued her by climbing on top of her and pinning her legs down with his knees. Hence the deep bruising to her thighs.'

Silence settled over the room and the Professor continued to stare back from the screen, ominously. Mrs Woodbine eventually summoned up the courage to speak.

'Can I ask a question?' she said to Inspector Follett.

'Please do,' he replied.

She looked at the screen. 'Professor, I believe we followed the correct procedure at Fern Lea and the GP examined Audrey's body not long after we found her. There was no mention of any bruising at all anywhere, let alone any suggestion of physical violence. How is that possible?'

'That's a very good question', said the Professor. 'But the simple fact is that bruising often doesn't occur in such circumstances until anything between twelve and twenty four hours after death. It's probable that a number of cases of suffocation go undetected for precisely this reason.'

The meeting eventually broke up and Marjorie and Mrs Woodbine headed off to the car park.

Claude found himself following Inspector Follett to the Chief Constable's office. They walked in silence and Claude spent the short journey wondering if the Inspector would have ordered the post mortem himself if the Chief Constable hadn't intervened. Probably not, he thought. They arrived at the office and the Inspector knocked on the door frame.

'Excuse me, sir. You wanted to see Mr Simmons before he left.'

The Chief Constable got up from his desk. 'Ah yes, thank you,' he said as the Inspector departed. 'Claude, please come in. Have a seat.'

It was a large, well appointed office with its own meeting area and he gestured towards the sofas. They both sat down.

'I just wanted to say thank you for the incredible thing you've achieved here. This was a very nasty murder and it was almost the perfect crime. So nearly undetected but for you, Claude.'

'Well, thank you for putting your faith in an old timer, Peter,' Claude replied. 'You're almost the only one that did.'

'Which brings me on to my next subject. I'm asking Inspector Follett to head the murder enquiry and I was hoping he might be able to use you for wise counsel ....'

Claude sensed a 'but'.

'But I'm afraid HR and Health and Safety have rather ganged up on me. You know, eighty year olds in harm's way and all that.'

He was trying to let Claude down gently.

'You mean that Inspector Follett is having none of it?' Claude responded.

The Chief Constable looked at his shoes, embarrassed.

'Listen, he's headstrong but we all were in our day, weren't we? Plus we're very stretched at the moment and I'm afraid I don't have any other options.'

Claude weighed things up. Realistically, he knew there was no place in a murder enquiry for two pensioners with a combined age of a hundred and sixty years. Also, he was pleased that Audrey's murder was now going to be properly looked into. Nonetheless, he had felt a twinge of disappointment when the Chief Constable had actually spelt things out. He and Marjorie's mini-investigation had re-invigorated him and he had started to feel some of his old certainties returning. With apologies to poor Audrey, it had been extremely therapeutic.

The Chief Constable accompanied him back to the car park.

'We're going to be seeing a bit more of you anyway,' he said, trying to end on a positive note. 'We're interviewing all the staff at Fern Lea. I believe the ploy is we're part of a government inspection team, so as not to frighten the residents.'

At the door they shook hands, a little stiffly.

'Goodbye Peter.'

'Goodbye Claude. And thank you again.'

It had finally stopped raining as Mrs Woodbine drove the three of them home. However, Storm Marjorie was very much raging inside the car.

'Stood down? How can we have possibly been stood down?' she fumed, hearing Claude's news. 'We've just brought them a murder investigation on a plate, for heaven's sake. Stupid man!'

'Which man?' asked Claude, watching his own sense of disappointment being positively dwarfed. 'The Chief Constable?'

'No! . . . . Inspector . . . . Inspector . . . .' she said, searching for the name in exasperation. 'Inspector Fuckwit!'

'Mrs Watson, really,' said Mrs Woodbine.

'Well, I ask you. I expect you're delighted anyway, Mrs Woodbine. Now that you've got us back under your iron rule.'

'I'm not, actually,' she replied. 'I feel terrible about what's happened with Audrey and everything and I feel I should apologise to you both.'

This took Claude and Marjorie completely by surprise.

They waited at a red traffic light. Mrs Woodbine hadn't finished.

'It's not easy for me to say this,' she continued. 'I think I'm going to have to, well . . . . you know, loosen up a bit.'

The traffic light had turned green while she was talking. The car behind sounded its horn.

CHAPTER FIVE

"Retirement Homes Regulatory Authority. Private" read the laminated sign stuck to a large oak door which led off the Fern Lea entrance hall. In front of the door, a row of chairs had been set out and three members of staff sat waiting.

Eventually, the door opened and Constable Deacon came out, dressed in plain clothes, followed by another member of staff who had clearly just been interviewed. The Constable consulted his clipboard and addressed the three seated members of staff.

'Ms Kovac?' he enquired.

A young woman in carer's uniform got up and followed Constable Deacon back into the room. The door was closed behind them.

Claude and Marjorie were sat on a sofa on the far side of the hall, watching events with interest.

'He's a nice young lad,' said Marjorie.

'Who is?' replied Claude.

'Constable Deacon – I've been having a few chats with him. He's a big fan of yours.'

'Have you? Is he?'

Arthur shuffled past with his Zimmer frame.

'Morning Psycho! Morning Marjorie!' he called out.

'Morning Arthur!' Claude and Marjorie chorused.

'I think he's been looking you up on the internet. He was telling me about your theory about the key to a murder being the three . . . .' she racked her brains, unsuccessfully. 'The three something-or-others.'

'Ah yes. The three M's. Motive, motive and motive. I think that one might be a bit of a cliché now.'

'Anyway, I've got his phone number now and he says I can WhatsApp him if I need to.'

'Who's the dark horse now, Marjorie?' said Claude, surprised.

The door opened again and Constable Deacon reappeared with his clipboard. The next member of staff got up and followed him back into the room.

'You don't happen to know what WhatsApp actually is, do you?' asked Marjorie.

Notwithstanding her new relationship with Constable Deacon, Marjorie remained cross about being side-lined from the police enquiry. Even a week later, she was still unable to let it go.

'Are you still convinced it's an outsider?' she asked Claude as they strolled around the garden.

'Who? The murderer?'

'Obviously the murderer.'

Claude ignored her tetchiness. In fact, he did still feel that the murderer was likely to be an outsider.

In his experience, smothering with a pillow usually suggested family or friends. It had always been the murder weapon of choice if you were trying to bump off an unwanted relative without being discovered.

They were about to sit down on the patio under a sun umbrella when Mrs Woodbine arrived at the double, huffing and puffing.

'Claude, Marjorie, there you are. Inspector Follett has just rung – they've arrested someone. Can you come?'

They followed Mrs Woodbine back to her office and she shut the door behind them. Claude and Marjorie sat down while she paced anxiously around the room.

'Heaven knows what management is going to say. The suspect is one of the staff.'

Claude was taken aback.

'A member of Fern Lea's staff, you mean?'

'Yes, one of the carers – Stefan Wisniewski.'

'Sweet little Stefan?' said Marjorie. 'Has he admitted it?'

'He's saying nothing apparently. Completely clammed up.'

'Did the Inspector say what evidence they had?' asked Claude.

'Unfortunately he did. Stefan had apparently worked at two other residential homes before Fern Lea and both showed unexplained spikes in the death rate during his time there.' Mrs Woodbine continued to pace. 'Worst of all, they're now regarding another death at Fern Lea as suspicious as well – Mrs

Grainger, four weeks ago.'

'Ah yes, died in her sleep we thought,' said Marjorie.

Claude seemed unimpressed. He'd heard all the stuff about spikes in death rates before, but in the end statistics weren't the same thing as proof. And they certainly weren't enough to start making judgements about serial killings. Not in his opinion, anyway.

'Is there actually any hard evidence?' he asked, bluntly.

'How do you mean?' asked Mrs Woodbine.

'Well, the autopsy on Audrey was carried out quite quickly and it revealed the bruising – that's evidence of suffocation. But Mrs Grainger died four weeks ago. And what sort of funeral did she have?'

Mrs Woodbine sat down at her computer and started to tap away.

'Hang on . . . . here we are . . . .' She scrolled through a series of pages. 'Cremation.'

'Not much evidence left there then,' said Claude, dryly.

They eventually left Mrs Woodbine to pace around on her own and headed for the privacy of the faraway bench behind the birch trees. Claude remained lost in thought for some time, digesting the news.

'I'm not saying the police are wrong,' he said, eventually. 'After all, they have all the facts and we don't. But I must confess, I'm surprised.'

'Your judgement's been pretty good so far,' said

Marjorie, encouragingly for once.

'I mean, have all the other avenues been explored before we jump to the conclusion it's a serial killer?' he said, as much to himself as to Marjorie. 'Heavens, the world's obsessed with serial killers.'

'You might have something to do with that, Claude.'

He shrugged.

'Listen, if you're this unsure, perhaps we should do a bit more investigating ourselves?'

Claude allowed his frustration to show. He pointed out that the modern police force had forensics, DNA testing, state of the art computers and who knows what else. He also pointed out that he and Marjorie were trapped in an old people's home.

'Do you see the difficulty?' he asked.

Marjorie was undeterred. 'We'll be fine, Claude. We've got your vast experience and my big mouth. We're unstoppable.'

The mechanical digger worked steadily, excavating the grave. It was illuminated by bright spotlights and surrounded by a three-sided tarpaulin tent.

Inspector Follett and Chief Constable Selby stood to one side in the surrounding darkness, watching in silence.

'This is a very drastic course of action, Inspector,' said the Chief Constable, eventually.

'I know, sir. But I think it will provide Professor

Ross with the forensic evidence we need.'

The digger reversed back from the grave. Two men in forensic all-in-one suits stepped forward. They climbed into the grave and secured straps around the coffin.

'Particularly distressing for the relatives as well,' the Chief Constable continued.

'I know sir. I've taken care of all of that.'

The straps were attached to the mechanical digger and the coffin was slowly raised from the grave. It emerged into the light, covered in mud and seeping water.

'You know you're betting that this is an Angel of Mercy killing, don't you, Inspector?'

'I suppose I am, sir,' he replied.

'And you know who christened it that?'

The Inspector paused. 'I'm guessing Claude Simmons?'

'Exactly right. Bit ironic, isn't it?'

The coffin was lowered onto an awaiting trolley and the two men removed the straps. They pushed the trolley off towards an unmarked black van parked nearby.

In truth, the Chief Constable had visited the graveyard because he remained in two minds about the investigation. Like Claude, his instincts told him that identifying the murder of Audrey Patterson as a serial killing was just a bit too convenient. On the other hand, he had a duty to allow his Inspector some space, perhaps enough space to make a few mistakes. No point in having a dog and barking yourself, as someone had once taught him.

'Let's get on with it then,' he said to the Inspector.

'Yes sir.'

'But if this fails to produce any forensic evidence then the suspect needs to be released. Are we agreed?'

'Sir.'

Inspector Follett set off after the trolley.

The next day, Claude and Marjorie were sat in Mrs Woodbine's office. Mrs Woodbine was pacing around again.

'Exhumed?' said Claude, surprised. 'How do you know that?'

'I found out this morning from some colleagues in the business. I'm told there were five suspicious deaths at the other retirement homes where Stefan worked and four were cremated.'

'So the poor old fifth one's been dug up,' said Marjorie.

Claude looked thoughtful. 'It sounds like Inspector Follett is betting it's Angel of Mercy Syndrome.'

'Angel of what syndrome?' asked Mrs Woodbine.

'Angel of Mercy. You know, someone who believes they're doing the world a favour by putting the old and the infirm out of their misery. I was involved in a case here and there have been several in America. Perhaps the Inspector's right.'

'Let's hope he's wrong!' said Mrs Woodbine anxiously. 'I've got management on my back and the residents are about to find out we've been blithely employing a serial killer for the past year. What on earth am I to do?'

'Well, you could always join the rebel army with Claude and me,' said Marjorie, half joking.

Actually, Mrs Woodbine gave this some serious thought. 'And what would that entail exactly?' she asked.

Fifteen minutes later, they were all gathered around Mrs Mayer's computer, watching as she lined up the footage from the security cameras. Mrs Woodbine had officially gone over to the other side.

Marjorie couldn't resist a dig before they got started. 'It's a funny old world isn't it Mrs Mayer? Here we are looking at the CCTV footage after all.'

'Yes indeed, Mrs Watson,' said Mrs Mayer. 'Umm, sorry.'

'Okay, let's get on,' said Mrs Woodbine, still capable of lapsing into officiousness. 'Mrs Mayer, start at 11.30 PM on May 2nd please.'

She tapped away on her computer and CCTV footage of the front door appeared on the screen. 'There,' she said.

'And shuttle forward, please.'

More tapping and the footage began to fast forward.

'Have the police seen this?' asked Claude.

'I sent them a copy straight away after the autopsy,' said Mrs Mayer. 'We didn't hear any more.'

'There!' said Claude pointing at a flurry of activity on the screen. 'Go back please Mrs Mayer.'

She reversed the footage and then ran it forward at normal speed - the time code read 03 MAY 00:06 AM. They watched as a member of staff left through the front door. Just as the door was about to close, a person wearing a black hoody squeezed back in through the gap.

'Exactly as Claude predicted,' said Marjorie, triumphantly. 'And five minutes before he heard the commotion in Audrey's room.'

Mrs Woodbine was peering at the screen. 'But who is it?'

'Someone who knew what they were doing,' said Claude. 'Hood pulled down, face turned away from camera. Shuttle forward again please Mrs Mayer.'

She tapped away on her keyboard and the footage fast forwarded. There was a second flurry of activity and she reversed the footage and ran it back at normal speed again. The person in the hoody reappeared and exited through the front door. The time code now read 03 MAY 00:15 AM.

'Fifteen minutes past midnight and he's gone,' said Claude. 'I hesitate to say he's a professional but he's certainly very efficient.'

'But is he a member of staff?' said Mrs Woodbine, looking at Claude.

He took a while to answer, trying for a moment to put himself in the attacker's shoes. 'The police obviously think he is but I'm afraid I don't,' he said, eventually. 'Why would this Stefan chap dress up like a . . . . well, like a comedy villain and risk being spotted prowling about? If he were the murderer, he'd wear his carer's uniform and hide in plain sight, wouldn't he?'

Nobody could disagree.

'So, what happens next?' asked Mrs Woodbine, now almost entirely deferring to Claude.

Claude looked at Marjorie. 'Well,' he said, 'at the risk of incurring Peter Selby's wrath, I think Marjorie and I are going to have to do a bit more investigating.'

'Which means we're going to have to pop out again,' added Marjorie.

'Oh lord,' said Mrs Woodbine.

They set off immediately for Mrs Owen's house. They arrived and opened the front gate. They walked up the path towards the front door.

'You do realise that this is the scene of our greatest defeat, don't you?' said Marjorie.

Claude pressed on regardless. He climbed the front steps and rang the doorbell. Eventually, the door was opened, not by Mrs Owen but by a female nurse. He was taken by surprise.

'Oh . . . . umm . . . . we were hoping to have a word with Mrs Owen, please,' Claude said, stammering again.

'Yes, I'll see if . . . .' The nurse herself was interrupted by Mrs Owen shouting grumpily from the back room.

'Who is it?'

Before anyone had a chance to answer, Mrs Owen

appeared in the corridor, looking even more frail. She now trailed an oxygen cylinder on wheels behind her.

'I knew it. You two again,' she said.

After they left Mrs Owen's house, Claude and Marjorie walked in silence back towards the bus stop again. But this time, they only went as far as a Ford Fiesta parked in the road. They got in and found Mrs Woodbine waiting for them.

'You've been gone quite a while,' she said. 'It can't have been a total disaster.'

'It wasn't,' said Marjorie. 'Considering how ill she now is she was actually very helpful.'

Claude sat quietly in the back of the car, reflecting on what they'd heard from Mrs Owen. She had clearly been hugely affected by Audrey's murder and seemed keen to have it resolved. In the end, she had told them pretty much everything she'd told the police.

'What next then?' asked Mrs Woodbine, starting the engine.

'Well, I think we've got some old-fashioned detective work to do,' said Claude.

They drove back to Fern Lea and Mrs Woodbine led them to a disused bedroom on the first floor. Inside, the bed itself had been stripped, the curtains had been taken down and the whole room smelt, to put it politely, as if it needed airing. Marjorie walked straight over and opened a window.

'You can make as much mess as you like,' said Mrs Woodbine. 'The whole room is being refurbished next month.'

'Thank you, we will,' said Claude.

Marjorie sat herself down at the table. She had a pad of over-sized Post-It notes, a number of magic marker pens and some Blu Tack. She began sketching.

Claude had with him a large photo of Audrey. 'Our victim is Audrey Patterson,' he said, taking some Blu Tack and sticking it right in the middle of the wall. He borrowed one of Marjorie's pens and wrote Audrey's name and her date of death underneath.

He was beginning a makeshift crime investigation board.

To the left of the photo he wrote "£2.5 million".

'And here's the headline news from Mrs Owen yesterday: Audrey left two and a half million pounds in her will,' he said.

'Crikey!' said Mrs Woodbine, who had seated herself in the armchair.

'Motive, motive, motive,' said Marjorie, without looking up from her sketching.

'Indeed,' said Claude. 'Now, moving on to the rest of the family, starting with Audrey's husband George.'

He turned to Marjorie and she handed him a Post It note on which she had caricatured a picture of an elderly man. He took it and stuck it on the wall next to Audrey.

'That's actually very good,' he said.

'Oh you know, the old skills – Art A level, 1956.

Plus I sneaked a look at all the family photos when we were at Mrs Owen's house.'

'Anyway, this is George Patterson. He pre-deceased Audrey in 2014. Obviously not a suspect.' He wrote George's details on the wall.

'Which brings us on to their only child, Catherine Patterson – now Mrs Catherine Owen, of course. Sole beneficiary of Audrey's will.'

Marjorie gave Claude her sketch of a gaunt and haggard looking Mrs Owen. He placed it directly below Audrey's photo and wrote in her details.

'Presumably not a suspect either?' asked Mrs Woodbine.

'I very much doubt it,' said Claude.

'Sadly, she's hardly got the strength to open a bottle of aspirin, let alone suffocate someone,' said Marjorie.

Claude picked up Marjorie's next sketch. It showed a man with bleary eyes, cartoon stubble and unruly hair. It was almost worthy of the Beano.

'Moving on to Catherine Owen's ex-husband, Stephen Owen.' He stuck the picture on the wall. 'A drunk. Abusive, violent. Living in Germany for the past ten years. Interestingly, Mrs Owen thinks Audrey might have paid him quite a lot of money to leave the country.'

'Suspect?' asked Mrs Woodbine.

'We're definitely not ruling him out,' Claude replied.

He waited for Marjorie to finish the next caricature. It was of a young woman with spikey hair and wild, staring eyes. He stuck it underneath Stephen Owen and added her details.

'So now we come to Mrs Owen's two children,' he said. 'This is the daughter, Stephanie. Following in her father's footsteps she was having trouble with alcohol in her early teens before graduating to heroin in her twenties.'

'She's gone straight to the top of my list,' said Mrs Woodbine.

'Except that her addiction took such a toll on the family that Mrs Owen stopped all contact with her five years ago. In the end, she cut Stephanie out of her will. Very traumatic, not least because Audrey and Mrs Owen fell out about it.'

'Oh,' said Mrs Woodbine, immediately failing her audition as a detective.

He collected the final family portrait from Marjorie. It showed an intense looking young man with rimless glasses. She had made him look like a young Wittgenstein.

'Which brings us to the son, Andrew Owen.' He added him to the collection on the wall, just under Mrs Owen. 'Currently in his third year at Edinburgh University, reading mathematics. Apparently very bright but accordingly a bit, umm, what's the politically correct phrase . . . ?'

'A bit Mr Spock,' said Marjorie.

'Thank you. And also now the sole beneficiary of his terminally ill mother's will,' said Claude.

Marjorie handed Claude a final portrait.

'Here's young Stefan,' she said, 'just to complete

the collection.'

Claude stuck Stefan on the wall and wrote in his details. Then he stepped back a few paces and weighed things up for a moment.

'Good. A strong looking board, don't you think?' he said.

Neither Marjorie or Mrs Woodbine had a clue what a strong board should really look like, but that didn't stop Marjorie from chiming in, having seen this sort of thing on the TV a few times.

'Shouldn't it have some of those red lines that make sinister connections between people?'

Claude picked up a red magic marker pen from the table.

'Well, one line suggests itself immediately.'

He drew a red line from Audrey's £2.5 million down to Mrs Owen and on to Andrew Owen.

'Although it's probably far too obvious,' he said.

At the police station, Inspector Follett was no less pleased with his investigation board. After all, he currently had seven potential victims and the board was criss-crossed with numerous connecting lines.

The Inspector was standing in front of the board admiring his handiwork when Constable Deacon arrived with a folder.

'Sir, Professor Ross asked for this to be given straight to you. It's the autopsy report on the body that was exhumed.'

'Thank you, Constable,' he said. He took the folder and opened it. He read the first page with a deepening frown. He read the remaining pages at an accelerating rate.

'Shit,' he said.

Claude and Marjorie sat together in the TV lounge, with a handful of other residents. The main BBC news at ten o'clock was just coming to an end and the local news was about to begin.

Claude started to get up. 'The local news is always my signal for bed,' he said. 'Plus we've got a very big day ahead of us tomorrow. I'll see you in the morning, Marjorie.'

'But you'll miss the story about the missing sheep and the local councillor who got caught with his . . . .'

Marjorie stopped abruptly and grabbed Claude's arm as he was about to leave.

'Oh lord,' she said.

On the TV screen was a picture of Fern Lea. It was followed by a picture of a young Audrey.

Claude sat back down and they both stared at the TV.

' . . . . police investigating the murder of Audrey Patterson at the Fern Lea residential home have been forced to release the man they arrested earlier, due to conflicting evidence,' said the newsreader.

A medley of pictures of Fern Lea appeared on the screen ending with the front gate clanging shut, as if keeping out reporters.

'Inspector Ben Follett, the investigating officer, said a number of other lines of enquiry are being followed . . .' continued the newsreader.

'That's it. Now all the residents know,' said Marjorie. 'Poor Mrs Woodbine.'

Claude looked around the room. Every other resident was asleep in their armchair.

'Oh, I think the secret's safe at least until morning,' he said.

CHAPTER SIX

T he pretty Norman church was full of flowers and the spring sunshine streamed in through the beautiful stained glass windows. An oak coffin sat in front of the altar, bedecked with lilies. Next to it was a large easel which carried a photograph of a smiling Audrey.

Claude, Marjorie and Mrs Woodbine were sat in a pew near the back, listening attentively as the vicar came to the end of his address.

' . . . and so I would encourage you to see past the tragic circumstances of her death and remember instead a life well lived. Today is a celebration of that life, of Audrey's countless friendships, her love of family and of the many kindnesses she bestowed on all who knew her.'

He paused briefly, to give everyone a moment to reflect.

'And now, we will please sing hymn number fifty two.'

The organ struck up with the opening chords of Abide With Me. Claude found it a difficult hymn to sing at the best of times, let alone at the funeral of his friend. He gave up and studied the Owen family in the front pew instead. Fortunately, the choir carried the day.

The eulogy was to be delivered by someone called Alexander Kaplan, according to the Order of Service booklet. He looked distinctly nervous as he stepped up to the lectern and he read mostly from his notes, only occasionally raising his head to look at the congregation. Claude sat forward and listened intently.

' . . . and although I was primarily a business associate of her husband George, I can honestly say that Audrey never treated me as anything other than family,' he intoned. 'When I found myself in personal difficulties a few years ago she was the first person to stand by me, a loyalty which sadly I had not been able to fully repay by the time this terrible tragedy occurred.'

After he'd finished, they sang Lord Of All Hopefulness and then moved outside for the committal.

Mrs Owen, now in a wheelchair, made a huge effort to stand when she reached the graveside. She coughed persistently and her nurse had to support her as the coffin was slowly lowered into the grave.

Claude and Marjorie watched from a respectful distance, particularly interested in her two children. Andrew stared at the coffin, frowning slightly, as if he was trying to work out what the correct reaction should be to his grandmother's death. Stephanie looked entirely lost in her own world. She gazed off into the middle distance.

In turn, the family members threw a handful of earth into the grave and the vicar offered the final blessing.

Claude and Marjorie intercepted Mrs Owen as the nurse pushed her in her wheelchair back towards a waiting limousine.

'Mrs Owen, can we say again how sorry we are about Audrey? She was our very good friend,' said Marjorie.

'Yes I know. And thank you both for all you've done,' she replied.

'Not at all.' said Claude. 'Umm, would it be okay If I offered my condolences to your son, Andrew? I know that Audrey was very fond of him.'

'Please do. He's still at the graveside, I think. Struggling to make sense of it all.'

Claude wandered off and left Marjorie and Mrs Owen hanging in silence for a while. Eventually Mrs Owen spoke.

'Unlike you to bite your tongue Mrs Watson. Come on, out with it.'

'Well, it's probably none of my business but I was surprised to see your daughter Stephanie here today. Is there a chance of some sort of reconciliation between the two of you?' Marjorie was as blunt as ever.

'My daughter who's currently on probation again for possession of heroin, you mean?' Mrs Owen snapped back, immediately seeing red. She paused for a moment and then thought better of her outburst. 'I'm sorry, you're probably right to ask. Given everything that's happened, we'll have to see. The fact that we sat together in church today without causing a thunderbolt was at least a good start.'

At the graveside, Claude and Andrew Owen finished their conversation. Claude offered a handshake which Andrew took a moment to accept. He walked back and found Marjorie.

'What was he like?' she asked.

'Oh, perfectly polite. Just as you'd expect.'

They walked back towards the car where Mrs Woodbine was waiting. The three of them drove back to Fern Lea, each lost in their own thoughts.

The next morning, Claude and Marjorie were seated in the disused bedroom again, staring silently at the investigation board. The door opened and Mrs Woodbine came in.

'I'm afraid I can only spare fifteen minutes today,' she said. 'The papers are full of the news about Audrey and I have a lot of anxious residents to reassure. Sorry.'

'The truth is, we're a bit stuck anyway,' said Claude. 'Our board points clearly in one direction but the police don't seem to agree at all. What are we missing?'

They all stared at the board.

'I think I might have found a way forward,' said Marjorie.

Claude looked surprised.

'Really?'

'Yes, I've been WhatsApping with my new best friend, Constable Deacon,' she said. 'Reading between the lines, I don't think he's delighted with the way the investigation's going. He's very smart so he's never going to give anything away and he's certainly never going to criticise his boss. But my intuition says he's a bit . . . frustrated.'

'Probably even more so now Stefan's been released,' said Mrs Woodbine.

'Shall we agree a plan of action then, Marjorie?' asked Claude, apprehensively.

'Oh I've already agreed it,' she replied. 'You and I are meeting him at the pub tomorrow.'

Claude walked back from the bar, slipping his wallet into his inside jacket pocket. 'They'll bring the drinks over in a minute,' he said to Marjorie and Constable Deacon. He sat down.

'I think Constable Deacon . . . umm . . .Tom, might like to hear about a couple of your successful cases, Claude,' said Marjorie. 'How about starting with the Dulwich Dentist?'

'You mean you want to hear about it, Marjorie?'

Constable Deacon smiled.

'In any case,' Claude continued, 'are you sure you want to know the details? There were body parts strewn all over the Home Counties by the time we caught him.'

'And was he just an ordinary dentist?' asked Marjorie, undaunted.

'No, he wasn't a dentist at all, that was just the

nickname the newspapers gave him. He was actually a school janitor.'

'Was he? Why dentist then?'

'Okay, you did ask, Marjorie. His nickname referred to the fact that he had a fascination with, how can I put it? . . .umm, the surgical possibilities of electric drills.'

Claude mimed with his forefinger the action of revving up an electric drill and made a passable impression of its high speed noise.

'Okay, perhaps we'll leave that there then,' said Marjorie.

Fortunately, at that moment the drinks arrived.

'Gin and tonic?' said the barman.

'Yes that's me. Thank you,' said Marjorie.

He set down two pints of Guinness as well.

Claude took the opportunity to change the subject. 'Now what about you, Tom? Marjorie tells me you're on the police fast track.'

'I am. I'm enjoying it.'

'I'm assuming that these days that means you've got a university degree?'

'A computer science degree, yes. From Durham.'

'Really? Most impressive.'

'Then straight on to police training college. Are you aware that you feature prominently in the current police training manual?'

Claude was surprised.

'Do I?'

'Yes, relating to your famous motto: "Results first, rules second".'

'Infamous more like. Surely they're not teaching cadets that's the correct way to behave?'

'Umm no, they're teaching cadets that's now precisely the wrong way to behave.'

Claude laughed.

Marjorie chimed in. 'We're not going to ask you to break the rules, Tom, But would you consider . . . . gently bending them?'

Constable Deacon smiled. He knew how much they'd both been involved in the case and he knew that Marjorie wouldn't be able to resist asking him for information. Fortunately, he'd worked out an answer that didn't compromise the police enquiry.

'Obviously, I can't tell you anything confidential about the case,' he said. 'But perhaps I can tell you some things that are already a matter of public record that you may not yet know.'

'How clever you are,' said Claude, genuinely impressed.

'Let's start with the most obvious suspect - Mrs Owen's son, Andrew.' He tapped something into his mobile phone before explaining that Andrew had been taking part in a student union debate in Edinburgh on the evening of May the second. The debate hadn't finished until an hour before Audrey Patterson's murder, some 330 miles away.

'The video of the debate is on YouTube,' he said, turning his phone around to show them. They stared wide-eyed at Andrew Owen on the screen.

'In other words?' said Marjorie, hoping she was missing something.

'In other words,' said the Constable, taking a sip of Guinness, 'there is no chance he could have committed the murder. Not even if he had a helicopter.'

'Mmm,' said Claude.

'Then there's Mrs Owen's daughter Stephanie,' the Constable continued. He described how she'd been in and out of police custody for a number of years and at the time in question had been duly under arrest again. She had spent the night of the murder in the cells.

Claude sipped his pint, lost in thought.

'And in respect of Mrs Owen's ex-husband Stephen Owen, you may or may not know, he now resides in Germany. In any event, he also has a UK court restraining order preventing him being within 100 yards of both Mrs Owen and Mrs Patterson. How can I put it? There is nothing to suggest that public order has been breached.'

Claude and Marjorie looked at each other.

'All three with perfect alibis,' said Claude, taken aback.

'I know,' said the Constable. 'Hard to believe, isn't it?'

In the pub car park, the Ford Fiesta was waiting for them again.

'Can I just point out that once this murder investigation is over, I'm no longer your mini-cab driver?' said Mrs Woodbine as Claude and Marjorie clambered in.

'We're very grateful Mrs Woodbine,' said Marjorie. 'And please drive carefully because we've already hit one brick wall tonight.'

They returned to Fern Lea and everybody called it a day. Back in his room, Claude poured himself a glass of whisky and reflected on Constable Deacon's comprehensive evidence. Eventually he put on his pyjamas, hooked his walking stick over the bedside table and climbed into bed.

Two hours later he was abruptly woken by a pillow being violently forced on to his face. He found himself thrashing around wildly in self-defence, desperately trying to come to his senses. He managed blindly to land a couple of glancing blows on his assailant but this only succeeded in causing the assailant to increase the pressure with the pillow while quickly climbing on top of Claude. His knees dug painfully into Claude's thighs as he pinned him down.

Claude was losing. But he still flailed around with his right arm. He banged into his bedside table, he knocked over his alarm clock. He reached out and reached out. And eventually his hand fell upon his walking stick. He grabbed it and swung it as hard as he could at where he guessed the assailant's head might be. Direct hit.

Claude swung twice more and there was a distinct cry of pain. He shaped to swing a fourth time and the assailant instinctively lifted his hand to protect his face. The pressure on the pillow weakened and

Claude started to wriggle free. It was over.

The assailant had no choice but to give up and run. He threw open the door and Claude caught a brief glimpse of his black hoody in the corridor light as he fled.

'Help! Help!' Claude called out, as loudly as he could.

Claude dozed in the hospital bed. He was attached to various bits of medical equipment which bleeped intermittently. A police officer was stationed outside his door.

Chief Constable Selby and Inspector Follett came striding into the room and Claude sat up.

'Claude, how are you?' asked the Chief Constable anxiously.

'Oh, a bit battered and bruised but otherwise no harm done,' said Claude.

'That is a huge relief. And you've been fully checked over?'

'Indeed I have. I think I'm going home this afternoon.'

'You'll be pleased to know we're in the process of re-arresting our initial suspect, Stefan Wisniewski,' said Inspector Follett. 'He should be back in custody by the time I finish taking your statement.'

'I can give you my statement straight away,' said Claude. 'I don't believe he did it.'

'I'm sorry?'

'I've been sceptical about the serial killer theory all along. Now I'm convinced it's wrong.'

The Chief Constable could feel his authority slowly starting to be questioned. He pointed out that Claude couldn't possibly know all the facts of the case.

'No, but I know a scam when I see one,' said Claude, undaunted. 'Serial killers always end up with a nickname, don't they? What are you going to call this one? "The murderer who methodically worked his way along the retirement home corridor with a pillow?" Very catchy, isn't it?'

'Claude, really.'

'It's ridiculous. I've never seen such a ham-fisted attempt to hoodwink the police. Carry on with this Inspector and you'll soon find yourself on the TV again explaining why you're releasing your only suspect for the second time.'

Claude had no intention of trying to take command, but it seemed to be happening anyway.

'What would you have us do?' asked the Chief Constable, attempting to restore some calm.

'Believe it or not, I'm trying to help,' said Claude. 'I've already done you a huge favour by providing you with some actual hard evidence for a change.'

'How do you mean?' asked the Inspector.

'I managed to survive thanks to my faithful walking stick. I gave the assailant three good cracks on the head with it – I was pleasantly surprised by how much oomph I still have in my swing, actually. Trust me, I will have done him some damage. So perhaps you might see how your suspect Stefan looks this morning? Any cuts and bruises, for example?'

The Chief Constable gave the Inspector a look which basically said 'Get on with it then' and the Inspector turned to leave. Claude, however, hadn't finished.

'Oh Inspector, you might like to take my walking stick. The assailant was wearing a hoody so you might not find any DNA but it's worth a try. I managed to preserve the evidence with a sterile dressings bag that Mrs Woodbine found for me.'

Claude pointed to his walking stick which stood all alone in the corner of the room, wearing a plastic bag.

CHAPTER SEVEN

Claude and Marjorie were staring at the makeshift investigation board again. Nothing had changed except that Claude now sat in a wheelchair and had an NHS walking stick laid across his legs. The door opened and Mrs Woodbine came in, carrying a sheath of papers.

'Two things,' she said. 'Firstly, Stefan has been released again. It's becoming quite a regular celebration.'

Claude and Marjorie looked pleased.

'And secondly, I've got the information you wanted, Claude.' She shuffled through the papers. 'Yes, here we are . . . Andrew Owen visited Audrey during Easter weekend this year.'

'In other words, about a month before the murder?' said Claude. 'Do the police have this information?'

'Yes. Mrs Mayer sent them the whole visitor's log.'

Claude thought about this for a second. 'And when was the last time he visited before that?'

Mrs Woodbine worked her way through the papers again. 'I think that might be the only time he ever visited.'

Claude got up stiffly from his wheelchair and shuffled to the window. He gazed out, lost in thought.

'I'm sorry to pour cold water on your musings, Claude, whatever they may be,' interrupted Marjorie. 'But Andrew Owen has a cast iron, chromium plated alibi.'

'That's right . . . .' said Claude, distractedly.

'Plus how was he supposed to know about all this money in Audrey's will anyway?' asked Mrs Woodbine. 'I can't imagine her telling him that. I mean, Mrs Owen apparently only found out herself after Audrey's death.'

Claude turned away from the window. 'Actually, that's a fair point Mrs Woodbine.' He walked slowly back to his wheelchair and sat back down.

'What did you say about the log?' he asked. 'Did Audrey have any other visitors?'

She rifled through the papers yet again. 'Let me see. A number of visits from Mrs Owen, trailing off more recently for obvious reasons. Then there's someone called Alexander Kaplan. Visited three times in the last year.'

'Where do we know that name from?' said Marjorie, pondering. 'Oh yes, the funeral. He read the eulogy. You remember, he was the chap who hadn't managed to repay Audrey's loyalty.'

'Of course,' said Claude. 'Do we know anything else about him?'

Mrs Woodbine shook her head. 'Nothing at all, I'm afraid.'

They were slightly lost as to what to do next.

'We could always doodle him,' said Marjorie.

Claude and Mrs Woodbine looked at her, confused.

An hour later, the three of them were gathered around Mrs Mayer's computer again.

'Google has rather a lot of Alexander Kaplans,' said Mrs Mayer, peering at the screen. 'Thirty seven in all. Is there a middle name or an initial?'

'I'm afraid not,' said Claude. 'Perhaps add 'solicitor' to the search?'

Mrs Mayer googled again.

'Nope. No solicitors of that name.'

Claude pondered. 'How about 'chartered accountant'?'

'Ah yes, here we are. Alexander Kaplan, chartered accountant . . . specialising in inheritance tax.'

'Audrey's will!' exclaimed Marjorie.

'And if Kaplan visited her three times, perhaps she was in the process of changing it,' said Claude. 'Is there anything else Mrs Mayer?'

'Yes lots. There's a biography here – public school, read history at university and then straight into military college. All very posh. He's officially a Captain, retired.'

Claude asked about his business career.

Mrs Mayer scrolled down on her computer.

'Ah, not quite so good. Several newspaper articles here. He was a member of a property consortium which failed spectacularly in 2015 with losses of over £60 million. Several members of the consortium went to jail. Kaplan himself was acquitted.'

'Oh lord,' said Mrs Woodbine. 'How on earth did Audrey get mixed up with him?'

'Perhaps we should pay him a visit and see what he's got to say for himself?' said Marjorie. 'Is there an address Mrs Mayer?'

Mrs Mayer began scrolling again.

Claude had to intervene and point out to Marjorie that this was a terrible idea. Not being the police, there was no prospect of them knocking on his door and asking him if he was the murderer.

She liked Claude's new-found authority, except where it disagreed with her own plans. A strategy was quickly forming in her mind.

'You're right Claude,' she said, all sweetness and light. 'And in any event, you need to stay here and rest after your ordeal. No sense in over-exerting yourself.'

She leant in to see what Mrs Mayer had discovered on her computer screen.

Several hours later, Claude was kicking himself. Marjorie had suddenly become reasonableness itself in Mrs Mayer's office and he hadn't spotted it. Marjorie, for heaven's sake. What on earth was he thinking of?

She had missed dinner. She wasn't in her room. He scoured the rest of the house and garden but to no avail. It was getting dark.

Eventually, he was forced to track down Mrs Woodbine who, up to that moment, had been enjoying a glass of wine in her apartment.

'For pity's sake, not again. I thought you were in charge of all this now, Claude?' she said, a little harshly.

'Well . . . .'

She looked at him askance. 'Please don't tell me we've got to contact the police again?'

Claude shrugged.

At that precise moment, Marjorie was half-hidden behind a large plane tree in a quiet, suburban street. Her taxi had just driven away and she was studying the large, detached house on the other side of the road.

There appeared to be no-one around so she hurried across the road as fast as she could and took refuge behind one of the gateposts. Her heart raced. She felt quite intoxicated even though she'd been nowhere near the gin.

She popped her head up and looked around furtively. Nobody in sight. She set off across the large front lawn in what could best be described as a low, crouched scuttle. She made a beeline for a conifer tree some way off and hid behind it. She was starting to hum the Mission Impossible music.

She paused behind the tree for a moment to check the coast was still clear. Then she hurried towards a flower bed in front of the house's bay window. She clambered in, flattening several small shrubs as she did so. She reached a large sash window and pushed it to see if it was open. It was.

She took a deep breath and lifted up the window slowly. And immediately triggered a security floodlight. She jumped back, startled, and a second and equally bright floodlight came on. She stopped humming.

'Bollocks!' she said, out loud.

Before she could decide what to do the front door opened and out came Alexander Kaplan, carrying a torch. He had a large Boxer dog on a short leash and he struggled to restrain it.

Marjorie, still stranded in the middle of the flower bed, put her hands up as if she had been caught escaping from Stalag Luft 3. Alexander Kaplan approached.

'Who on earth are you?' he asked, astonished.

Marjorie kept her hands up. 'I'm Marjorie Watson and I'm investigating the death of Audrey Patterson. I'd like to ask you a few questions, please.'

The duty Sergeant shot back the inspection hatch on the cell door. He peered inside and found Marjorie seated primly on the edge of the bed. He moved aside to allow Claude to peer in.

'Morning Marjorie!' said Claude, trying to be cheery. No reply.

The Sergeant shut the inspection hatch and then unlocked the cell door itself. Marjorie stood up.

'Apparently, Mr Kaplan will not be pressing charges. You're free to go, Mrs Watson,' said the Sergeant.

Marjorie walked towards the door looking thoroughly unrepentant. She walked straight past the Sergeant and stopped in front of Claude.

'Why do my hunches never come off, Claude, and yours always do? It's bloody annoying.'

They waited at the police station while Claude ordered a taxi and when it arrived they set off for Fern Lea. Eventually, Marjorie broke the silence.

'A night in the cells certainly focuses the mind, doesn't it?'

'I believe it does,' said Claude, wondering where this was going.

'The truth is, I've had a lot of time to think and I've seen the error of my ways.'

'Really?'

'Yes, I should never have gone to see Kaplan . . . .' Marjorie paused. 'I should have been much more devious.'

Claude raised an eyebrow. He didn't entirely follow.

'You were right all along Claude, he was never going to tell us anything. But if he was involved in jiggery pokery with Audrey's will then who is the other person most likely to know about it? Who should I really have gone to see?'

Claude frowned for a moment, thinking about this 'Actually, that's not a bad idea at all, Marjorie,' he said, realising what she meant. He immediately reached into his pocket for his mobile phone. 'I'll get the details from Mrs Woodbine.'

Ten minutes later they were being ushered into the wood-panelled office of Edward Randall, an affable looking man in his early sixties.

'Well, I thought I'd seen it all,' he said, directing them towards the sofa, 'but two octogenarian private detectives is a new one even for me.'

'Thank you,' said Marjorie, taking this to be a compliment. 'And we're very grateful for you seeing us without an appointment, Mr Randall.'

'Oh not at all, I'm keen to help. I was Audrey's solicitor for about twenty five years and I was extremely fond of her. Plus I was always a keen follower of the Chief Superintendent's career.' He looked at Claude. 'You probably don't remember but I defended a man you'd charged with murder when I was a young, upstart solicitor.'

'Really?' said Claude, surprised. 'Did you win?'

'No, I'm afraid you did.'

They both smiled.

'Actually, what we'd really like to ask you about is Audrey's tax accountant,' said Claude, getting on with it.

'Alexander Kaplan? Why am I not surprised?'

'Can you tell us about his relationship with Audrey, please?'

'Well, he'd looked after the family's tax affairs for years. Went back a long way with Audrey's late husband George, I think. Might have been in the army together or something?'

Marjorie joined in.

'And was Audrey aware he nearly went to prison for a dodgy property deal in 2015?'

'She was, but in the end she came down on Kaplan's side, against my better judgement I must say. Audrey was a very decent person and she put a huge premium on loyalty.'

'He visited Audrey at Fern Lea three times last year. Any idea why?' continued Marjorie.

Mr Randall was at pains to point out that Audrey's will was headed for the High Court, given the circumstances of her death. This meant there was a limit to the amount of information he could give. He apologised.

'Let's just say he was her tax advisor and she had an estate worth two and a half million pounds,' he said.

'But you were her solicitor and you didn't visit once,' Claude persisted.

'I didn't feel the need to. Kaplan claimed he was being diligent about Audrey's affairs but to my mind he was making a song and dance about everything.'

'You mean about the rewriting of her will?'

Mr Randall looked at Claude, clearly taken aback by the question. 'I can't confirm that I'm afraid. Anyway, in the end, the will was never rewritten,' he said, cryptically.

Changing tack, Claude asked about Andrew Owen and whether he'd ever met with Kaplan.

'Oh yes, he met with Andrew and also with Stephanie, on a number of occasions.'

'To do with Audrey's will?'

'Again, I can't confirm that. Sorry if this all sounds a bit of a riddle.'

Claude and Marjorie finished the meeting and returned to Fern Lea. They summoned Mrs Woodbine for a team conflab in the disused bedroom. There was a great deal to catch up on.

Marjorie sat at the table drawing a Post It note portrait of Alexander Kaplan. She seemed to be giving it even more attention than usual.

'There you are, Alexander Kaplan. Drawn from bitter personal experience,' she said, handing the portrait to Claude.

'Now that's what I call a doodle,' said Claude, grinning. He stuck the picture to the wall.

'Ha bloody ha,' said Marjorie.

'Obviously, he's a suspect?' asked Mrs Woodbine.

'Definitely,' said Claude. 'He was effectively bankrupt so he clearly had motive. We just need to work out how he would have actually benefitted from Audrey's death.'

Mrs Woodbine thought about this. 'But he did meet with Andrew Owen, didn't he?'

'The Andrew Owen with the perfect alibi you mean?' Marjorie interjected.

'Mmm . . . .' said Claude, musing to himself.

She wasn't letting it go. 'What do you mean "Mmm"?'

'Sorry, but the alibi's annoyingly perfect isn't it?'

Marjorie set off on a mini-rant.

'We're not doing very well are we? We've got one suspect in Alexander Kaplan who we still don't know enough about – that might be partly my fault. And we have a piece of Irish logic that says Andrew and Stephen Owen might be guilty because they couldn't possibly have done it.'

Claude got up and walked to the investigation board.

'I don't think you can say that any more,' said Mrs Woodbine.

'Say what?' asked Marjorie.

'Irish logic.'

'Can't you? Why not?'

Their debate about political correctness was interrupted by Claude who was staring at the board.

'That's it.'

'What's it?' asked Marjorie.

'Ireland. It's been staring us in the face.'

Marjorie and Mrs Woodbine looked at Claude, baffled.

CHAPTER EIGHT

They sat at their usual table in the corner of the pub. Constable Deacon was under siege from Marjorie and cradled his pint of Guinness, as if it might afford him some protection.

'But we all want the same thing, don't we Tom?' said Marjorie, insistently. 'We all want to find Audrey's killer.'

'Of course we do, Mrs Watson,' the Constable replied. 'But this remains a confidential police enquiry and I can't just throw open the police database for you. I'm sorry, I can't.'

'Confidential even for the Chief Superintendent here?' Marjorie persisted, trying to pull rank again. 'I mean, we only need a few tiny details investigating. A quick tippety tap tap on your computer and the whole thing's done.'

Claude intervened to save Constable Deacon further punishment. As far as he was concerned there was a simple way round all of this. He tried to reassure Marjorie.

'It's very straightforward, Marjorie,' he said. 'We'll just have to act as informants. We'll have to give the Constable here an old-fashioned tip off.'

The Constable shrugged, as if he thought that might work. Marjorie took a little more time to think about it.

'Police informants? Sounds very illicit and under-hand, doesn't it?'

She broke into a smile.

'I like it.'

Marjorie had finished her gin and tonic so Claude went off to the bar to buy another round. He took the opportunity to collect his thoughts while he waited to be served. His tip off was actually quite compli-cated. When he returned, Constable Deacon had his notebook at the ready.

'Okay,' Claude said, sitting back down. 'Can we begin with our German resident, Stephen Owen, please?'

Constable Deacon looked surprised.

'I'm sure you've been very thorough with his alibi,' Claude continued. 'I'm sure you're certain he hasn't entered the UK because you've checked every port of entry – airports, Channel Tunnel, ferry ports, everything.'

Constable Deacon raised his eyebrows, as much as to say 'I can't possibly comment, but yes.'

'But what about Ireland?' asked Claude, bluntly.

'How do you mean?' asked the Constable.

'What if Stephen Owen flew from Germany to Ireland?'

'Sorry, not following you, Chief Superintendent.'

'The border with Northern Ireland is soft isn't it? It's what all the Brexit fuss was about,' said Claude.

'So, Owen flies to, say, Dublin and makes his way to the border. Then he walks straight across without even needing to show his passport. Bingo, he's in the UK.'

The penny dropped with Constable Deacon. 'And there's no passport control on the ferry to Liverpool. Only photo ID. Damn!'

'Exactly. After that he makes his way to Fern Lea by train, coach, hire car, whatever. Bit of a palaver, I know. But not if you're aiming for a share of two and a half million pounds.'

Three days later, Claude and Marjorie were enjoying a lunch of poached salmon in the dining room at Fern Lea. They had been waiting impatiently for news from the police station and had now officially exhausted the subject of Audrey's murder. Claude was keen to move Marjorie on to a new subject.

'I'm sorry Marjorie,' he said. 'My life's become an open book, what with the "Psycho" thing and all. But what about you? I realise I don't know anything about Marjorie Watson before Fern Lea.'

'There's nothing much to tell,' she said, in a matter of fact tone. 'I had the same job for about twenty five years.'

'And what was that?'

'Oh, I was in the Diplomatic Service.'

Claude choked on his salmon. He took a moment to collect himself, with the aid of a glass of water.

'The Diplomatic Service? You're having me on.'

'I'm offended, Claude. Do you think I'm not bright enough?'

'Oh, you're more than bright enough, Marjorie. It's just that you're not really . . . how can I put it? . . . diplomatic enough.'

Marjorie thought about this. She pointed out that she had worked for the same diplomat for twenty years and he apparently always claimed to value her forthrightness.

'Did he?' asked Claude, still struggling with the story.

'Yes, he said I made a refreshing change from all the other over-educated bullshitters he had to work with.'

'And he actually called them over-educated bull-shitters?'

'Well, now I come to think of it that might be my phrase. But it was definitely what he meant.'

Mrs Woodbine arrived at the table. 'Are you two in the middle of something?' she asked.

'If I told you, you wouldn't believe me,' said Claude.

'Anyway, brace yourselves,' she went on, 'we've been summoned to the Chief Constable's office.'

'For what reason?' asked Marjorie.

'They didn't say. We'll set off in about half an hour if that's okay.'

Mrs Woodbine headed back to her office. As she left, Claude and Marjorie became aware that Arthur had been standing behind her, trying to listen in to the conversation.

'Any news Chief Superintendent?' he said, trying to look innocent.

'We're off to the police station shortly, Arthur. We'll let you know,' said Claude, not wishing to start a rumour.

To no avail. Arthur shuffled off with his Zimmer frame and almost immediately bumped into Margaret, going slowly with her walking stick in the other direction.

'There's been a development,' he said to her.

Margaret continued on and came across Doris, carrying a bowl of apple crumble and custard.

'Claude's made a breakthrough,' she said as they crossed paths.

Doris headed back to her table, passing Harry in his wheelchair.

'Claude's cracked it,' she said.

It was a beautifully orchestrated exchange. Almost balletic, in a slow-motion, Zimmer frame, walking stick, wheelchair kind of way.

Oblivious to the goings-on of his fan club, Claude set off with Marjorie to meet Mrs Woodbine. They drove to the police station and found themselves waiting in the Chief Constable's ante-room. The tense silence was punctuated by the noisy typing of his secretary.

Eventually, the door opened and out came Inspector Follett, with a face like thunder. He gave Claude and Marjorie a disdainful look before turning on his heel and striding off.

A moment later, the Chief Constable appeared at the door and ushered them into his office, where Constable Deacon was already waiting. No reference was made to Inspector Follett's abrupt departure. They all sat down on the sofas, except Constable Deacon who remained standing.

'Thank you all for coming. We have some news,' said the Chief Constable. 'First of all, it transpires that Constable Deacon has an informant. An anonymous informant.' He was clearly not best pleased that the informant's identity was being kept from him. He looked at Constable Deacon and then at Claude and Marjorie.

'I don't suppose you two would know anything about that, would you?'

'Absolutely not!' said Claude and Marjorie, accidentally together.

'Thought not,' said the Chief Constable. 'Anyway, it transpires the informant does actually know what he – or she – is talking about.'

Marjorie was still trying hard to look innocent.

'I'm pleased to tell you that, based on the information received, Stephen Owen was arrested yesterday in Germany for the murder of Audrey Patterson. He's now in our custody.'

'Excellent!' said Mrs Woodbine. 'It's not a serial killing after all, it's a proper old-fashioned murder. The residents will be delighted.'

'You're starting to sound like me, Mrs Woodbine,' said Marjorie.

Claude sat quietly, listening.

'Anyway,' said the Chief Constable, trying to get things back on track, 'perhaps you can fill in some of the details please, Constable?'

Constable Deacon consulted his notebook. He played back the fact that Stephen Owen had appeared to have the perfect alibi, not having passed through any UK port of entry. And he played back the suggestion about Ireland. Marjorie was now having trouble suppressing a grin

'Ireland? How would that have helped Stephen Owen?' asked Mrs Woodbine.

'It's the soft border, apparently,' said Marjorie, interjecting. 'You know, the Good Friday thingy.'

Mrs Woodbine looked none the wiser. To be honest, so did Marjorie.

Constable Deacon boxed on. 'A quick records check showed he took a Lufthansa flight from Munich to Dublin the day before Audrey Patterson's murder. And then a return flight to Munich the day after.' He consulted his notebook again. 'And then he made a further round trip that exactly coincided with the attack on the Chief Superintendent.'

The Chief Constable looked pleased. He couldn't resist joining in. 'You might also be interested to know, Claude, that he has a number of cuts and bruises to his head, including a particularly nasty gash over his left eye. And the DNA we recovered from your walking stick is . . . .' He picked up a lab report from the coffee table and handed it to Claude. '. . . . a perfect match for Stephen Owen.'

'Bravo Claude!' said Marjorie.

'Yes, bravo,' said Mrs Woodbine.

Claude looked pleased, although not exactly over-joyed. He put the lab report back on the table. He folded his arms.

The Chief Constable looked him up and down. He knew the signs.

'Okay Claude, what is it?'

'Sorry Peter, it's very good news. Congratulations to everyone. It's just that it's not even half the story yet.'

'Isn't it? We now know he was the murderer.'

'Of course. But I'm afraid that Stephen Owen had absolutely no motive himself for killing Audrey,' said Claude. 'He was hardly going to be mentioned in Audrey or Mrs Owen's will, was he? They both had restraining orders against him. What was he supposed to gain by the murder?'

'What are you suggesting?' asked the Chief Constable.

'Come on, Peter. Stephen Owen was doing the dirty work for someone else.'

'Who?'

'For his son, Andrew Owen, of course. The person who stood to make two and a half million pounds from Audrey's death.'

Marjorie was struggling to keep up with Claude. 'So Andrew Owen's perfect alibi is . . . .?'

'Entirely irrelevant,' said Claude. 'He wasn't the murderer so he didn't need an alibi. He was the mastermind.'

'And what evidence is there for that?' asked the

Chief Constable.

Claude paused. All of his instincts told him Andrew Owen was guilty but at the moment he had to admit he had precious few facts to back it up. He tried to impress the Chief Constable with what little he had. He told him about Andrew Owen's visit to Fern Lea one month before Audrey's murder and how, in Claude's opinion, he was playing the part of the dutiful grandson whilst actually checking out the CCTV and security arrangements in advance of his father's visit.

The Chief Constable looked sceptical. 'Anything else?'

'Well, Stephen Owen has been a drunk for the past twenty years so the chance of him working out how to tap dance around UK passport control is extremely remote,' said Claude, trying again. 'It had to be his son, the clever mathematician. I doubt Stephen Owen could even organise his own flights.'

'Hardly your strongest case,' said the Chief Constable.

A thought occurred to Claude.

'Constable Deacon, can I ask, have you checked Stephen Owen's bank account details? Did he actually pay for the flights?'

'I have,' said the Constable, 'and he absolutely did not pay for them. All of his credit cards are completely maxxed out.'

'See?' said Claude.

'Yes I do see,' said the Chief Constable. 'But it hardly proves Andrew Owen's guilt.'

'I'm sorry that Marjorie and I can't tie up all the evidence with a neat bow, Peter,' said Claude, frustrated and slightly cross. 'We don't have access to any of this financial information. Trust me, the answer will be in Andrew Owen's financial records, because it always is.'

The Chief Constable thought about this for a moment. His inclination was to trust Claude's instincts but he was frankly embarrassed by the lack of progress of Inspector Follett's squad. He swallowed what was left of his pride.

'Constable, presumably we have Andrew Owen's financial records?'

'I believe we do, sir. But I don't think the team has got round to, umm, processing them yet.'

'Shall we get round to processing them now?' he asked, tersely.

They decamped to the open-plan office where Claude and Marjorie had first been interviewed by Inspector Follett. Constable Deacon sat down at his desk and started up his computer. He linked it to the large TV screen on the wall and after a minute or so, Andrew Owen's bank statement appeared on the screen. Everyone peered at the screen as he scrolled up and down, examining the details.

'Well, for a student his bank account looks extremely tidy . . . .' said the Constable. He hovered the cursor over a number of items to highlight them. '. . . standing order to the University for rent . . . . food bills at the refectory . . . . books . . . . no large sums going in or out . . . .'

'Nothing out of the ordinary then?' asked the Chief Constable.

'Not that I can immediately see, sir.' The Constable started to scroll through again.

'Stop a second please, Constable. Who's that there?' asked Claude, pointing with his walking stick at an item on the screen. 'M O'Connor: £75?'

Constable Deacon peered at his own screen. 'Umm, it's a standing order I think. I'll request the details.'

They left him to it for a moment. 'What are you thinking, Claude?' asked the Chief Constable.

'Don't know. Bookmaker possibly?'

'Why on earth would you say that?' asked Marjorie, intrigued.

'Just another hunch I'm afraid, Marjorie. But given the family's problems with addiction, it wouldn't be surprising to find that Andrew had a weakness for the gee gees, would it? Plus he's a maths whizz. Probably believes he can beat the odds with an algorithm.'

Constable Deacon was still peering at his screen. 'He certainly hasn't beaten the odds. Mr O'Connor is indeed a bookmaker and Andrew Owen owes him . . . .'

Everyone looked at the big screen as the bookmaker's statement appeared.

' . . . . eighteen thousand pounds.'

'Heavens!' said Marjorie.

'Good grief!' said the Chief Constable. He turned to the next desk where a uniformed Constable was seated. 'Where's Sergeant Pearson?' he asked.

The Constable jumped up a scurried off to find him.

The Chief Constable turned back to talk to Claude but found him still staring intently at the TV screen. Constable Deacon had put Andrew Owen's original bank statement back on the screen and Claude was studying it quietly, ignoring all the commotion.

'And what about this one?' asked Claude, pointing at another item which read 'Miles and More: £40'.

'Also a standing order. I'm assuming it's a petrol station,' said the Constable.

'But who pays a standing order to a petrol station? Can we check, please?'

Constable Deacon looked to the Chief Constable for approval and he duly nodded. If he was being honest, the enquiry had slipped out of his control a while ago and it was a bit late to start worrying about procedure now. Results first, rules second.

Mrs Woodbine's phone rang noisily and she rummaged around for it in her handbag. 'I'm sorry, I'll take this outside,' she said, setting off for the corridor.

She passed Sergeant Pearson who was on his way in. He presented himself to the Chief Constable.

'Ah, Sergeant. The Audrey Patterson murder – Andrew Owen needs to be brought in for questioning immediately. Liaise with the Edinburgh police, please and . . . .'

Constable Deacon cleared his throat loudly, interrupting the Chief Constable and Sergeant Pearson.

They turned to look at him.

'I think you might as well just arrest him, sir.' He tapped a key and a credit card statement appeared on the big screen. 'Miles and More is not a petrol station, it's a credit card – actually it's Lufthansa Miles and More. And it's been used recently for four flights .... between Munich and Dublin.'

There was a stunned silence in the room, eventually broken by Marjorie.

'We're doing rather well, aren't we? And we haven't even got on to Alexander Kaplan yet,' she said, beaming.

By contrast, the Chief Constable looked as if his head might explode.

Claude noticed that Mrs Woodbine had come back into the room, putting her mobile phone away in her handbag. She looked a little upset and he asked if she was okay.

'No, I'm afraid not,' she said. 'That was Mrs Mayer ringing to let me know that Mrs Owen passed away in her sleep last night.'

'Thank goodness for that!' said Marjorie.

'Really Marjorie, you are the limit,' said Mrs Woodbine, crossly.

'No, I'm being serious for once. Mrs Owen had years of dealing with her daughter's addiction and her husband's abuse. Let's be grateful that she didn't have to face the fact that her son masterminded her mother's death.'

Everybody looked at Marjorie.

'Fair point,' said Claude.

CHAPTER NINE

'I thought murder debriefs were supposed to take place in a wood panelled library, with the famous detective confronting all of his suspects,' said the Chief Constable.

'I'm afraid you're going to have to make do with the Fern Lea way,' Mrs Woodbine replied. 'In the TV lounge, with Claude confronting his adoring fan club.'

She and the Chief Constable were standing at the back of the lounge which was full to bursting. Four rows of chairs had been set out and each one had been filled by an eager resident. The overspill area for wheelchairs was grid-locked.

At the front of the room, Claude and Marjorie's makeshift murder investigation board had been lovingly re-created. Every Post It note and every written detail had been painstakingly transferred from the disused bedroom wall to a whiteboard on wheels. Even the red line connecting Andrew Owen to the money had been added back in.

Marjorie sat to one side of the board, facing the audience. She was trying hard not to look pleased with herself.

Claude stood in front of the board, casually leaning on his walking stick. He began by briefly reminding everyone of the circumstances of Audrey's death. He hadn't got very far before Arthur put up his hand.

'Yes Arthur.'

'Thank you, Claude. Can you tell us why you didn't think it was a serial killing?'

Claude was expecting this. 'Well, from the start it felt to me that the motive for the murder was money and that turned out to be right. Also, as I keep saying, every other TV drama these days is about serial killing when in fact they're incredibly rare. In my old murder squad we used to joke that you could count the number of serial killers on the fingers of a dismembered hand.'

This produced a slightly bloodthirsty laugh from Arthur and some of his mates.

Claude turned towards the board. 'I mean, two and a half million pounds is an awful lot of motive. Admittedly, Andrew Owen had to pay his father a quarter of a million pounds for doing the dirty work and he had to pay Alexander Kaplan as well.' He pointed his walking stick at each of the co-conspirators as he mentioned them. 'Nonetheless, Audrey's murder was going to pay off all of his gambling debts and make him a very rich young man.'

Claude looked back at the audience. He seemed to have lost some people already. Harry put his hand up.

'Sorry Claude. Who's Alexander Kaplan?'

'A very unpleasant character,' said Marjorie, butting in. 'Audrey placed her trust in him and he repaid her by conspiring to have her murdered.'

'He was Audrey's tax advisor and she asked him to help her rewrite her will,' said Claude, taking over again. 'Given the terminal illness of her daughter, Mrs Owen, Audrey wanted to bring her granddaughter back into the settlement.' Claude pointed to Stephanie with his walking stick. 'So she asked Kaplan to tailor a trust fund for Stephanie and for Andrew, to share the estate.'

Claude looked at the audience again. They were sitting forward in their seats, straining to follow this rather complicated story. Violet had nodded off.

Claude explained that Kaplan had completely ignored Audrey's instructions. Instead he had gone straight to Andrew Owen and told him about his two and a half million pound inheritance and about the fact that he was going to lose half of it unless he acted quickly. Kaplan had then deliberately delayed the rewriting of the will while Andrew devised a plan to get his father to Fern Lea.

Claude was acutely aware of the fact that he sounded like he was delivering a lecture in criminology, with a bit of arithmetic thrown in. He decided to try and bring things back down to earth.

'But let's not forget there a few were mishaps along the way. I mean, Marjorie managed to get herself arrested and spent a night in the cells.' He smiled.

This attempt at honesty produced a slightly unexpected response.

'Well done, Marjorie!' Arthur called out.

'Excellent work, Marjorie!' shouted someone at the back.

Marjorie gave the audience a regal wave.

Claude pressed on with another attempt at self-effacement.

'And I haven't had the heart yet to tell Marjorie or the Chief Constable that I made a terrible mistake in the middle of the case. Almost got myself killed.'

'Wait, what?' asked Marjorie.

'Well, to be honest I had my suspicions about Andrew Owen from the word go so I thought I'd goad him, push him out of his comfort zone. See if I could get him to make a mistake.'

The Chief Constable looked on from the back of the room. He shook his head.

'Where? At the funeral?' asked Marjorie.

'Yes. When I was offering him my condolences I let him know that it was me who'd uncovered Audrey's murder in the first place and how dreadful it was. Then I managed to drop into the conversation the fact that I used to be a police officer. And for good measure I made him a promise that I would find the person who murdered his grandmother, come what may.'

'And the next thing you know he sent his father to suffocate you?' said Marjorie.

'I'm afraid so.'

'So, at the ripe old age of eighty you thought the best thing to help the case was to endanger your own life?'

'Sorry, Marjorie,' he said, expecting her and everyone else to be cross.

'Oh, I don't think there's any reason to be sorry.' She turned to Claude's fan club. 'Is there?'

Arthur started to clap, quickly followed by Margaret and Harry. Pretty soon, everyone was clapping and cheering. Zimmer frames and walking sticks were banged on the floor enthusiastically. There were a couple of unsuccessful attempts at whistling.

Marjorie, Mrs Woodbine and the Chief Constable were all applauding loudly.

Claude looked plain embarrassed.

Claude reflected on his strange time at Fern Lea. When he'd arrived he was still dealing with the after shocks of a fairly major stroke and he'd felt completely lost. Then he'd found himself caught up in, of all things, his friend Audrey's murder investigation. He knew it was a bleak irony, but he'd come out the other side of it almost completely rehabilitated.

He continued to pack his suitcase and he put in his iPad and his alarm clock. He closed the lid and zipped it up. He had one final look around the room and set off for the corridor.

Outside the door, Stephan Wisniewski stood waiting for him.

'Good morning, Claude,' he said. 'Can I carry that for you, please?'

'Thank you Stefan, that's very kind,' said Claude, handing over the suitcase.

Together, they walked along the corridor, into the entrance hall and out through the front door. Outside in the sunshine, Claude's son and daughter-in-law were waiting by their car. Mrs Woodbine and Marjorie stood to one side.

'David, Alice, thank you for coming,' said Claude.

'Not at all, dad. Can I take the suitcase?' David took it and put it in the boot of the car. Stefan shook hands with Claude and left.

Mrs Woodbine stepped forward. 'Well this is a first, Claude. I've never heard of anyone going back out of a retirement home before.'

'Unless it's in a pine box,' added Marjorie.

Everyone managed a laugh at this, dispelling the slightly awkward atmosphere.

'Seriously though,' said Mrs Woodbine, 'I know we got off on the wrong foot, but I'm very grateful for everything you've done.'

'Not at all Emily,' Claude said. 'Thank you for taking care of me.'

They gave each other a brief hug.

Claude turned to Marjorie.

'Marjorie, I think we deserve a hug, don't we?'

They gave each other a proper, big hug. Marjorie tried to hide the fact that she was welling up.

'Obviously, I'm going to come back and visit,' Claude said to Marjorie, 'but David and Alice reckon I should be moved into my new flat in a month so you can come and visit me.' He turned back to Mrs

Woodbine. 'Is it okay if Marjorie pops out every now and then?'

'Oh don't start that again,' said Mrs Woodbine, smiling.

'Claude, I know I don't always sound the world's most sincere person,' said Marjorie, 'but please take care of yourself. We're all going to miss you.'

Claude walked to the car and opened the back door. He turned back to Marjorie and Mrs Woodbine and blew them a kiss. David started the engine and Claude climbed in.

Marjorie and Mrs Woodbine watched in silence as the car set off up the meandering drive.

'I think we're going to need a lot of cheering up,' said Mrs Woodbine, eventually.

'Another murder. That's what we need,' said Marjorie.

PART TWO:
THE PENSIONER'S
SUPERPOWER

CHAPTER ONE

The examiner made a note on his clipboard as the Volkswagen Polo drove along at precisely thirty miles an hour. He looked across at the driver.

'In a moment, I'm going to ask you to perform an emergency stop,' he said. 'Bring the car to a halt as quickly as you can, please.'

They were driving along in a quiet housing estate and the examiner quickly looked over his shoulder to check for other cars. He waited for several seconds.

'Stop!' he said loudly, slamming the palm of his hand on the dashboard at the same time.

The car screeched to a halt with a suddenness that took the examiner by surprise. He shot forward violently against his seat belt and then slammed back hard against his seat. He took a moment to recover, pretending to adjust his tie.

'Thank you. Drive on, please,' he said, with a slight wobble in his voice.

Further down the road, the examiner requested a three point turn. This was followed by parallel parking. Both executed with geometric precision.

He gave directions back to the DVLA Centre and they eventually pulled up in the car park. He made a final note on his clipboard.

'Given the unusual circumstances of this driving test, I have thoroughly examined every aspect of your driving ability and could find no fault,' he said. 'I'm pleased to tell you that you've passed, Mr Simmons.'

Claude Simmons sat in the driver's seat, smiling broadly. 'Thank you very much. That's very good of you.'

Claude drove home, minus his L-plates. Inside his flat, he searched around for something to celebrate with and settled on a generous measure of single malt. He selected his favourite album, flopped down in an armchair and indulged a moment of quiet satisfaction.

David and Alice, his son and daughter-in-law, had helped him to find his new home and Alice had helped him to furnish it. It was a Victorian mansion flat with high ceilings and the light flooded in through huge sash windows. The living space had been converted into one large, open-plan room. It was solid and spacious and, six months after he had left Fern Lea, he felt settled.

The doorbell rang.

He heaved himself back out of the armchair and went to answer it. He was surprised to find Marjorie Watson and Emily Woodbine waiting on the doorstep.

'Marjorie, Emily, how lovely to see you,' he said.

'Do come in.'

They hung up their coats and settled themselves on the sofa while Claude went off to organise some drinks.

'Sorry to turn up unannounced,' Marjorie called out. 'We did try and ring earlier but you were obviously out gallivanting about.'

'Gallivanting? Not me,' he called back from behind the kitchen island. 'I was taking my driving test.'

'For a minute there I thought he said he was taking his driving test,' said Marjorie to Mrs Woodbine, loud enough for Claude to hear.

'That's exactly what he said,' she replied.

Claude reappeared with a gin and tonic for Marjorie and a cup of tea for Mrs Woodbine and set them down on the coffee table.

'Sorry to doubt you Claude,' Marjorie went on, 'but I thought they might have got the digits the wrong way round. I mean, you're nearly 81 not 18. Is it even legal?'

He told them that his doctor had been happy to write a letter saying he had effectively recovered from his stroke – he waggled both arms exaggeratedly to show he was no longer using his walking stick. That meant the DVLA were happy for him to retake the test. And he had passed.

Mrs Woodbine congratulated him. Marjorie was still frowning.

He sat back down in his armchair and picked up his glass of whisky.

'Anyway, enough of that,' he said. 'To what do I

owe the pleasure of you two's company?'

Mrs Woodbine sat forward on the sofa, looking anxious. 'I'm not sure pleasure is the right word. I'm afraid we bring news of another murder.'

'Heavens. What, at Fern Lea?'

'Thankfully, no.'

She outlined the details of the murder. The victim was apparently the cousin of an old school friend of Mrs Woodbine's. The body had been found unceremoniously dumped on a piece of wasteland. She'd been strangled.

Claude was immediately curious.

'Really? Strangled with what?'

'Well . . . . with . . . .' Mrs Woodbine squeamishly mimed putting her hands around someone's throat.

Claude was surprised. As far as he was concerned, anyone who strangled someone with their bare hands was almost certainly a gang member. It was what was usually referred to as a signature killing.

'Was she involved in anything illicit? Drugs? Prostitution?' he asked.

'No, no, quite the opposite. She was a fifty five year old widow living quietly on her own. The only thing she was involved with was the local church.'

'And the police?'

Mrs Woodbine explained that it was now two months since the murder and that the police had made little or no progress. There was very little information, but as far as she could tell they seemed to be treating it as a random and motiveless killing.

'Which is where we come in, Claude,' said Marjorie.

Claude sipped his single malt. Somehow he thought it might be.

'Obviously, Emily's friend has heard about our role in solving Audrey's murder,' she continued. 'She wondered if we could possibly help out with this case.'

'That's very flattering, Marjorie. But don't forget how hard it was to get the police to listen to us about Audrey's murder. And we were the ones that uncovered the whole thing.'

'I couldn't agree more, Claude. Which is why I've come up with an idea that means they'll have to take us seriously.'

Claude looked anxious. Marjorie paused for dramatic effect.

'We're going to start a detective agency.'

He opened his mouth but no meaningful words found their way out. Marjorie pressed on.

'I've taken the liberty of designing us a business card,' she said, producing a card from her handbag and presenting it to Claude.

It read, "Claude Simmons and Marjorie Watson. Partners in crime." He looked at Marjorie and then at Mrs Woodbine. He was still speechless.

'What do you think?' asked Marjorie, eagerly. 'I've included my phone number so you won't have to be bothered with any admin.'

Claude knew from past experience that he had two choices here: go along with it or risk a serious bust-up with Marjorie.

'I think it's an excellent idea, Marjorie,' he said, smiling bravely.

Claude tried to hand the card back but she snapped her handbag firmly shut.

'You can keep that one,' she said. 'I've had another five hundred printed.'

Mrs Woodbine tried to return the discussion to normality. She asked if Claude would be interested in taking on the case.

'What's your friend's name?' he asked.

'Edith. Edith Fairchild.'

'Perhaps we should pay Mrs Fairchild a visit.'

Claude arrived the next morning at Fern Lea in his Polo. He found Marjorie with her coat on, seated on a sofa in the entrance hall. She explained that they were waiting for Mrs Woodbine who was finishing something up. Claude sat himself down.

Almost immediately, Arthur came wandering by with the aid of his Zimmer frame.

'Morning Psycho!' he said, enthusiastically.

'Good morning Arthur!' Claude replied.

'Pleased to see that you two are an item now.' Arthur looked from Claude to Marjorie, smiling broadly.

'An item?' queried Claude.

'Or "partners" I think they call it these days.'

Marjorie intervened. 'No, no, no, Arthur. We're not partners in the lovey-dovey sense. We're partners in a detective agency.'

'Of course you are!' said Arthur, with a lascivious chuckle. He wandered off.

'This place, honestly,' said Marjorie. 'It's an absolute hotbed of gossip.'

'I know. I can't imagine who let the story out in the first place,' said Claude.

Marjorie was saved by the arrival of Mrs Woodbine. They all headed for the car.

They climbed into the Polo and set off. Mrs Woodbine sat in the passenger seat, busy with Claude's mobile phone.

'So, I'm programming the address into the satnav on your phone, Claude.' she said. 'If you have to come back, just look under Recent Journeys. There . . .'

She pressed the final button on the screen and after several seconds the satnav spoke.

'Continue on the current road.'

Claude thanked her, having not entirely followed what she'd said.

Mrs Woodbine rested the phone in one of the coffee cup holders. She turned to face Claude and Marjorie.

'So the victim's name is Rosemary Fuller and it's her house we're going to. My friend Edith will meet us there.'

Marjorie wrote Rosemary Fuller's name down in her notebook. She asked why the house hadn't been sold yet.

'Because everything's frozen while the police investigation is on-going,' said Mrs Woodbine. 'Edith is the executor but there's nothing she can do.'

'In half a mile, turn left,' the satnav interrupted.

'And is Mrs Fairchild pleased she has a detective agency working for her?' asked Marjorie.

The truth was, Mrs Woodbine had told her friend that Claude and Marjorie might be able to help with the case but she had left out the bit about the detective agency. It was somehow too difficult to explain, not least because the agency was going to be run by two octogenarians.

'To be honest, I think she's a bit, umm, confused by that. But she's very pleased to be getting some help,' said Mrs Woodbine, trying to be as diplomatic as possible.

'Perhaps she's concerned it might cost money,' Marjorie persisted. 'I think we should make it clear it won't cost her a penny. I'm sure Claude agrees, we're going to do this pro .... umm, what's the phrase? .... pro-bonio.'

'I think you mean pro-bono,' said Mrs Woodbine.

'Do I?'

Claude was listening to this exchange with interest. 'I used to have a dog once,' he said in a dead-pan voice. 'He was very pro-Bonio.'

Mrs Woodbine tried to suppress a snigger.

'Bugger off the pair of you,' said Marjorie.'

'Your destination is ahead,' said the satnav.

They pulled up in front of a terrace of houses where they found Mrs Fairchild waiting.

She led them inside to what was a modest house which, if not run down, was starting to look a little threadbare. They made their way into the lounge and she invited everyone to sit down while she opened the blinds.

'Sorry, the house has been shut up for two months,' she said, releasing a cloud of dust which hung in the air as the late autumn sunshine streamed in. She settled herself into an armchair and addressed Claude and Marjorie.

'And after two months I'm afraid we're no closer to finding Rose's killer. I'm grateful for you coming today but do you really think you might be able to help?'

Mrs Woodbine intercepted the question before Marjorie could get a word in.

'If I can speak for Claude and Marjorie, I think they are keen to do whatever they can, Edith.'

Marjorie got a word in anyway.

'And we've got a one hundred per cent track record at the moment,' she said, enthusiastically.

Mrs Fairchild looked confused.

Claude intervened. He was keen to find out the circumstances of Rosemary's death. He asked Mrs Fairchild if the police thought that Rosemary had been murdered there, in her own house.

'Well they haven't ruled it out but I don't think they really know,' she answered.

'No signs of a disturbance then?'

'I don't want to be critical of the police but there are no signs of anything, anywhere.'

Claude moved on to his favourite subject: motive. He asked if Rosemary had had any problems recently. Or major disagreements with anyone.

Mrs Fairchild shifted in her chair. 'Ah, that's where I haven't been much use, I'm afraid.'

She explained that she and her husband had been in Australia for the six weeks immediately before the murder, on a long planned trip to see their son and his family. That meant she hadn't been able to have any of her normal heart-to-hearts with Rosemary. If there had been a problem, she hadn't been there to hear it. She seemed quite upset about it.

Claude allowed her a moment before continuing. He asked if there was anyone else she might have confided in.

'You could try the vicar,' she said. 'Rose was church warden at St Michael and All Angels. Oh and there's some strange business about the vicar's car being involved in all of this. You'll have to ask him for the details I'm afraid.'

Marjorie made a note in her notebook.

Claude was keen to hear about Rosemary's finances and about who stood to benefit from her death.

'Well, nobody really,' said Mrs Fairchild, flatly. 'They weren't able to have children and, in any case, there really isn't any money. Rose struggled financially after her husband died and she was doing a couple of part-time jobs just to make ends meet. There may be some value in this house but it rather depends on what we can get for it. The mortgage is very large.'

Marjorie asked about Rosemary's will.

'There is no will so whatever there is passes to her next of kin,' said Mrs Fairchild.

'Which is you?'

'No, which is her mother.'

Claude and Marjorie were both surprised by this. They looked enquiringly at Mrs Woodbine.

'Her mother?' asked Marjorie.

'Yes, Mabel. Rose's mum, my aunt.'

'Sorry!' interjected Mrs Woodbine. 'That's why I'll never make a detective. I completely forgot to mention her mother with all the other stuff going on. I mean, she's so obviously not the murderer.'

'Indeed,' said Claude. 'But where is she? What's her situation?'

'She was living in a bungalow about a mile away which meant Rose could keep an eye on her,' said Mrs Fairchild. 'She suffers from vascular dementia, poor old thing. But she had seemed to be just about struggling by.'

'And now?' asked Claude.

'As ever with these things, Rose's death has revealed just how serious the dementia is and there's no way she could carry on living on her own. Fortunately, with Emily's help I've been able to get her into a good residential home nearby. We're about to put the bungalow on the market to help pay for it all.'

'Could we visit her if we need to?'

'Of course, but I'm not sure I'd recommend it. When I go she asks me at least five times where Rose is and I don't have the heart to keep telling her over and over that she's dead. I've had to start making things up.'

'I see. I'm sorry,' said Claude.

Mrs Fairchild got up from her armchair and walked over to the bookshelf, keen to move on to something less upsetting. She took down an over-stuffed box file, releasing more dust into the air.

'On a more positive note,' she said, 'let me give you some things you might find useful. These are Rose's financial records – bank statements, mort-gage papers, everything. The police have finished with them so you're welcome to have them.'

She took down a smaller, ring-bound folder. 'And these are her mother's finances. Have a look through them. You never know.'

Marjorie stood up straight away and took the folders. 'I'll have those, thank you Mrs Fairchild. Fo-rensic accountancy is more my area than Claude's.'

Everybody stared at her.

'What?' she asked.

CHAPTER TWO

Claude sat on the sofa in his lounge. He was wearing a white linen shirt, black linen trousers and a pair of sandals. In his right hand he held a wooden staff of about five feet in length. He tapped the staff distractedly on the floor.

The doorbell rang.

Claude picked up his keys from the bowl in the hallway and opened the door. Outside stood his Aikido teacher. It was hard to determine his age but he had a shock of grey hair, tied up neatly in a top knot. He was similarly dressed to Claude and he carried an identical staff.

'Good morning, Shihan,' said Claude, addressing his teacher by his correct title and bowing slightly.

'Come on then,' replied the Shihan, in a voice that was more Glaswegian than mystically Eastern. 'Let's get on with it.'

Claude closed the front door behind him and they walked down the stairs and out into the communal gardens which surrounded the mansion flats. They made their way to the centre of the lawn, turned towards each other and bowed deeply.

They took up a position side by side and began

their routine. Claude mirrored the actions of his teacher as they started slowly, reaching forwards and backwards rhythmically with their staffs. The tempo gradually quickened and the movements became more complex and demanding.

They finished with a considerably faster, more staccato routine, appearing to parry the blows of an imaginary foe and responding with jabs and thrusts. This was only Claude's third lesson. He was already good at it.

'In one mile, turn left,' said Marjorie.

They were driving through the countryside the next day. Marjorie was peering at a map that was spread out in front of her.

'Can I ask?' said Claude. 'When you decided on "Partners in crime" as our slogan, did you have any other ideas that you rejected?'

'I did, let me think. There was "Simmons and Watson. With 160 years of experience." You know, you're in your eighties, I'm in my eighties. Might have made a bit too much of the age thing, though.'

Claude turned left onto another country road. Marjorie peered at the map again. 'Continue on the current road,' she said.

'You're starting to sound like the satnav, Marjorie,' said Claude, rather pleased with his observation.

Marjorie looked at him disdainfully over her

reading glasses. They continued on their current road in silence for a while.

Eventually, Claude ventured forth again. 'Any other slogans?'

Marjorie thought about it. 'Ah yes. "Simmons and Watson. The new, improved Holmes and Watson". That was my favourite but unfortunately it was a bit too long to get on the business card.'

Claude found himself driving along with both eyebrows raised. ' "Partners in crime" it is then. Good choice, Marjorie.'

A church spire appeared ahead. They drove towards it and pulled up opposite a large maroon sign with gold lettering which read "St Michael and All Angels Church". They had rung ahead and the vicar met them at the lych gate. They introduced themselves and the three of them set off for a walk around the churchyard.

'Had Rosemary seemed particularly anxious or agitated about anything?' asked Claude, getting the ball rolling.

'Well, she had the on-going concern about her mother, of course,' the vicar replied. 'The dementia certainly wasn't getting any better and Rose knew she was putting off the decision about residential care. Was she a little more preoccupied than usual? . . . . possibly.'

'Frightened about something perhaps?'

The vicar shook his head emphatically. 'Given Rose's situation, it's very easy to see her as a timid little thing but she really wasn't. She had a very strongly developed sense of right and wrong and you soon knew about it if she disagreed with you.'

'How, for example?'

'Well, her most recent crusade had been to get the church to open a women's refuge. It's hard to believe but there are increasing problems in town with, ahem . . . . sex trafficking.'

Claude was surprised. He asked if the rest of the parish council had agreed with her.

'Not all of them, I'm afraid. We had an extremely spirited debate about it and, how can I put it? . . . . Rose ganged up on the rest of us.'

They reached a bench under the shade of an enormous old yew tree. They sat down. Marjorie took the opportunity to get her notebook out. She asked about the vicar's car being involved in the murder.

'We believe it may have been but we're not really sure,' said the vicar. 'Rose asked my wife and me if she could borrow it and of course we said yes.'

'And what happened?'

'You tell me. The next thing we knew she was dead and the car was missing. The police eventually found it three days later.'

'Where?' asked Claude, sitting forwards.

'Parked in a service station on the M4, I believe.'

He pondered this. 'And what did the police say?'

'Nothing at all, I'm afraid. They kept it for about a week and then it was simply delivered back by a police Constable. No explanation whatsoever.'

Claude frowned. He was confused by the lack of information from the police. He could see no reason why everyone should be kept so much in the dark.

They chatted a while longer and then walked back to the lych gate.

'Thank you so much for seeing us, vicar,' said Marjorie, handing him one of her business cards. 'Please don't hesitate to ring me if you think of anything else.'

Claude and Marjorie set off back to Fern Lea. The vicar was left staring at the business card. Partners in crime? He shook his head.

'Are you starting to develop one of your theories?' asked Marjorie on the way back.

'Not yet, I'm afraid – there's still a lot to take in.' said Claude. He was worried about Marjorie jumping to lurid conclusions about sex trafficking. Perhaps Rosemary had stumbled into something like that but his instincts told him they should be starting their investigation somewhere closer to home.

'I have a hunch that Rosemary's mother and her dementia will be tied up with this somehow,' he said. 'If there's no point in visiting her in person, why don't we take a trip out to her bungalow tomorrow? Might be a good place to start.'

'Good idea,' said Marjorie. 'I'll alert Mrs Woodbine.'

He dropped her back at Fern Lea and she spent the evening sifting through the financial documents Mrs Fairchild had given her. When she'd been working, she'd looked after the business and travel expenses of not only her boss but also of the whole section he supervised. Needless to say, most of them were on the fiddle, as a matter of course. That meant that, while she was certainly no forensic account-ant, she had an eye for spotting when things didn't quite add up.

The next morning, Claude duly arrived back at Fern Lea. He found Marjorie and Mrs Woodbine seated on a sofa in the entrance hall. Marjorie was wearing her coat.

'Taxi for Marjorie Watson,' he said.

'Very droll, Claude.' she replied.

'Yes, good morning Claude,' said Mrs Woodbine, business-like as usual. 'Now, Edith popped over with the key to the bungalow this morning.' She handed him the key which had a name tag attached to it. 'The address is on the tag so just programme that into your satnav.'

Claude looked at the name tag and then at Mrs Woodbine. He frowned.

'Ah, you haven't used the satnav yet, have you?' she asked.

'Not as such,' said Claude.

'It's very straightforward. Just pop in the post code and it does everything else for you.'

Half an hour later, Claude and Marjorie were parked in a layby as the traffic thundered past on a busy dual carriageway. They were both staring at Claude's phone.

'Make a U-turn immediately,' said the Satnav.

They limped on for a while and eventually found themselves at a crossroads, somewhere in the middle of nowhere. They stared at a road sign which offered them a choice of four possible directions.

'You have arrived,' said the satnav.

They gave up and resorted to Marjorie's tried and trusted map reading. Eventually, they made it to the bungalow.

'Shackleton is turning in his grave,' she said, unlocking the door.

The bungalow was gloomy and in need of airing. In the lounge, Claude drew back the curtains and he and Marjorie began a methodical examination of the room. They studied the framed photos, took down books from the bookshelf and peered into the sideboard.

'By the way, I finished going over all the financial documents that Mrs Fairchild gave us,' said Marjorie.

'Good. Anything interesting?' asked Claude, blowing the dust off an old black and white photo.

'Rose's stuff just confirms the picture of her struggling to make ends meet. I could find nothing untoward – no strange payments or huge debts or anything like that.'

They moved into the bedroom. Marjorie opened the curtains and Claude turned his attention to the wardrobe.

'But Rose's mum's accounts are an entirely different story. In the months before Rose's death she was taking out quite large sums on a regular basis.'

'How large?' asked Claude.

'Hundreds of pounds on occasion. Much more than she could afford.'

They moved into the kitchen.

'I'm afraid she'd made a serious dent in her savings. Hard to think that Rose hadn't spotted it.'

'And nothing to suggest what she was spending it on?'

Marjorie opened the cutlery drawer. 'No, I'm afraid not. Always cash withdrawals.' She pulled out a handful of bent and misshapen knives and forks, all with yellowing handles. 'But I think we can safely assume she wasn't spending it on the house.'

They worked their way back to the front door having found nothing of any particular interest. Marjorie retrieved the key from her handbag and opened the door. Claude hesitated.

'Sorry . . . . I feel like I'm missing something,' he said, turning and walking back into the lounge. Marjorie followed him.

He looked around the room and then laughed. 'We're literally missing something,' he said, pointing to a length of aerial cable lying on its own on the carpet. 'There's no television set.'

Marjorie stared at the cable. 'Perhaps there's been a burglary?'

'Somehow I don't think so,' he said.

Marjorie locked the front door and they walked back down the path towards the car. They immediately bumped into a lady carrying a bag of shopping who was about to cross the road. She stopped.

'Hello,' she said. 'Are you relatives of Mabel?'

'Well, more like friends of the family,' said Claude, trying not to give too much away. 'We're just looking over the bungalow before it's put on the market.'

'I'm Marion Grey, by the way. I live opposite,' she said, putting down her shopping for a moment.

Claude and Marjorie introduced themselves.

'It's a shocking business, isn't it? I mean, what with Rose and all,' Mrs Grey continued.

Claude agreed. He asked if she and Mabel were friends.

'Oh yes. We'd both lived here for years and years. Poor old girl hadn't been herself for a long time, though.'

'How do you mean? Forgetful?'

'To say the least. And it was starting to get a bit out of hand.'

'In what way?' asked Marjorie.

Mrs Grey pointed to Mabel's front garden which, in truth, was the size of a postage stamp. Apparently, Mabel had had a gardener working on it every other day.

'Why?' asked Claude.

'You tell me, he didn't even do a very good job. Just taking advantage of her we all thought. Rose was very upset about it. She couldn't get any sense out of Mabel so she came over to my house a couple of times to . . . . well, to spy on the gardener.'

Claude and Marjorie exchanged a glance, surprised.

Unfortunately, Mrs Grey had no idea how interesting her revelations were to Claude and Marjorie.

As far as she was concerned she was just idly gossiping. She picked up her bag of shopping again.

'Anyway, I can't really stop, my peas are starting to defrost,' she said. 'Nice to have met you.'

She set off across the road to the house opposite leaving Claude and Marjorie hanging in suspense.

They drove back to Fern Lea with Claude lost in thought for most of the way. Eventually, they arrived at the front gate.

'I'll come in for five seconds if I may,' said Claude. 'I want to have a word with you and Emily together, if that's okay.'

'About Mrs Grey?' asked Marjorie.

'Oh no, about something else.'

'As you wish,' she said, intrigued.

They found Mrs Woodbine in the conservatory and the three of them sat down together. Claude got straight to the point.

'I think this is going to be a very long and complicated case and there's a great deal of work ahead of us,' he said.

'Oh dear,' said Marjorie. 'You're not getting cold feet are you?'

'Not at all. But I have a practical concern that you and I are going to spend our lives in the car, travelling between Fern Lea and my flat, Marjorie. So I'm just going to say it: I've got a very nice spare room and I think it would be much more sensible if you came and stayed with me until the case is solved. You can think of the flat as the headquarters of the detective agency.'

Mrs Woodbine broke the silence that followed this bombshell. 'I think it's an excellent idea. We'll have to cover things off with a bit of paperwork but I see no problem apart from that. Marjorie?'

In truth, Marjorie was excited by the suggestion but thought it was inappropriate to appear too keen. She had a brief go at clambering up onto the moral high ground.

'It might be a good idea but I do have my reputation to think of. I've only just stopped everyone gossiping about us after we formed our partnership, Claude. They seem to have finally forgotten about it.'

At that point, Lorna and Sylvia, two of the residents, came walking round the corner.

'Ah, here's the two love birds,' said Lorna, beaming at Claude and Marjorie.

'It's wonderful to have a proper romance at Fern Lea. People talk of nothing else,' said Sylvia.

They continued on, leaving Claude and Mrs Woodbine staring at Marjorie.

She went off to pack.

Half an hour later, Claude opened the front door to his flat and wheeled in Marjorie's suitcase. He headed for the spare room. Marjorie followed behind but paused in the doorway. She peered into the umbrella stand, searching for Claude's old walking stick.

'I'm sure you'll agree that we're going to have to start as we mean to go on, Claude,' she said.

Claude stopped in his tracks. 'Are we?'

She fished out the walking stick and held it aloft.

'I've been meaning to say this for a while: you're going to have to start using your walking stick again.'

He reminded her that he was fine and had no need of it anymore.

'It's not a question of needing it. It's actually part of your brand, Claude – it's one of those icon thingies.'

She thrust the walking stick into his hand. 'We have to think about these things now that we're running a business.'

'Welcome to the flat, Marjorie,' said Claude.

CHAPTER THREE

Marjorie stood at the window watching Claude and his Shihan walk out into the centre of the communal gardens. She was fascinated. They turned to face each other and bowed deeply. She gave a little bow herself. They began their routine with each using his staff to parry imaginary blows, first from the right and then from the left. It all seemed to take place in elegant slow motion.

Marjorie picked up her handbag and attempted to mimic the movements. Unfortunately the bag was large and made of soft leather and flopped around limply as she tried to swing it backwards and for-wards. She looked around the room for something to weight it down. On the window ledge she spot-ted one of those artistic arrangements of polished stones, precariously balanced in a pile (a design flourish by Claude's daughter-in-law). She took the largest stone, which you could be forgiven for think-ing was a small boulder, and placed it in her hand-bag.

She tried again to mimic Claude and the Shihan. They were now parrying blows and then thrusting forwards. She swung the handbag back a short distance to one side and then swung it forwards again. Much better. She tried it on the backhand. Perfect.

Her confidence buoyed, she drew the bag back as far as she could and then swung it forwards with considerable gusto. Unfortunately, she had entirely underestimated the centrifugal force created by the weight of the stone and it swung her round, like an Olympic hammer thrower. The bag crashed into a wicker fruit bowl on the nearby table and sent the apples and oranges flying into the air.

In the garden, Claude and the Shihan continued their exercises serenely, oblivious to Marjorie's mayhem.

Later that evening, the two detectives were sat in the lounge, Marjorie with a gin and tonic and Claude with a glass of beer. Claude was wrestling with a problem. Thirty years ago, he would have had a squad of twenty officers to help him work every aspect of the case. Now there was just him and Marjorie and a distinct lack of options.

'Is everything alright?' asked Marjorie, eventually.

Claude came to from his reverie. 'Yes, sorry. I'm just trying to work out a way to move this forward.'

'And?'

'Well, I've got a plan but unfortunately . . . .'

'What?'

'Unfortunately, it puts us slightly in harm's way.'

Marjorie was delighted.

'Do go on,' she said.

Claude asked her if they still had the key to the bungalow.

'Yes, I've got it in my handbag.'

'Well, I think you and I should spend a few days there, perhaps. See what happens.'

Marjorie was intrigued. Did he actually mean they should move in?

'Well, pretend to move in,' said Claude. 'My instinct is that this gardener or one of his mates will be back quite quickly when they get wind of some new prospects.'

Marjorie pondered on this. What were they supposed to do when the gardeners actually arrived?

'I think we should just play along and let them think we're a soft touch, like Rose's mum.'

'Act as if we're senile, you mean?' asked Marjorie.

'Well, yes, we ought to be able to do that, didn't we?' said Claude with a wry smile.

Marjorie was too busy contemplating her upcoming acting role to be offended.

'Let's be honest,' he continued, 'the gardeners were simply taking advantage of Mabel's absent mindedness. They came back day after day and charged her for gardening work they probably weren't even doing.'

Having worked her way through Mabel's finances, Marjorie couldn't disagree.

'I doubt they had any qualms about completely cleaning her out,' Claude continued. 'I bet that's where the television's gone. Yet more payment for gardening.'

'Oh lord,' said Marjorie.

'Quite. Which is why we must take no risks with these people. They are potentially very dangerous,' said Claude, emphatically. 'Will you promise me that please Marjorie?'

'Of course, Claude.'

She absolutely intended to follow Claude's advice.

They set off for the bungalow bright and early the next morning. Claude remained anxious. In truth, he could see no way of making progress on the case except by them planting themselves right in the middle of things. But, notwithstanding Marjorie's bravado, it was undoubtedly risky. He also had a nagging concern about Mrs Woodbine. She had secured the bungalow key for them in good faith and, well, they were now taking advantage of that. Shouldn't they have tried to explain their plan to her? He weighed things up and decided not to pester Marjorie any further with his concerns for the moment. By way of light relief, he tried an entirely different conversational tack.

'You never talk much about your husband, Marjorie,' Claude said. 'What happened to him?'

She looked at him, surprised.

'There's a reason I never bring him up,' she said, bluntly.

'Which is?'

'Which is that everyone automatically assumes I

drove him into an early grave. It's bloody rude.'

In Claude's defence, he was only half-thinking that.

'Actually, we had a very happy marriage,' she continued. 'But then, out of the blue, he had a massive brain haemorrhage, about a year before he was supposed to retire. Very sad.'

'I'm sorry,' said Claude. 'And what happened?'

'Well, they put him on a machine for a while but there was no real hope. In the end, I had to switch him off.'

Claude had to admire Marjorie. Even when she was talking about an act of undoubted kindness, she had the knack of making it sound magnificently heartless.

They arrived at the bungalow and set about trying to make it look inhabited. They drew back all the curtains, opened a window in every room and left the front door ajar. Claude found a recycling box in the back garden. He filled it with old newspapers and copies of the Radio Times from Mabel's magazine rack and placed it on the pavement next to the front gate. Eventually, they settled themselves down in the lounge.

'Our first stake-out,' said Marjorie, enthusiastically. 'Now what?'

'We just wait, I'm afraid,' said Claude, ignoring the fact that it wasn't strictly speaking a stake-out.

It quickly transpired that Marjorie wasn't very good at waiting. She drummed her fingers loudly on the side table. She spent about half an hour trying to get comfortable in the armchair. She fidgeted endlessly and sighed loudly.

'How about a cup of tea?' asked Claude after a while, keen to relieve the tedium. They had a brought a bag of provisions with them, including milk, tea bags and a Tupperware box of tuna sandwiches. He disappeared off into the kitchen to boil the kettle and eventually returned with two mugs.

'I'm not sure police work is all it's cracked up to be,' said Marjorie, sipping her tea.

'Patience, Marjorie, patience,' said Claude.

'I'd be a lot more patient if Rose's mum hadn't sold the television,' she said, grumpily.

Somehow, what with lunch and an afternoon doze for Marjorie, they managed to struggle their way through to six o'clock. They closed all the windows and drew the curtains. They left the hall light on, locked the front door and headed back to Claude's flat.

The next morning they were back again at eight o'clock sharp.

'It's a bit like Hawaii five-O but without the beaches, isn't it?' said Marjorie sarcastically as they traipsed back up the bungalow's path.

This time they had brought a portable radio with them and a pack of cards, in addition to their bag of provisions.

Claude plugged the radio in and tuned it into

Radio Four. They sat down and listened to the last hour of the Today programme followed by Desert Island Discs. Marjorie repeatedly disagreed out loud with the radio and Claude eventually turned it off.

He disappeared into the kitchen to make a cup of tea. Marjorie got up and went to the window to check for possible visitors. Nothing. When she had finished her tea, she went to the front door to peek out. Nothing. Bored, she delved into the bag for the sandwiches. She opened the Tupperware box and offered it to Claude.

'Cheese and tomato?'

'I would, thanks, but it's only half past ten,' he said.

Eventually, they settled on a game of "Snap!" into which Marjorie was able to put all of her pent up frustration.

Outside, a white van was driving past. The driver spotted the recycling box and pulled up at the kerb. He leant across the passenger seat and peered out, surveying the bungalow's open door and windows. He put the van back into gear and drove away.

'Snap!' said Marjorie loudly, making Claude jump.

On day three, they found themselves back in the lounge, tuned into the Today programme again. Even Claude was starting to feel a bit bored. He lasted until Woman's Hour and got up from his armchair. He picked up his walking stick.

'Right, I'm going to do something useful for once,' he said. 'I'm going to nip over the road and have another chat with that lady – Mrs Grey is it? I'd like to know a bit more about Rosemary spying on her mother. Back in a minute.'

'Of course,' said Marjorie, engrossed in Woman's Hour.

He set off across the road and knocked on the door. Mrs Grey seemed pleased to have a visitor and invited him in.

'Would you like a cup of tea?' she asked. 'The kettle's already on.'

'Well, I can't really stop . . . .' said Claude, worrying about Marjorie being on her own. 'But okay, yes please.'

She disappeared off into the kitchen leaving Claude to size up the excellent view of the bungalow from Mrs Grey's bay window. This had been Rosemary's vantage point for observing the gardener.

'What brings you back here then?' she called out.

'I didn't want to say too much before,' Claude replied, 'but my friend Marjorie and I are investigating Mabel's daughter's murder.'

Mrs Grey emerged with the tea tray and set it down on the dining table at the back of the room. She looked a bit surprised.

'Really? I don't want to sound rude but aren't you both a bit old for detective work?'

'Well, it's a long story . . . .' said Claude.

They sat down at the table, out of view of the bungalow. Mrs Grey poured.

Meanwhile, Marjorie was still listening to the radio, joining in loudly with the interviewer and the contributors.

There was a knock at the door.

She sat up with a start and reached over to turn the radio down. Her mind raced. She knew that Claude would not have wanted her to answer the door. But what was the problem, really? She just needed to act a little bit absent-minded and she had more than enough friends at Fern Lea to base her performance on. What could possibly go wrong?

There was a second, louder knock. She got up and walked purposefully to answer it.

'Can I help you?' she said, affecting a voice that sounded as if she wasn't entirely with it.

Opposite her stood a man in his late twenties. He was scrawny and unshaven and dressed in jeans and a T-shirt. Parked behind him in the road was his white van.

'I help you, I hope,' he said, his English uncertain.

'How's that dearie?' asked Marjorie, getting into the part.

'I look after garden for Mabel, lady before.'

'Yes, that's my cousin. She's had to go in a home now, poor old girl – gone a bit soft in the head I'm afraid. And what's your name?'

'Is Grigor.'

'Grigor? Very unusual. I shan't forget that dearie.'

Across the road, Mrs Grey had brought out a plate of chocolate digestives and she and Claude were deep in conversation.

'Rose came over two or three times,' she said. 'The last time, she got very agitated.'

'Did she? Any idea why?'

'Well, the gardener was at Mabel's, as he always was. Then a second man arrived. For some reason this seemed to really bother Rose.'

'Any idea who he was?'

'No. She wasn't giving anything away but she clearly knew him. I just assumed he was the foreman or something, checking on the gardener's work. But I'm afraid I'm guessing.'

Back at the bungalow, Marjorie and Grigor had moved out into the garden, deciding on the work that needed to be done.

'I'd like to be looking after the garden myself,' said Marjorie, 'but the doctor says I shouldn't be lifting anything heavier than a cup and saucer.'

'Is okay. I come tomorrow with equipment, make everything nice.'

'That's very kind of you . . . . er, what's your name dearie?'

'Is Grigor,' he said, now convinced he'd found another soft touch.

'Ooh, that's very unusual. I shan't forget that.'

Claude put down his tea cup. He had stayed too long and got up to leave.

'Thank you very much Mrs Grey, that's very helpful and . . . . oh, for heaven's sake!' Through the bay window, he was confronted by Marjorie and the gardener standing next to the white van, shaking hands. 'Claude, you stupid idiot!' he said.

He was forced to wait until the gardener had driven off and then he rushed out of the front door and down the drive. Mrs Grey appeared in the doorway behind him.

'If you'd like to come back and do a bit of spying yourself then you're more than welcome,' she called out.

Claude and Marjorie drove home largely in silence. Back at the flat, Marjorie tried to muster a defence.

'I don't understand why you're quite so cross, Claude,' she said.

'Because we discussed it Marjorie and specifically agreed we wouldn't put ourselves in harm's way.'

'But I don't think I did. You saw him – if he's the strangler then I'm Brigitte Bardot. In any case, I didn't have much choice. If I hadn't answered the door then he might have been gone for good. Then where would we be?'

Actually, this was a fair point. Claude made his way to the kitchen and poured them each a drink. He handed Marjorie a gin and tonic by way of a peace offering. He had to admit that he was probably mostly cross with himself. He had allowed himself to be waylaid by Mrs Grey's chocolate digestives.

'You worry too much, Claude,' said Marjorie. 'Don't forget that I played Portia in my school's production of the Merchant Of Venice, to very good critical reviews. The gardener is entirely under my spell.'

◆ ◆ ◆

Marjorie took her card from the cash point and waited for the money to come out. She put everything in her handbag and walked back to the car. She got in.

Claude indicated and pulled out. He had been stewing on the day ahead and was unable to hide it from Marjorie. She, by contrast, didn't seem to have a care in the world.

'Can we at least agree a couple of rules, please?' he asked.

'If we must.'

'Firstly, please do not allow the gardener, or anyone else for that matter, into the bungalow under any circumstances.'

She agreed.

'And secondly, if you're in the slightest bit worried about anything, simply walk away. Just walk across to Mrs Grey's where I'll be waiting.'

'Okay, dearie.'

Claude looked at her, askance.

'Sorry, just getting into character,' she said.

They arrived at the bungalow. Marjorie went inside and settled herself into an armchair. She started to play a game of Tetris on her phone, becoming more and more animated as the pieces sped up. She lost quite quickly.

'Bugger,' she said out loud.

Claude had walked across the road to Mrs Grey's.

He took up residence in the bay window, with his old Leica camera around his neck. Mrs Grey had brought him a cup of tea.

'Thank you for putting up with all this inconvenience, Mrs Grey,' said Claude.

'Wouldn't miss it for the world,' she replied, looking over Claude's shoulder nosily.

Half an hour later, the white van arrived and Claude snapped a picture of it. Grigor got out and walked to the front door. He knocked and Marjorie eventually answered the door, appearing to be confused.

'Can I help you?' she said.

'Yesterday, we speak about garden,' Grigor replied.

'Did we? Well, it does need doing, I suppose.'

He set off to unload the equipment from his van and Marjorie went inside to make him a cup of tea. He pulled out an old petrol engine lawnmower and yanked several times on the starting rope. It sprang noisily into life.

He ran it backwards and forwards several times over the tiny expanse of grass and then stopped. He kept the engine running but pulled out his mobile phone and started to scroll through his messages.

'Told you. Not exactly Percy Thrower is he?' said Mrs Grey, looking on.

Eventually, Marjorie returned with the tea and Grigor quickly put his phone away and turned off the lawn mower.

'There you are, two sugars wasn't it?'

He looked at the cup. 'Er, no sugar.'

'Oh, sorry dearie. Anyway, nearly finished?'

'All done today. Tomorrow I come finish everything more. Is forty pounds today.'

'Ooh, you have worked hard. I'd better get my handbag.'

Claude and Mrs Grey watched from across the road as Marjorie went back inside.

Grigor immediately tipped his tea into the flower bed. After a minute, Marjorie returned with her handbag.

'How much, dearie?'

'Is forty pounds.'

Claude took several photos as Marjorie counted out the money and handed it over. Grigor loaded the lawnmower back into the van and drove off down the road.

Claude jumped up immediately and hurried out of the front door to watch the van go. Surprised, Mrs Grey followed him. The van went no further than a hundred yards down the road and then stopped again. Grigor got out and walked to the van's back door. He pulled out the lawnmower.

'Thought so. Another unsuspecting customer,' said Claude.

Mrs Grey looked on.

'Oh dear . . . . Mrs Davis. I said hello to her in the street the other day and she didn't recognise me.'

After locking up the bungalow, Claude and Marjorie drove back to the flat, discussing the events of the day and the plan for tomorrow. Claude had been developing a new strategy.

'I may come to regret this . . . .' he said.

'What?'

'Well, I think we need to gather as much evidence as we can. So, after your man Grigor has done his five minutes work tomorrow, I think we should try a bit of extra surveillance.'

'How do you mean?'

'Sorry, I think we should follow him.'

'Excellent!'

CHAPTER FOUR

It was approaching lunchtime the next day and there was still no sign of the gardener. Claude sat in his usual seat in Mrs Grey's bay window. Mrs Grey looked over his shoulder, nosily.

'Do you have a local pizza delivery service, Mrs Grey?' Claude asked.

She looked surprised. But yes, she did.

'Well, can I treat us to pizza today please, as a thank you for all your hospitality?'

'There's no need Claude. But I'll get the menu.'

Half an hour later, a moped with a large pizza safe on the back pulled up outside. The driver rang the doorbell and Claude set off for the front door.

Desperate not to miss anything, Mrs Grey stepped forward and peered round the side of the bay window. She watched as Claude took the two pizzas from the delivery man and gave him twenty pounds. Then he appeared to ask him a question and the man nodded. Claude gave him another twenty pounds. Then there was a further question, a further nod and twenty pounds more. Sixty pounds for two pizzas?

At the bungalow, Marjorie had had a busy morning of Tetris, Candy Crush and Angry Birds. She had tucked into a late lunch of ham and pickle sandwiches and Hula Hoops, with an apple for afters. Feeling tired, she stretched out on the sofa for just a moment and fell asleep.

She was woken by a loud knock at the door. She took a second to come round and eventually got up. When she opened the door, she saw that Grigor had already gone back to unload his van. She went to the kitchen to make some tea.

Grigor started by roughly pruning a shrub with a pair of shears. Claude was watching from across the road and could see no discernible difference in the shrub once he had finished. He gave a second shrub the same cursory treatment. Claude snapped a photo.

Grigor stopped and checked his messages for some time before moving on to a rose bush. He deadheaded a couple of old flowers, leaving a number of others still in place. He made no attempt to clear up the rubbish. He eyed up two wilting geraniums and wondered whether to bother with them or not.

Marjorie re-appeared carrying a mug. 'Here's your tea, Gregory. One sugar, wasn't it?'

'Is Grigor. And no sugar.'

'I know, dearie. Nearly finished?'

'All garden done. Very tidy,' said Grigor, now bluffing brazenly.

'I'm sure it is – your eyes are much better than mine. What do I owe you?'

'Is one hundred and twenty pounds.'

'Crikey!' said Marjorie, almost slipping out of character.

'Is special price. Not come back til two weeks.'

Claude snapped another picture as Marjorie produced her handbag and paid the gardener. He counted the money before climbing into his van and driving off.

Claude said a quick goodbye to Mrs Grey and went off to sit in his car. Further down the road he could see that the gardener had stopped at Mrs Davis's again. He was taking out the lawnmower from the back of his van.

Marjorie arrived and got into the passenger seat.

'Good work, Marjorie,' said Claude. 'How much did he charge?'

'Have a guess,' she replied.

'Double. Eighty pounds.'

'Nope, treble. But he says he won't be back for two weeks.'

Claude scoffed. 'Two days more like.'

The pizza delivery man arrived on his moped and parked in front of the car. He gave an exaggerated nod with his crash helmet to Claude and Marjorie.

'Who's he nodding at?' said Marjorie.

'Oh don't worry. He's working for us,' Claude explained.

'Is he? I've already had lunch.'

'No, no, he's going to run a bit of interference for us – make sure your gardener friend doesn't spot we're following him. It's an old police trick.'

Further down the road, Grigor had already finished his work and he got back into his van. As he drove away, the pizza delivery man started his moped and set off in pursuit. Claude followed suit and they trundled along to the traffic lights at the end of the road.

The lights changed and all three turned left onto the main road. The moped drove right behind the van and Claude hung back a little. Grigor was oblivious to the fact that he was in a makeshift convoy.

After about a mile, the delivery man decided he should ring the changes and overtake. He waited deliberately until the van was about to pull out and pass a row of parked cars. This made it dangerously tight for the two of them with the oncoming traffic but the moped got its nose ahead and, in a classic pizza delivery man manoeuvre, he cut sharply across in front of the van. Grigor was forced to slam on the brakes.

The delivery man hadn't finished yet. Now in front, he slowed right down and rode one-handed while he struggled to retrieve an address from his back pocket. The van pulled out to overtake but the moped veered violently across the road. Grigor sounded the horn and shook his fist.

'I'm enjoying this,' said Marjorie, watching from the safe distance of Claude's car.

The moped was now doing about ten miles an hour and the delivery man was still driving one-handed. He held the address in his other hand and studied the houses passing by, apparently trying to read their numbers. He weaved from side to side erratically.

Fortunately for Grigor, his turning eventually appeared. He signalled left and turned onto a quieter road, bringing the pizza delivery man's brilliant performance to an end. Claude, who had been about fifty yards back, turned left and followed the van.

They hadn't gone very far on the new road when an old banger aggressively overtook Claude, causing him to swerve slightly. It had about eight spotlights attached to the front grille and an enormous spoiler hanging off the boot. As it went past, its air horns played "La Cucaracha".

'What on earth is that?' exclaimed Marjorie.

'Don't worry,' said Claude. 'That's the pizza delivery man's brother. He works for us as well.'

The old banger took up a position right behind the van. It was starting to get dark and Grigor switched on the van's headlights. There was a brief pause and the old banger switched on its array of spotlights. Temporarily blinded, Grigor was forced to grab the rear view mirror and twist it away from his eye line.

They drove on like this for some time with Grigor cursing angrily to himself. The houses along the road began to give way to farmland and eventually he slowed down and signalled right. He turned onto an unmade road leaving the old banger to accelerate away, playing one last rendition of "La Cucaracha" as it went.

Claude and Marjorie pulled up briefly at the junction with the unmade road. They watched the van bump along through the potholes and then turn off into what looked like it might be a floodlit caravan site where a number of other vehicles were already parked. Claude put the Polo back into gear and drove a short distance until he found an entrance to a farmer's field. He pulled the car off the road and parked next to the gate.

They both set out across the grassy field in the encroaching darkness and Marjorie switched on her phone torch. Claude was on his phone as well but appeared to be typing something.

'This is hardly a time to be checking your messages, Claude,' said Marjorie, picking her way carefully through the field and trying to avoid cow pats.

'No, sorry. I'm just trying to put this location into my satnav. You never know.' He stopped for a moment while he completed the task. 'There, I've done it. Wonders will never cease.'

Marjorie turned off her torch as they approached a scraggy hedge which bordered the floodlit area. They peered through the hedge and realised that what they had thought were caravans were actually two large, static mobile homes. They stood in front of some old, derelict farm buildings and were surrounded by wonky stacks of wooden pallets, piles of hardcore and several abandoned fridges.

There were four white vans, including Grigor's, parked in front of the left hand mobile home. A smart looking black van with tinted windows stood in front of the other home.

As they watched, a fifth white van arrived. The

driver got out and went up the steps and into the left hand home. Raucous laughter spilled out briefly.

'Well, you did say it was a gangland killing from the word go,' said Marjorie. 'Don't six vehicles constitute a gang?'

Claude had brought his camera and was fiddling with it, making sure the flash was switched off.

'Possibly, but it's a gang of gardeners at the minute, isn't it?' he said, snapping a photo of each of the number plates. 'I can't quite make that add up. No-one gets strangled over a gardening dispute, do they?'

At that moment, the door to the right hand mobile home opened and two girls tottered down the stairs in high heels and not a great deal else. They were heavily made-up and it was hard to tell their age. Claude's guess was that they were fourteen or fifteen at the most. He took their picture. They were followed out by a man in a dark suit, very possibly their minder. The girls clung together nervously as he ushered them into the black van. He drove them away.

'How about getting strangled over a child prostitution ring?' asked Marjorie, pointedly.

She set off to circle round the back of the mobile homes to see if they could see anything more. Claude followed her reluctantly.

'Must we?' he hissed, struggling to clamber through a hole in the hedge. He tried to enlarge the opening with his walking stick and only succeeded in tangling his jacket in the thorns.

'You know we must,' Marjorie hissed back, pressing on ahead.

Out of range of the floodlights, they worked their way along stealthily to the back of the first mobile home. Through the picture window they could clearly see the merry band of bogus gardeners, with Grigor very much at the centre of things. They were all drinking beer and regaling each other with stories, doubtless of how easy it was to defraud little old ladies of their savings. They looked very pleased with themselves. Claude snapped a photo of each of them.

They moved on to the second mobile home. Inside, it was an entirely different story. There were four more girls, as heavily made up as the two who had just left and almost certainly all teenagers as well. They sat huddled together on a bed, clinging loosely to each other and staring vacantly at a portable TV. Another minder sat with a magazine on his lap, rolling a joint.

Claude thought he knew his way around the average gang. He'd dealt with drug rings, protection rackets and even organised prostitution. But in his day, people trafficking and child prostitution were almost unheard of. He snapped photos of everyone. He had to admit, he was shocked.

They stumbled back to the car and set off for Claude's flat, pondering on just how suddenly their little investigation had escalated.

'Well, that rather changes things, I'm afraid,' said Claude eventually.

'Oh dear, does it? I was just starting to enjoy myself.'

'We've got to be realistic, Marjorie. We're certainly looking at prostitution, probably child prostitution and very likely sex trafficking. We're miles out of our depth.'

'I suppose you're right, but I'm a bit confused. Now that we're seeing the full extent of it, how does it fit together with gardening, exactly?'

This particular aspect of gang organisation was not new to Claude. Seeing the whole picture, he knew that the gardening would just be a training ground for the new recruits. Gangs always had training grounds.

'In this case,' he said, 'you impress the boss with the amount you can bring in from defrauding little old ladies and, bingo, you get to play with the big boys.'

'And the young girls,' observed Marjorie, dryly. She gazed out of the window. 'So all of this means we're going to have to give up?'

Claude thought about this. 'No, I think we probably need one more visit from your friend Grigor to complete our little bit of the investigation. Three incidents of fraud from him make a compelling case. That means you've got time for one last virtuoso performance, Marjorie.'

Neither of them noticed the cash point as they drove past it.

'But after that we need to call it a day,' Claude continued. 'We need to collect up all the information and all the photographs we have and hand them over to the police. Agreed?'

'Agreed.'

CHAPTER FIVE

D ay six at the bungalow and intense boredom had set in. Marjorie got up from her armchair and turned on Radio Four.

'. . . and now it's time for thought for the day with the Right Reverend Basil . . . .'

She turned it off abruptly. She went and made yet another cup of tea and sat and read the paper for a while. She tried the radio again and re-tuned it to another station.

'German Bight, Humber – south westerly veering north westerly, six to gale eight, squally showers, mainly good . . . .'

She turned it off again. She tried the crossword but without a great deal of success. She dealt out a game of Patience but lost interest in it almost immediately. She gave the radio a last go and re-tuned it to Radio One.

' . . . . D J won't even play my jam, cos I am an enemy, if I wasn't then why would I say I am?'

Rap. She turned the radio off and unplugged it.

Day seven and Claude sat staring out of Mrs Grey's bay window. Having slightly run out of conversation, he had given Marjorie's business card to Mrs Grey to read and she looked at it with a puzzled expression.

'Partners in crime? Doesn't that mean you're actually the guilty ones?'

Claude was about to attempt a lengthy justification of Marjorie's slogan but was saved by the arrival of the white van. He watched Grigor walk up to the bungalow's front door and knock. Marjorie came to the door.

'Can I help you?' she said.

'I gardener. Is two weeks since I do work.'

It was two days not two weeks, just as Claude had predicted, and Marjorie had to try hard not to get cross with him.

'If you say so, dearie. I'm losing track of the days.'

Grigor set to work and this time Claude decided to make a list of what he actually did:

1 Starts lawn mower.

2 Runs lawn mower back and forwards across lawn twice.

3 Consults mobile phone for ten minutes.

4 Clips four leaves off shrub.

5 Pulls up two weeds.

6 Consults mobile phone again.

7 Deadheads one single rose flower.

8 Puts lawn mower back in van.

After what could only have been fifteen minutes at best, Grigor went back to the front door and knocked. Marjorie reappeared.

'Ooh, sorry dearie. I forgot to make you a cup of tea.'

'Is no matter. Garden all finish now.'

Marjorie disappeared inside for a moment to get her handbag. 'What do I owe you, dearie?'

'Is two hundred and fifty pounds for everything.'

'Ooh, I don't think I've got that much,' she said, taken aback. She rooted through her handbag but the truth was she had completely forgotten about getting more cash out from the cash point.

'I might have a bit put by somewhere in the house if you come back later,' she said, playing for time.

'I help look now,' said Grigor, stepping forwards.

Mindful of Claude's rules, Marjorie stood her ground in the doorway. 'No you can't come in. My late husband always used to say never let any strangers in the house. No offence, dearie.'

'My boss say no credit,' Grigor countered.

'I'm sure he does. I know what, I'll walk over to my neighbour Mrs Grey and she'll run me to the cash point. That's the best idea.'

Marjorie was trying her hardest but it was starting to get very awkward.

Grigor gestured towards his van. 'I take you cash point. Very safe.'

'Oh no, I don't want to be any more trouble, dearie.'

'Is no trouble, please.'

Across the road, Claude had got to his feet. He watched as Marjorie walked back to the bungalow's front door and locked it.

'What's she doing?' he said, to no-one in particular.

She walked towards the van. Grigor held the passenger door open for her and she got in.

'No Marjorie, No, NO!'

Claude rushed to the front door as the van disappeared off down the road. He scurried to his car, leaving Mrs Grey looking on in disbelief. He threw his walking stick on the passenger seat and set off in pursuit.

He reached the traffic lights at the end of the road and saw that the van had already turned right. He put his foot down as the lights changed and sailed across on amber, tyres squealing. He tried to catch up with the van but they were approaching the town centre and before he could do anything about it there were three cars between them. Up ahead, the van turned left at another set of traffic lights leaving Claude stranded as the lights turned red.

'No. no!' he said, again to no-one in particular.

After what seemed an age, the lights turned green and Claude turned left, urgently scanning the road ahead for any sign of the white van. He drove on for a while before he spotted it some way ahead, parked in front of a bank. Marjorie and Grigor were already out of the van and had arrived at the bank's cash point.

Marjorie delved into her handbag and pulled out her purse. Unbeknown to her, she accidentally pulled out one of her business cards as well and it fell on the pavement. She turned her back on Grigor deliberately, took her credit card from her purse and put it in the machine.

'Sorry, I don't want you seeing my pin number, dearie,' she said, trying to keep her acting performance up in the increasingly difficult circumstances.

Grigor bent down and picked up the business card from the pavement. He read it slowly, not quite believing what he saw. He took out his phone and dialled the number on the card and after several seconds the phone in Marjorie's bag began to ring. Flustered, she reached into her bag to find the phone but Grigor ended the call.

'Sorry, must be one of those nuisance people,' she said, as the ringing stopped.

The machine finally dispensed the cash and Marjorie put it in her purse.

Claude had parked about four cars back and was half out of the car when he saw Marjorie and Grigor heading back to the van. He was forced to get back in and start the engine.

In the van, Grigor started the engine and set off up the road. After the revelation with the business card at the cash point, he paid particular attention to his rear view mirror as he drove. He watched as Claude's car pulled out and settled in behind him. Grigor turned left and watched the car follow him. He turned right and watched the car follow him again.

Suddenly, he put his foot down and accelerated away as fast as the van would go.

'Ooh, bit quick, dearie,' said Marjorie.

Grigor took no notice and sped towards a set of traffic lights. They turned red when he was still some way off but he ignored the signal and threw the van violently left at the junction. The tyres squealed and the gardening equipment crashed around in the back. Several cars had set off from the other side of the lights and had to take evasive action, sounding their horns angrily.

Claude arrived at the red light and was forced to stop.

Marjorie was gone. He slammed his fists on the steering wheel.

'Damn, damn, DAMN!'

It took him a moment to collect his thoughts but then he reached into his pocket and produced his mobile phone. He tapped away furiously at the screen but he only had one bar of signal and the phone was very slow.

'Come on, come on!' he said.

The traffic lights turned green and the car behind politely beeped its horn. Claude ignored it and continued on with his phone, scrolling down in search of something. More car horns joined in.

'Okay, okay!'

Finally, he found what he was looking for and pressed the screen, just as the green light turned amber.

'Turn left,' said the satnav.

Claude threw the phone on the passenger seat, put the car in gear and turned left, using up the last millisecond of the amber light. He left behind a cacophony of car horns.

Grigor was a little out of his league. He had effectively taken Marjorie prisoner on the spur of the moment but now had no idea what to do with her. Instinctively, he had driven to the derelict farm for help but when they arrived the mobile homes were both deserted. Worst of all, Marjorie herself was proving to be completely unmanageable. She seemed not to be in the slightest bit frightened and happily followed him into the mobile home, largely so she could continue to harangue him. She had scrapped her acting performance and reverted to full-throttle Marjorie.

'Grigor, have you thought this through?' she asked. 'At the moment, you just keep adding years to your prison sentence with everything you do. Conning money out of old ladies. Kidnapping old ladies. Hoping to graduate to a bit of sex trafficking, are you?'

Grigor decided his only hope was to phone the boss. He pulled out his phone and scrolled through the numbers.

'Quiet. I make call,' he said, trying to sound tough.

'Good idea,' said Marjorie. 'Phone the strangler. He'll definitely know what to do.'

He dialled the number and put the phone to his ear. He put his other hand out to Marjorie to signal her to be quiet and turned away from her.

Marjorie saw her chance. Grasping her handbag with both hands, she swung it backwards a little and then swung it forwards. She did it a second time, feeling the rhythm. Then she took aim at Grigor and swung it back as far as she could. . . .

'Is Grigor. Big problem.'

. . . . and swung it forwards again with all her might. It hit him squarely on the back of the head, making a hollow noise rather like a coconut being dropped onto a stone floor. He crumpled forwards and crashed down with a bang which made the mobile home shake.

Marjorie had no time to be either pleased or shocked about what she'd just done. She inched past Grigor's prostrate body and hurried out of the door. She rushed past the white van and started back down the unmade road, going as fast as her eighty year old legs would carry her. By the time she eventually got to the country lane she was seriously out of breath and had to stop for a moment.

Back in the mobile home, Grigor moaned and lifted his head off the floor. He tried to sit up.

Marjorie looked up and down the lane and tried to decide which way to go. She saw a car parked a short distance away on the left with two men inside. They seemed to be watching her. Not taking any more chances, she turned right and set off up the lane, huffing and puffing with the effort.

Grigor had managed to struggle to his feet. He took a moment to regain his balance and then stumbled down the caravan steps and into his van. He started the engine.

Marjorie managed about another fifty yards but after that could go no further. She was absolutely out of oxygen. She looked back down the lane anxiously and saw a vehicle speeding towards her.

'You have arrived,' Claude's faithful satnav had said as he screeched round the corner, narrowly missing the parked car. He saw Marjorie up ahead and drove on, skidding to a halt next to her. He leant across and opened the passenger door.

'Quick! Get in! Get in!'

Marjorie fell into the car and Claude accelerated away, spinning the wheels slightly as he did so. They drove on with Marjorie still fighting to get her breath.

Claude was extremely agitated. 'Thank God, Marjorie. Are you okay?'

'I'm fine thank you Claude, never better,' she said, eventually. 'Poor old Grigor might have a bit of a headache, though.'

Marjorie removed the large stone from her handbag. She replaced it on the windowsill and tried to pile all the other stones back on top of it. Half of them slid off immediately. She tried again with even less success.

'Bugger,' she said, abandoning the attempt and walking back to the sofa. She sat down next to

Claude.

Chief Constable Selby had been waiting for this little performance to finish. He stood with his arms folded, crossly.

'Would there be any point in lecturing you about taking such absurd risks?' he asked.

Marjorie looked totally unrepentant.

'In Marjorie's defence . . . .' Claude started to say.

The Chief Constable cut him off. 'I was talking about both of you, Claude. Correct me if I'm wrong but not six months ago you were goading someone into suffocating you with a pillow.'

Claude looked chastened by this. Marjorie did not.

'See, we're as bad as each other, Chief Constable,' she said defiantly. 'But the thing is we get things done, unlike the police. How many months have you been on the Rosemary Fuller case?'

The argument was interrupted by Acting Sergeant Deacon. He had been standing in the kitchen, talking on his phone.

'Sorry sir, but uniform have searched the two mobile homes and it seems everyone's gone. The whole site has been completely cleared out.'

'Good job we've already found you some proper evidence, then,' said Marjorie. She picked up a folder from the coffee table and handed it to the Chief Constable. She explained that it contained the details of Grigor's activities and the money he'd been demanding, plus the vehicle registrations of him and the rest of his aficianados.

'And photographic evidence of what to us looks

like a child prostitution and trafficking ring,' added Claude.

'Really? Very impressive,' said the Chief Constable. 'We'll see if we can pass it on to the investigating team.'

Claude was taken aback. Which investigating team was he talking about?

'This is not our case, Claude. Never has been. It's part of a big on-going Regional Crime Squad investigation that we're supposed to know nothing about.'

Claude frowned. He was trying to put the pieces together in his mind.

'I suppose that explains something,' he said. 'When I found Marjorie in the country lane there were two men in a parked car watching us. Police officers if I'm any judge. But not two of yours, then?'

'Absolutely not,' said the Chief Constable. 'The Regional Crime Squad took control of the Rosemary Fuller murder immediately and we've been told to mind our own business. I have no idea what they're thinking or what they're doing. It's an information black hole, I'm afraid.'

'But you must know something about it, Peter?'

'Only what I hear. The gossip confirms most of what you've been saying – that it's a gang involved in child prostitution, human trafficking, and perhaps drugs.'

'Don't forget gardening,' said Marjorie, making a half-decent attempt at irony.

Claude ignored her. He asked if the Chief Constable had any idea who was running the investigation.

'That I do know,' he replied. 'It's our old mate Charlie Wainwright.'

'Is it indeed? Well, well – grumpy Charlie. He's not going to be best pleased when he finds out we've wandered onto his patch.'

'Probably not. But for the minute, I'm more worried about this gang. Assuming there's a gang master somewhere, he's just been made to look a complete fool by an eighty year old woman. I doubt he's going to take kindly to that.'

Everybody looked concerned except Marjorie. She looked thoroughly pleased with herself.

CHAPTER SIX

Claude and Marjorie emerged from the local Tesco having stocked up after their extended manoeuvres at the bungalow. They set off slowly up the road, Claude carrying a shopping bag and Marjorie towing a basket on wheels. They retraced their steps to the flat.

After a while, Claude stopped to look in a shop window. He appeared to be looking at his reflection in the glass. He straightened his tie. He wasn't normally this vain and Marjorie looked at him curiously.

'Thought so,' said Claude.

'Sorry?' she said. 'Thought what?'

'I had my suspicions on the way here, but now I'm certain.'

'Well go on. What?'

'Don't look now but we're being followed.'

Somehow, Marjorie managed to resist the urge to turn round.

'How exciting. By who?' she said.

'As far as I can tell, it's your old friend Sergeant Deacon.'

'Is it? Why on earth would he be following us?'

'Because the Chief Constable is worried about our safety, I should think,' said Claude.

Marjorie pondered this for a second.

'What, you mean we've got a bodyguard? How posh!'

Back at the flat, Marjorie went off to put the kettle on. She emerged with two mugs of tea, handed one to Claude and then set off for the front door.

'Where are you going?' asked Claude.

She explained that she was taking a mug of tea out to the Sergeant. Claude pointed out that they weren't supposed to know he was there.

'I know, it'll be just like that scene in Los Angeles Cop,' said Marjorie, grinning.

'Do you mean Beverly Hills Cop?'

'Exactly!'

She made her way downstairs and out into the street. She found Sergeant Deacon sat in his car, parked a little way up the road. She tapped on his window and he reluctantly wound it down. He didn't look at all pleased to have been discovered.

'Don't look so worried, Tom, it's only a cup of tea,' said Marjorie. 'I'm not going to ram a banana up your exhaust pipe.'

'Sorry?' said the Sergeant, confused.

'It's a film reference. You're probably too young.'

'Right, yes.'

'And tomorrow, don't spend the day out here on your own,' she added. 'Come up to the flat. You're supposed to be looking after us anyway, so why not?'

The Sergeant thought about this. Now that he'd

been discovered he could see no reason not to follow Marjorie's advice.

Bright and early the next morning, he was duly seated on the sofa in Claude's flat. Marjorie had gone off to the kitchen to make them each a coffee. She returned with two mugs and a plate of shortbread biscuits. She sat herself down on the sofa.

'Claude's got a Feng Shui lesson this morning so you and I can have a good chat, Tom,' she said.

Claude was in his bedroom getting ready, but not out of earshot. 'It's Aikido, thank you Marjorie,' he called out.

There was a knock at the door.

'And that'll be my teacher. Will you let him in, please?'

Marjorie disappeared off to the door. She quickly reappeared, being marched backwards across the room by the rapid approach of a large and unpleasant looking man. He carried on marching until she bumped into the sofa and fell back onto it. He was followed into the flat by three equally unsavoury looking men.

Marjorie, needless to say, was undaunted by her rough treatment.

'Claude, you might like to know that four thugs have just walked in,' she called out, casually.

A number of things then happened quite quickly.

Claude emerged from the bedroom, doing up his last shirt sleeve button. He quickly took in the scene and reached out for his walking stick which he'd left hooked over the kitchen worktop.

Sergeant Deacon jumped up from the sofa and produced his warrant card from his back pocket. 'I'm a police officer and you all need to leave immediately,' he said, urgently.

Thug number one took a step towards the Sergeant and shoved him hard in the chest. 'And if not?' he said, contemptuously.

At which point, Claude's Shihan arrived, wooden staff in hand.

'If not, we'll have to politely show you out,' he said in his broad Glaswegian accent. He smiled benignly.

Rashly, thug number four decided to up the stakes by pulling out a knife and brandishing it at the Shihan. This was a serious tactical mistake. The Shihan struck him two lightening quick blows to the side of the head with his staff, followed by a sharp upward blow to the groin. He groaned audibly and bent double, dropping the knife on the floor. The Shihan kicked the knife under the table.

This was the cue for a general free-for-all.

Thug number one threw a punch at Sergeant Deacon who managed to duck inside it and land a hefty right cross in return. Followed by a straight left. The thug staggered backwards, knocking over a table and the plate of biscuits.

Thug number two lunged at Claude who managed to parry the blow, using his walking stick as if it was an Aikido staff. In the background, he could see that his Shihan's staff was a blur as he set about thugs three and four simultaneously.

Marjorie, meantime, got up from the sofa and quickly scurried off behind the kitchen's island unit. If it looked like she was taking refuge, she most certainly wasn't.

Frustrated, thug number two lunged at Claude even harder. He overreached and lost his balance as Claude deftly parried the blow again. He hooked his walking stick under the thug's trailing leg and yanked it sharply upwards. The thug crashed to the floor, landing in a potted plant.

Marjorie stepped forward with a saucepan and banged him hard on the head. She briefly considered a high-five with Claude but thought better of it.

The assailants decided to cut their losses. They picked each other up and limped out of the front door. The Shihan stepped aside politely to let them go.

Silence descended on the room. Claude, Marjorie and Sergeant Deacon looked at each other, shocked. By contrast, the Shihan looked like this was just a normal day's work.

'That's coming along nicely, Claude,' he said, in his Glaswegian accent. 'I'll see you same time next week.' He turned and left.

They set about clearing up the damage and standing the over-turned furniture back up.

'That was impressive Tom,' said Marjorie, picking up the broken biscuits.

'Thanks. I boxed a bit at university and at . . . .'

He was rudely interrupted by the arrival of three more people. Claude's lounge had turned into Piccadilly Circus. They walked straight in through the open front door, uninvited, and stopped in the middle of the room.

'Hello Charlie,' said Claude. 'I was wondering when we might see you. How are you?'

'Bloody annoyed Claude, thank you,' he replied. 'And it's Chief Inspector Wainwright now.'

Marjorie was unimpressed by the Chief Inspector's grand entrance.

'If you're the cavalry then you're a little bit late, I'm afraid. We've just been attacked by four very unpleasant characters.'

'Perhaps that's because you've wandered right into the middle of an on-going Regional Crime Squad investigation,' the Chief Inspector responded, forcefully. 'Do you realise how much damage you've done?'

'We're all fine Chief Inspector, thank you,' said Claude, pointedly.

Marjorie eyed up Wainwright's two companions. She recognised them.

'And while we're at it, it was nice of your officers to sit and watch the other day while an eighty year old lady was being kidnapped. Very decent of them.'

Wainwright ignored Marjorie and turned to Claude.

'Do I really need to lecture you about the way this goes, Claude? You and your best mate here have very nearly blown a two year undercover operation. If you continue I won't hesitate to charge you both – wasting police time, obstruction of justice or anything else I care to think of. And I don't give a toss if you're eighty or a hundred and eighty.'

Sergeant Deacon drove Claude and Marjorie to Fern Lea. He had informed the Chief Constable about the fight at Claude's flat the previous day and had been told to continue with his protection duty and to leave the four thugs to the Regional Crime Squad. He had also told him about the abrupt arrival of Chief Inspector Wainwright himself. This had been greeted by complete silence from the Chief Constable.

Marjorie leaned forward from the back seat. She had a question for Claude.

'Not a great deal of love lost between you and Chief Inspector Wainwright, then?'

Claude shrugged.

'Can I ask, were you his commanding officer?' said Sergeant Deacon.

'I was,' said Claude. 'He and your boss the Chief Constable were in my squad at the same time. And that was the problem really.'

'How do you mean?'

'You might be surprised to know, Tom, that Chief Constable Selby was an enthusiastic adopter of our old philosophy of results first and rules second. He knew how to take a risk did Peter. But I'm afraid that Charlie Wainwright had no time for the rules at all.'

Marjorie looked surprised. She asked if Claude

was suggesting that Wainwright was corrupt.

'Oh no, not at all,' said Claude. 'But he always knew best. And he was extremely hot headed. I lost count of the number of suspects who accidentally fell and banged their heads while Charlie was questioning them.'

'So what happened?' asked Marjorie, intrigued.

'What happened is that when it came time for promotions, I chose Peter Selby and not Charlie Wainwright. Not really a difficult decision. But one that Charlie took rather badly.'

Sergeant Deacon pulled into Fern Lea's drive. He wound down the window and pressed the intercom. The gate opened and they drove through.

Marjorie gazed out of the window at Fern Lea's beautiful grounds.

'Remind me again why we're going to see Mrs Woodbine?' she asked, confused.

'Because we need the key to Rosemary Fuller's house. I feel like we're missing something and I want to have a good look round, just to make sure.'

'But I thought we were off the case?' said Marjorie.

Claude hadn't taken kindly to he and Marjorie being threatened by Wainwright the day before. Given their past history, it had sat badly with him and had only served to strengthen his resolve.

'Off the case? Whatever gave you that idea?' he asked.

Sergeant Deacon raised his eyebrows.

'Pleased to hear it,' said Marjorie. 'But I think that means we're going to have to come clean with

Mrs Woodbine about the bungalow and all the, you know, goings on.'

Claude was still feeling bad about their deception but he knew it had been necessary. In any event, they had already upset a gang master and a Chief Inspector. As far as he was concerned, Mrs Woodbine could do her worst.

She certainly had a good try. Sergeant Deacon sat outside Mrs Woodbine's office in disbelief as she harangued Claude and Marjorie for fully five minutes. He couldn't hear every word she said through the closed door but her tone and volume didn't leave much to the imagination. She banged the table repeatedly for punctuation.

Eventually, there was a pause and the door opened. Claude and Marjorie trooped out.

Mrs Woodbine hadn't finished.

'And this is absolutely your last chance, the pair of you! One more juvenile incident and you're both fired!'

'Stupid bloody woman,' said Marjorie as she passed Sergeant Deacon.

Claude followed on behind, seemingly unperturbed. He had the key and he swung it around his finger, triumphantly.

They walked to the car and climbed in. Sergeant Deacon drove them straight to Rosemary Fuller's house and then waited for them outside. He leant on the bonnet of his car, surveying the scene.

Claude and Marjorie went in and began a thorough search of the house. They started upstairs in the main bedroom, delving into the bedside tables and the wardrobe.

'I've had a bit of a revelation, Claude,' said Marjorie.

'About the case?' he asked.

'No, about myself.'

'Go on.'

'It happened when I was in that caravan place with Grigor. He started to threaten me and I realised I wasn't in the slightest bit bothered. It was strange – like I had some sort of force field around me.'

'Really?' said Claude, intrigued.

They made their way into the second bedroom.

'I know Grigor's a wimp, but it's more than that,' Marjorie continued. 'It's something to do with the fact that I've lived my life to the full and, at the age of eighty, I don't have much to lose. I'm supposed to be fearful and frail but I feel just the opposite.'

'Funnily enough, I know what you mean.'

'I almost feel like I've got a . . . how can I describe it? . . . an old age pensioner's, umm . . . .'

'An old age pensioner's superpower?' asked Claude.

'Exactly!'

Downstairs, they started a search of the lounge. Claude began with the bookshelf and took down a couple of dusty box files. He began reading them.

'That's interesting,' said Marjorie.

She was peering at an old school photo hanging on the wall. She looked surprised.

Claude wandered across and looked over her

shoulder.

'St Catherine's school prefects, 1982. Look, there's Rosemary, smiling away at us . . . .' said Marjorie, pointing to the picture. Rosemary was sat in the middle of the front row. Her name was printed underneath.

'But who's this?' she said, pointing to someone on the extreme right of the photograph.

Claude leant in to get a closer look. He peered at the person and then down at the name.

He turned and looked at Marjorie.

They eventually locked up the house and Sergeant Deacon drove them back, with both of them lost in thought. About a mile away from the flat, they came to Goscinski's, a grocery store that Claude had used once or twice. There were two white vans parked outside.

'Slow down please, Tom,' said Claude, sitting forwards.

Two scruffily dressed men were standing outside, chatting to someone who Claude recognised as the store owner. They were all drinking coffee.

'I think we know the two scruffy ones,' said Marjorie. 'They're a couple of Grigor's mates, aren't they?'

'Hmm,' said Claude, pondering. 'The gang's obviously got itself a new rendezvous.'

'Why does it need one of those?' asked Marjorie, trying to understand what he meant. She peered through the back window as they drove past.

'Well, you know, it's somewhere to collect a package or pay in the day's takings if you need to. Have you forgotten you rather ruined their last meeting place, Marjorie?'

'So I did,' she said, smiling.

The Sergeant dropped them off at the flat and they settled in for the evening. Marjorie sat down with a gin and tonic and read the paper. Claude paced around for a while, frowning with concentration. Eventually, he sat himself down in an armchair.

'I think I might have worked out a new plan, Marjorie,' he said.

She lowered the paper.

'Good. I hope it's dangerous.'

'I'm afraid it is. Not least because we have to get it past Chief Constable Selby first.'

CHAPTER SEVEN

'Y ou want to do what?' asked the Chief Constable, in disbelief. He pointed out, somewhat crossly, that he'd only just been torn off a strip by his commanding officer for allowing Claude and Marjorie anywhere near the Rosemary Fuller case. Not that it had actually been anything to do with him, of course.

'Did I realise how vitally important Charlie Wainwright's investigation was?' he said, mimicking the rebuke he'd received. 'Did I know the Chief Inspector was liaising directly with the Home Office? Had I heard of modern slavery? By the end of it, I thought he might transfer me to the proverbial job in traffic.'

Claude, Marjorie and Sergeant Deacon were seated opposite the Chief Constable's desk, weathering the storm. Marjorie eventually responded. As ever, she was unrepentant.

'Welcome to the "I'm Constantly Being Shouted At Club", Chief Constable. Claude and I are founder members,' she said. 'Look, all we're trying to do is get to the bottom of Rosemary Fuller's murder since no-one else seems to be. Can Claude at least explain please?'

The Chief Constable sat back in his chair and very deliberately folded his arms.

'He can try.'

Claude collected his thoughts. He tried to explain that the only thing they really knew about the gang master was that he didn't take kindly to having the details of his operation revealed. Rosemary Fuller had clearly stumbled across his identity and had been undoubtedly threatening to expose him. He suggested that they try and do exactly the same thing.

'What, and get someone else strangled?' asked the Chief Constable, unhelpfully.

'But we can minimise the risks, Peter, knowing what we know,' Claude insisted.

'Go on.'

'I thought we might send in someone posing as a journalist. You know, a proper investigative journalist, looking to uncover the truth about a nasty gang defrauding little old ladies. Get him to ask some seriously awkward questions.'

There was a flicker of interest from the Chief Constable.

'And you presumably have someone in mind?'

'I thought dear old Douglas Carlisle might play the part well.'

The Chief Constable laughed, derisively.

'Douglas Carlisle? Also known as Britain's favourite conman?'

'Well . . .'

'Correct me if I'm wrong Claude, but isn't Sir

Douglas currently serving five years in the Scrubs for his latest acting performance? What do you want me to do, help him escape?'

'The good thing is you don't need to do anything, Peter. He's up for early parole and if the police offer no objections he'll be out straight away. Charlie Wainwright need never know.'

The Chief Constable mused on the attractiveness of this, tapping his pencil repeatedly on the desk. Yes, he was still smarting at the dressing down he'd received from his commanding officer. Yes, he would quite enjoy putting one over on Charlie Wainwright. However, neither of these was a reason to ignore orders or abandon police procedure. Certainly not for a Chief Constable.

But there was a third thing. He'd studied under Claude and he'd ended up inheriting a lot of Claude's instincts. And those instincts had been telling him for some time that there was something unusual about the Regional Crime Squad investigation. Something he couldn't quite put his finger on. Somewhere in the middle of it there was what, in the old days in Claude's squad, they would have called a bum note. He looked at Sergeant Deacon.

'Sergeant, I want our Mr Carlisle fitted with a state of the art tracking device.'

'Sir.'

He turned to Claude and Marjorie.

'And you two. He needs to text you every hour on the hour – set up an alarm on his phone. If he's as much as five minutes late, you alert Sergeant Deacon and we yank him straight out.'

Claude, Marjorie and the Sergeant left the Chief Constable's office before he could change his mind. They drove back to Claude's flat.

Sergeant Deacon expressed his astonishment at the boldness of the Chief Constable's decision.

'I told you before, Tom,' said Claude, 'Peter always knew how to take a risk.'

'Talking of risks, do you think I might have one of these trendy tracking devices please Tom?' chimed in Marjorie. 'I mean, I have been kidnapped once already.'

'Good idea, Mrs Watson. I'll sort it out.'

The main gate of Wormwood Scrubs opened and Douglas Carlisle emerged, blinking into the sunlight. He was dressed in the suit he'd obviously worn to his court sentencing and carried a plastic bag full of his possessions.

Claude and Marjorie were waiting for him.

'Douglas! Very good to see you,' said Claude.

They shook hands.

'Very good to see you, Chief Superintendent.'

'And thank you for agreeing to join our little troupe.'

'Not at all, I can't wait to get started,' said Douglas, looking up at the clear blue sky and smiling.

'Can I introduce you to my colleague, Marjorie Watson?' said Claude.

Douglas smiled warmly.

'Mrs Watson, may I say how delighted I am to meet you. I've heard so much about you from Claude.' he said, oozing charm.

He took Marjorie's hand and kissed it in exaggerated fashion. She was taken aback.

Claude, however, was not. 'Come on Douglas.'

'I don't know what you mean, Claude.'

'Hand it back.'

Claude held out his hand and Douglas reluctantly gave him back Marjorie's watch which he'd just stolen.

'Profuse apologies Mrs Watson,' he said. 'It's just so long since I've had anyone to practice on.'

For once, Marjorie was lost for words. She struggled to put the watch back on again.

Sergeant Deacon watched proceedings with interest. Everyone clambered into his car and he started the engine.

In a car fifty yards back from the prison gates, Chief Inspector Wainwright and his two plain clothes detective were also watching with interest.

'Are we going to arrest them, sir?' asked Sergeant Coyle, one of the detectives.

'No, let them have their fun for the minute – I'm quite enjoying it,' said the Chief Inspector. 'Besides, we might learn something.'

Under instruction from Marjorie, Sergeant Deacon drove to the nearest charity shop and Claude, Marjorie and Douglas Carlisle went inside. They emerged twenty minutes later with two large carrier bags crammed full. They proceeded on to W H Smith and then to the local phone store.

Back at the flat, Marjorie produced a sewing kit and took a brown corduroy jacket from one of the charity shop bags. She took the tracking device from Sergeant Deacon and started to sew.

'This is a bit like Mission Impossible and I'm playing the part of Q,' she said breezily.

Douglas thought about this for a second. 'Isn't Q in the Bond films?' he asked.

Marjorie pretended to concentrate on her sewing.

Claude returned from the kitchen with a coffee for everyone. He sat down with Douglas to discuss the plan of action.

'There's a grocery shop in the High Street that seems to be a meeting place for gang members,' he said. 'That's a good place to make yourself known.'

'Called what?' asked Douglas, notebook in hand.

'Goscinski,' said Claude. 'And push your luck a bit when you're in there – you know, put the frighteners on him. Promise him a starring role in your upcoming newspaper article about drugs and prostitution.'

This was an unusually aggressive approach for Claude, bearing in mind it was Douglas who was taking the risk. Douglas, however, seemed unperturbed and sat back, starting to contemplate his acting performance.

Marjorie finished her needlework. She handed him the jacket.

'There you are,' she said. 'Your jacket now has the tiniest tracking device ever, hidden in the lining.

And Sergeant Deacon has linked it to his laptop.'

'Thank you,' said Douglas.

'And it's essential you constantly text me,' Marjorie went on. 'We've set up a series of alarms on your phone so you'll be buzzed every hour. Okay?'

'Got it. I think,' said Douglas, slightly overwhelmed with all the information.

'The easy way to remember it is that when you get a vibration in your pocket, you think of Marjorie.' She grinned at her own joke.

Half an hour later, Douglas Carlisle was walking down the High Street, looking for all the world like a seasoned journalist – chinos, corduroy jacket, leather shoulder bag. All slightly second-hand and dog-eared.

He reached the grocery store and went in. Behind the counter stood Mr Goscinski.

'Good morning, I wonder if you can help me?' said Douglas, producing his notebook. 'I'm researching a newspaper article about a gang conning money out of old people in the area.'

'Sorry? What?' came the startled reply.

Douglas swept his hand in front of him as if imagining a newspaper headline.

'You know, "Heartless gang fleeces innocent pensioners". That sort of thing.'

Mr Goscinski started to look panicky.

'Why would I know anything about that?'

'It's just that I have it on very good authority that the gang members use this place to meet up.'

'No .... erm, absolutely not,' he stammered.

Douglas was unrelenting.

'You're sure? And what about the rumours of people trafficking and prostitution? Heard anything about that?'

Mr Goscinski decided the only thing for it was to tough it out.

'I'm afraid you've got the wrong shop. And you need to leave immediately, please.'

'Fair enough,' said Douglas, putting his notebook away and turning to go. 'I'll pop back when I've done a bit more research – give you another chance to tell your story in your own words.'

As soon as the shop door closed, Mr Goscinski reached into his pocket for his mobile phone and began to dial.

Douglas, meanwhile, set off in search of a café. He eventually found one and went in and ordered a coffee. He had no sooner sat down than his phone buzzed with the first of his reminders. He took out the phone and texted Marjorie, rather pleased with himself:

"Completely fell for it. Next?"

He waited for the reply. His coffee arrived and he sat sipping it. Eventually:

"Claude says brace for immediate response"

Douglas finished his coffee and set off to walk down the road. He hadn't gone very far when a black van pulled up next to him. It was the same one that Claude and Marjorie had seen back at the mobile home site. The side door of the van slid open and Douglas was dragged inside. The door was slammed shut again.

He remained inside for quite some time. Eventually, the door slid back again and Douglas was roughly thrown out. He stumbled across the pavement with the force of the ejection, windmilling his arms in order to stay on his feet. The van drove off.

Further back up the road, Chief Inspector Wainwright sat in his car with his two detectives.

'Dear, oh dear, oh dear,' he said, laughing.

Oblivious to the Chief Inspector's presence, Douglas made his way back to Claude's flat for a debrief on the events so far. He sat down with Claude and Marjorie and a cup of tea. Sergeant Deacon perched himself on a kitchen barstool.

'Were they rough with you?' asked Marjorie.

'I've had worse,' Douglas replied. 'I think they just wanted to read me the Riot Act. Or the gangland equivalent of it, anyway'

Claude seemed pleased with the way the plan was working out. Again, he seemed keen for Douglas to keep pushing his luck.

'Well, let's agree that you've definitely got their attention,' he said. 'Tomorrow I think it's time for you to meet Marjorie's old friend Grigor the gardener. Apparently he's resurfaced on the other side of town with a whole new list of victims.'

'And I should, what?' asked Douglas. 'Try and interview him?'

'Oh no, I think you can take a tougher line than that. You're an investigative journalist – doorstep him. Doorstep him with the fact that you're on to his little racket.'

◆ ◆ ◆

The next day, Grigor was at the home of Mrs Lloyd, yet another unsuspecting pensioner. True to form, he was giving the illusion of working on her front garden and waved his secateurs over a couple of shrubs. He started his lawn mower and gave it a cursory push across the tiny lawn.

Mrs Lloyd appeared with her handbag and he turned the lawn mower off.

'Everything good. Is two hundred pounds,' said Grigor, sweeping his arm across the garden as if he had transformed it.

'Is it?' said Mrs Lloyd, peering through her glasses. 'You are kind for helping me out.'

She counted out the money from her handbag. She just about had enough. She gave it to him and went back into her house.

Grigor wheeled the lawn mower back to the van. He found his way blocked by Douglas Carlisle, notebook in hand.

'Grigor, isn't it?' said Douglas. 'I'm writing an article about little old ladies being defrauded out of their life savings by an unscrupulous gang.'

Grigor was immediately rattled. He pushed roughly past Douglas and opened the van's back door. He threw the lawn mower inside.

Douglas pressed on regardless.

'I just saw you charge Mrs Lloyd two hundred

pounds for about fifteen minutes work.'

Grigor walked quickly to the front of the van and climbed into the driver's seat. He reached forward to start the engine.

Douglas shouted through the window.

'I make that eight hundred pounds an hour for gardening work, Grigor. Any comment for the readers?'

Grigor accelerated away as fast as he could. He screeched around the corner.

Douglas took out his phone and composed a text to Marjorie:

"Grigor wound up to fever pitch"

Marjorie had been waiting anxiously for the text. She read it out to Claude and then replied with three emojis: a rocket taking off, a bomb with the fuse lit and a ball of flames.

She put a kiss at the end of the message.

CHAPTER EIGHT

Marjorie sat on the sofa, sipping a mug of coffee. Unusually for her, she was quite agitated. She checked her mobile phone repeatedly.

The doorbell rang.

She got up and went to answer it, mobile in hand. She opened the door and discovered Sergeant Deacon waiting outside.

'Ah Tom, just in time,' she said. 'Claude's nipped out for a pint of milk and I'm here on my own waiting for Douglas's early morning text. Get your laptop ready.'

They both sat down on the sofa. Sergeant Deacon opened his laptop and Marjorie stared at her phone. Eventually it buzzed and a brief text arrived:

"Good morning"

'Excellent,' said Marjorie.

She replied with a sunshine emoji and another kiss.

A series of intertwined events began.

The black van, which Douglas had been dragged into the day before, was parked in front of a scruffy looking caravan on a piece of wasteland.

The caravan door opened and three men emerged. They walked purposefully to the van, climbed in and drove off.

Douglas emerged from a cafe. He put his phone back in his jacket pocket after his text exchange with Marjorie. He sipped his takeaway coffee and sauntered off down the road.

The van turned onto the main road and accelerated towards the town. As it did so, it passed a parked car. Inside the car, Chief Inspector Wainwright sat watching.

Douglas continued to wend his way down the High Street, evidently enjoying the early morning sun. He stopped and looked in a shop window.

The van joined a dual carriageway and gathered speed as it approached the outskirts of town.

Douglas turned a corner. Behind him, he heard a vehicle approach and pull up at the kerb. He turned to discover it was the milkman making a delivery. They acknowledged each other with an early morning wave.

The van drove through town. It turned a corner at speed, tyres squealing.

Douglas walked on. He reached into his shoulder bag and pulled out a packet of Rolos. He unwrapped one.

Claude walked on. He was on his way to the Tesco Local.

The black van screeched to a halt next to Claude. The side door shot back. Someone reached out and forced a cloth hood over his head. Two pairs of

hands grabbed him and Claude was hauled inside,
walking stick and all.

The van accelerated away.

Claude sat with his hands tied behind his chair
and with the cloth hood still in place. Footsteps
approached him and the hood was yanked unceremoniously from his head. He blinked briefly and
discovered he was in a caravan, confronted by three
men. Two of them he'd seen before during the attack
on his flat. The third, older and slightly better presented, looked like he might be the leader. He bent
down to bring his face closer to Claude's.

'You've become very irritating Mr Simmons,' he
said, with just a trace of an accent. 'We just want to
be left alone to run our business and you keep getting in the way.'

Claude didn't move a muscle, even though he
could feel the man's hot breath on his face. He stared
back implacably.

'I sent my friends all the way to your house to deliver you a personal message but you chose to ignore
it,' he continued. 'What are we to do?'

They were now almost nose to nose.

One of the other men garbled something, anxiously. He was looking through the caravan's window and almost immediately Claude heard a
car draw up outside. Doors opened and quickly
slammed shut. There was a brief pause and the cara-

van door burst open.

In marched Chief Inspector Wainwright followed by his two detectives, Sergeant Coyle and Constable Haines. He surveyed the room, taking in Claude and his three assailants. He turned to the man who looked like he might be the leader.

'Perfect, thank you,' he said. 'We'll see you three gentlemen outside in a moment.'

They left, quickly.

Chief Inspector Wainwright stood staring at Claude. Claude stared back.

'I'm so sorry, Chief Superintendent,' he eventually said. 'Have I upset your nicey nicey view of the police force?'

His tone was an unfortunate combination of the sarcastic and the patronising.

Claude remained expressionless. 'I could have used a lot of words to describe you over the years Charlie, but I never thought "bent" would be one of them.'

'Ooh, bit harsh. I mean, we can't all be a saint like you, can we Claude? I much prefer to describe it as "properly remunerated".' Wainwright pointed to one of his accomplices. 'Look at Coyle here, for example. He's worked very hard to get to the rank of Sergeant and he's had to put himself in harm's way, haven't you Coyle?'

'Yes, sir,' the Sergeant replied.

'And where have you told everyone you're going on holiday this year?'

'Bridgend, sir.'

Wainwright addressed Claude again. 'Bridgend – just what you'd expect on a copper's salary, isn't it? And where are you actually going, Sergeant?'

'Bridgetown, sir.'

Wainwright grinned. 'Bridgetown, Barbados! You see, I like my boys to have nice things. But enough about our good fortune. How about all these silly mistakes you've been making?'

The Chief Inspector started to walk around Claude, slowly and deliberately.

'Old age, I know, but believing there was an actual gang master in the first place and then trying to flush him out with dear old Douglas Carlisle. Really? We've had a bloody good laugh about that one boys, haven't we?'

Coyle and Haines were smirking.

'Just a wild guess here, but did sensible Selby suggest Douglas wear a tracking device and perhaps check in every hour?'

Claude stared back.

'And one more wild guess – did you forget to wear a tracking device yourself?'

Coyle and Haines stepped forward and grabbed Claude. They stood him up and ran a scanning device over every inch of him. They roughly forced him back onto his chair.

'Nothing, sir,' said Coyle. 'Completely clean.'

'Oh dear, Claude. You have let yourself down,' Wainwright continued.

He took out a Zippo lighter from his pocket. He repeatedly clicked it open and shut as he continued to pace around Claude.

'There is one thing you're going to be pleased about, though. We're not going to let your murder go to waste. Constable Haines here is a dab hand with forensics, if you'll pardon the pun. And he's been secretly collecting DNA and fingerprints from, erm . . . . what's his name?'

'Grigor, sir,' said Haines.

'Ah yes, Grigor. Your batty old girlfriend's gardener. And he's sprinkled just enough of it around the caravan here to make the forensic squad feel really clever when they discover it.'

Claude had had enough. 'Can I ask you a question, for my own peace of mind? Did you kill Rosemary Fuller as well?'

'Of course,' said Wainwright, without hesitation. 'Took your sage advice, Claude – never ask the troops to do something you're not prepared to do yourself.'

The Chief Inspector clicked open the Zippo lighter and lit the flame. He shut the lid and then did the same thing again.

'You'll be pleased to know we're making good use of that murder as well, though. Because everyone's complaining about the lack of progress on the case, we're going to re-examine the evidence. And, shock horror, we're going to find we made a mistake. There on Rosemary Fuller's clothing we're going to find the tiniest trace of – you've guessed it – Grigor's DNA. Genius, eh?'

'Genius? You've become grotesque Charlie,' said Claude.

'Well thank you, Claude. But I can't stand round here all day swapping compliments with you. We've got fish to fry. Toodle pip.'

The three of them trooped out and Claude was left alone. His hands remained tied behind his chair.

Outside, the caravan was parked next to a collection of derelict outbuildings. Wainwright found the three other men waiting, each holding a jerry can. He nodded to them and they began to splash petrol all around the base of the caravan.

When they had finished, Wainwright stepped forward and took the Zippo lighter out of his pocket. He flipped the lid open.

'Allow me to do the honours, boys,' he said.

'Well, if it isn't Charlie Wainwright! What a lovely surprise!'

Chief Constable Selby appeared from behind the derelict buildings. He was followed by Sergeant Deacon and a group of other police officers.

Wainwright and his accomplices were trapped.

'Shit!' said Wainwright, loudly.

A uniformed policeman stepped forward to handcuff him. The Chief Constable took the handcuffs from him.

'Allow me to do the honours, Constable,' he said. He fitted the handcuffs to Wainwright's wrists, as tightly as he could.

Not to be left out, Marjorie appeared from behind the buildings. She seemed pleased with herself.

'Is Claude okay?' she asked.

'Sergeant Deacon's checking now but I'm hoping

so,' the Chief Constable replied.

She turned her attention to Wainwright.

'Ah, former Chief Inspector Wainwright,' she said, with barely concealed disdain. 'May I say how good you look in handcuffs? They bring out the malice in your eyes.'

'Sod off!' said Wainwright, scowling.

'You always were compulsive Charlie,' said the Chief Constable. 'But help me out here – how did it come to this? Greed? Bitterness? Some warped sense of being hard done by?'

'Perhaps it was having to work with a self-righteous prick like you, Selby.'

'Ooh, grumpy Charlie,' said Marjorie. 'Still, I suppose you have just had your trousers taken down by two eighty year olds. It's a lot to come to terms with, isn't it?'

Chief Constable Selby had the final word. 'The good thing is, Charlie, you're going to have at least twenty years to come to terms with it.'

Wainwright was led away to join his henchmen in the back of a police van.

Marjorie and the Chief Constable walked across to the caravan and waited. The Chief Constable seemed perplexed.

'I don't suppose you'd care to enlighten me as to what's been going on here?' he asked.

'All in good time,' Marjorie replied.

Eventually Claude appeared, looking none the worse for wear. He walked down the steps as if nothing had happened. Sergeant Deacon emerged shortly afterwards, looking as puzzled as the Chief Constable.

'All in one piece, Claude?' asked Marjorie.

'Very much so, Marjorie. Thank you.'

The Chief Constable led them off towards the waiting ambulance to have Claude checked over. On the way, they passed the black van. Claude stopped.

'Excuse me,' he said.

He opened the back door of the van and rooted around inside. He emerged triumphant, walking stick in hand.

Five minutes later he was seated on the rear sill of the ambulance with the obligatory blanket over his shoulders. Marjorie was perched next to him. The Chief Constable could contain himself no longer.

'So, we get a mystery message from you, Mrs Watson, telling us that Claude is now wearing a tracking device and that you want us to follow him. And here we are,' he said. 'Apart from that I haven't got the first idea how any of this happened. But then I suppose I'm only the Chief Constable.'

'Where would you like us to start?' asked Claude.

'How about starting at the beginning with Douglas Carlisle?'

'Ah yes, ahem . . . . well,' stammered Claude. 'I have to admit, Douglas Carlisle hunting for a gang master was a complete double bluff by Marjorie and I. But there's nothing like playing to someone's arrogance is there? Charlie Wainwright swallowed it hook, line and sinker – couldn't wait to tell me how clever he was to have worked out Douglas's game.'

'So he was never really in danger?'

'Of course not. Dear old Douglas? You don't think he'd have done it otherwise, do you?'

The cogs were whirring in the Chief Constable's head. 'So . . . you were deliberately letting Wainwright know that you were behind the whole thing?'

'Exactly, Peter. And he simply couldn't risk the fact that Marjorie and I would carry on investigating and find the truth about him, just as Rosemary Fuller had done. So he grabbed me, right on cue.'

The Chief Constable shook his head, wearily. 'To sum up, you've conned Charlie Wainwright and in the process you've managed to con Sergeant Deacon and I, as well.'

Claude started to stammer again.

Fortunately, Sergeant Deacon changed the subject. He had been lost in his own thoughts for a while. He was, he said, still thoroughly confused about the tracking device.

'It's the one you gave me, Tom,' said Marjorie. 'Sorry, I gave it straight to Claude.'

'I assumed that was the case,' he replied. 'But . . . . were you wearing it when you nipped out for your supposed pint of milk, Chief Superintendent?'

'Of course, and we took the Chief Constable's advice about regularly texting in,' said Claude. He turned to Marjorie. 'When you didn't hear from me Marjorie, I assume you alerted Sergeant Deacon?'

'I certainly did,' she said.

The Sergeant held up Haines and Coyle's scanning device.

'But I found this scanner in the caravan. I'm assuming they used it to scan you for a tracking device?'

'Of course,' said Claude. 'We knew they would.'

Sergeant Deacon and the Chief Constable looked equally baffled. Why on earth hadn't they discovered the tracking device?

Claude handed his walking stick to Marjorie.

'Marjorie, would you like to show these gentlemen how it was done, please?'

'My pleasure,' she said. 'Tom hold out your hand, please.'

Sergeant Deacon held out his hand and Marjorie slowly unscrewed the bone handle of the walking stick. She shook the handle and nothing happened. She shook it again and a tiny tracking device fell out into the Sergeant's hand.

'Well I'm buggered!' said the Chief Constable.

'I just had to hang on to the walking stick when they put the hood over my head and dragged me into the van,' Claude explained. 'Then I flailed around with it until I hit one of them. Not surprisingly, they grabbed it from me and threw it into the back of the van.'

Sergeant Deacon shook his head, disbelievingly.

'It's called the pensioner's superpower,' said Marjorie, beaming. 'It never fails.'

CHAPTER NINE

Fern Lea's conservatory was filled with autumn sunshine. Claude and Marjorie were sat at a table, doing their best to debrief Mrs Woodbine and Mrs Fairchild on the complications of the case. Mrs Woodbine was struggling to understand how they'd come to suspect Chief Inspector Wainwright in the first place.

'Well, as you know, we went back to Rosemary's house to have a proper look round,' explained Claude. 'Just to see if anything had been missed.'

'And we stumbled across an old photo of Saint Catherine's school prefects when Rosemary was in the sixth form,' said Marjorie, picking up the thread. 'In the middle of the picture was Rosemary herself, smiling back at us. But on the extreme right was someone we hadn't expected to see: C T Wainwright.'

'Charlie Wainwright to you and I,' said Claude.

Mrs Fairchild shuddered, 'I had no idea,' she said. 'What are the chances of that?'

Claude explained that afterwards they had managed to get Rosemary's ancient computer going and found lots of emails about school reunions. Wainwright had agreed to attend a number of them.

'What's the significance of that?' asked Mrs Woodbine, frowning.

'It means they kept in touch, so Rosemary would have known about his career as a police officer.'

'Still not following.'

Claude thought about this for a second. He had given hundreds of debriefs in his time but was happy to admit he was a bit rusty.

'Ah sorry,' he said. 'We didn't tell you this: Mabel's neighbour, Mrs Grey, said Rosemary got very agitated when the gardener's boss turned up one day to collect money from him. We now know the boss was Charlie Wainwright.'

'And in that instant, she knew he was corrupt,' added Marjorie. 'Bent as a bugle.'

Mrs Woodbine was now following the story, but she wasn't very happy about it. She asked why they hadn't simply passed all this information on to Chief Constable Selby.

'Because if we'd told him he'd have been duty bound to alert Internal Affairs,' said Claude. 'Then he'd have been walking around in treacle for two years with Wainwright long gone. So we decided to find him some more evidence.'

'And put yourselves at incredible risk again.'

Mrs Woodbine was reverting to headmistress mode. Marjorie was having none of it.

'I believe "thank you for solving the case" is the phrase you're looking for,' she said, defiantly.

Mrs Fairchild intervened. 'Sorry Marjorie, we are

extremely grateful. It's just that Emily and I dragged you into this and we've been feeling responsible, not to say . . . . well, queasy about the risks you've been taking.'

'Well there's no need,' responded Marjorie. 'Claude and I are consenting adults.'

Claude looked at Marjorie. 'I think that might mean something else,' he said. 'Anyway, moving on . . . . what was it the vicar said about Rosemary? Oh yes, she had a strongly developed sense of right and wrong.'

'To say the very least,' agreed Mrs Fairchild.

'So, it looks like she borrowed the vicar's car, tracked down the gang and simply confronted Wainwright. Threatened to expose him and his mates there and then.'

'Oh lord,' said Mrs Woodbine.

'I'm afraid she'd completely underestimated the crimes he was involved in and completely misjudged how far he'd gone over to the dark side. Church warden versus gang master was never going to be a very fair fight . . . .'

Claude and Marjorie took a stroll around the Fern Lea gardens among the falling autumn leaves. Squirrels scurried around busily collecting acorns.

'Well, thank you for having me to stay, Claude,' said Marjorie. 'It was a very enjoyable break. Very relaxing.'

Claude wasn't entirely sure that he would have put it like that but decided to go along with it nonetheless.

'It was my pleasure,' he said. 'Actually, I was wondering about the detective agency thing, now that you're back at Fern Lea.'

Marjorie looked alarmed.

'We're going to keep it going aren't we? I'm already working on a new business card.'

'Are you? Why?'

'Because we've discovered a thing called pensioner's superpower – we'd be mad not to merchandise it. After I get it trademarked, that is.'

They walked on for a bit. Claude continued to play along.

'Any new slogans then?'

'Well, it's still a work in progress, but I've got a few I like.'

'Go on.'

'Um well, there's, "Pensioner's Superpower. Solves all stubborn crimes".'

Claude pondered on this.

'Might make us sound a bit like a washing powder. Or worse still, a toilet cleaner.'

'Good point, Claude. Good point. Okay, how about if we have a little dig at the police, then? You know, something like, "Forget the force, go with the power".'

'I'm not sure that's going to get you back into Chief Constable Selby's good books.'

They walked on in silence for a while.

'You may mock my attempts at brand management, Claude,' said Marjorie eventually. 'But who was it pointed out that your walking stick was a vital part of your image? And was I right?'

'Good point, Marjorie. Good point.'

Claude gave his walking stick a twirl as they walked on.

PART THREE: THE MISSING TESTICLES

CHAPTER ONE

The Polo drove along a pretty country lane, splashing through a puddle left behind by a late spring shower. Claude sat in the driver's seat, wearing a slight frown of concentration. Marjorie gazed out of the passenger's window, distractedly watching as the hedgerows hurried past.

She was hoping that they were on their way to be briefed on a new assignment but, to be honest, she wasn't entirely sure. She had received a call on her mobile phone from someone who had said he wanted to meet her and Claude to discuss a private matter. Mysteriously, he had refused to give any details about himself or even to disclose his address. The only thing she knew about him was his postcode.

'Your destination is ahead,' said the satnav on her phone.

She looked at the phone quizzically and then looked out of the window again. They were absolutely in the middle of nowhere, with no sign of civilisation whatsoever.

Claude drove on, rounding a bend in the lane. Almost immediately, the hedgerow on the right hand

side of the road gave way to a large brick wall. He followed the wall for a while and it eventually led to a very substantial pair of wrought iron gates, each with a gold crest in their centre. There was a gatehouse and, beyond it, a glimpse of a very grand house.

'You have arrived.'

Neither of them had been expecting this. Claude pulled up on the other side of the lane and peered out at the large sign attached to one of the gateposts. In gold lettering it read: "Beckwith Hall. Open to the public: Saturdays and Sundays"

Claude scratched his head. There was something about the name that was familiar. He pulled out his phone to try and google it but Marjorie had already beaten him to it.

'Beckwith Hall, ancestral seat of the Unsworth family,' she read out. 'Currently home to Lord Richard and Lady Camilla Unsworth.'

Claude still looked puzzled.

'And wasn't there some sort of drama?' he asked. 'Fifteen or twenty years ago, perhaps?'

Marjorie scrolled down further on her phone.

'Ah,' she said, surprised. 'Nearly fifteen years ago, Lord Unsworth's older brother Jacob . . .'

She looked up at Claude.

' . . . murdered.'

Now he remembered. It had been a lurid affair and the national newspapers had had a field day with it. He put the car into gear and drove up to the gates.

A man in a uniform bearing the Beckwith Hall

crest appeared straight away from the gatehouse. Clearly expecting them, he opened the gates and waved them through.

'At least we didn't have to pay to get in,' observed Marjorie.

They followed the meandering drive through the manicured gardens and eventually arrived at the house. It was a beautiful example of late Tudor architecture - half-timbered, with leaded windows and a roof that hosted a small forest of ornate, terracotta chimney pots. At the front door, a well-dressed man stood waiting for them. Marjorie, slightly overawed by the surroundings, nervously blundered into an early faux pas.

'Lord Unsworth, good morning,' she said, offering her hand. 'I'm Marjorie Watson. I'm very pleased to meet you.'

'Lord Unsworth is waiting for you in the study,' said the butler, politely ignoring the error. 'Please follow me.'

Claude tried to suppress a grin.

The word "study" hardly did justice to the room. It was enormous and wood panelled, dominated by a magnificent stone fireplace on one wall and a beautiful tapestry of St George slaying the dragon on another.

'Mr Claude Simmons and Mrs Marjorie Watson,' announced the butler, ushering them in.

An affable looking man in his early fifties stepped forward to greet them. He introduced himself as Richard Unsworth and steered them towards the

sofas.

'Your reputation goes before you,' he said, smiling.

Marjorie looked at Claude. What did he mean by that?

They sat down. Lord Unsworth began by apologising for the cloak and dagger nature of his phone call with Marjorie.

'You must think me very odd,' he said, 'but my wife and I have been social pariahs for so long that's it's become second nature. Sort of a defence mechanism, I'm afraid.'

Now Claude was confused. He was struggling to equate the opulence of Beckwith Hall with the fact that the Unsworths seemed to feel hard done by.

'Pariahs? Why? Because of the incident with your brother?'

'Thank you for putting it so politely Mr Simmons. Because of the gruesome murder of my brother, yes.'

Claude was still puzzled. He didn't remember either of them ever being charged. Lord Unsworth was at pains to point out that no-one was ever charged. After fifteen years, the case remained unsolved.

'You were the main suspects, though?' asked Claude.

'By some distance. Jacob had inherited the title, the house, the land, the vintage cars – everything. Then he was mysteriously murdered and lo and behold, everything passed straight to me.'

'Oh dear,' said Marjorie, looking up from her notebook. 'That's what Claude likes to call a cast iron motive.'

Lord Unsworth gave a weary smile. He explained that they hadn't just had a cast iron motive but a flimsy alibi as well. He and his wife had been living in a cottage on the other side of the estate at the time and on the night of the murder they were having a quiet night in with their one year old daughter. Their alibi was that they were watching TV together.

'Ah,' said Claude. 'So you were the two prime suspects and you were vouching for each other's stories?'

He gave a resigned shrug.

The door opened and Lady Unsworth came in.

'Ah, here's my co-conspirator now,' said Lord Unsworth.

Claude and Marjorie struggled to get up from the sofa but she gestured for them to sit back down.

'Please,' she said, 'I'm Camilla. It's good to meet you.'

Lady Unsworth was probably in her late forties. She seemed to share the affability of her husband and also his slightly confessional manner.

'So I take it that you've been discussing our little outcast problem?' she asked.

'Is it really that bad?' asked Claude.

'At the risk of sounding like we're feeling sorry for ourselves, I'm afraid it is. We were smeared with Jacob's death early on and I'm afraid we haven't been able to get rid of it. We now have only a handful of friends left. On the rare occasions we go out, people sometimes cross the street to avoid meeting us.'

'Heavens. After fifteen years?' asked Marjorie.

'For a while we held out the hope that the world would eventually move on,' Lady Unsworth continued. 'But the advent of social media has entirely put paid to that. Beckwith Hall's Twitter and Facebook pages are now a feeding ground for trolls where, you might like to hear, we're known as The Silver Spoon Murderers.'

She trailed off.

Lord Unsworth took over. The final straw, he told Claude and Marjorie, had been that the problems were now starting to follow their children to school. Their daughter had had several incidents with paparazzi at the school gates and their eight year old son was apparently in a punch-up with his classmates at least once a week, in defence of the family honour.

A silence descended, eventually broken by Marjorie.

'So what would you have us do?' she asked.

'Sorry, I thought you knew,' replied Lady Unsworth. 'We'd like you to reopen the case. We'd like you to find the murderer.'

Five minutes later, Claude and Marjorie found themselves tramping across the estate behind Lord Unsworth. They were headed towards a stone gazebo, standing at the edge of a large lake. He stopped for a moment and lapsed into tour guide mode. The gazebo was apparently Beckwith Hall's masterpiece, designed in 1722 by the renowned architect Josiah Pallant. For years it had attracted tourists from all over the world. Now, he told them, it attracted only ghouls.

'Ghouls?' Marjorie asked.

'Sorry, I always assume everyone is familiar with the details of the murder – this is where the police believe Jacob was attacked. People have a morbid fascination with it.'

They climbed the stone steps into the gazebo. Given the history, it felt particularly cold and empty. Claude paced around, looking thoughtful.

'So, if the attack took place here, then presumably the body was found here?' he asked.

'Good question but no, it wasn't,' replied Lord Unsworth. 'It was found over there in the lake.'

Claude was surprised. They climbed back down the gazebo's steps and walked to the water's edge.

'So the body had to be dragged all the way over here?' asked Claude. 'And then it was found, where? At the bottom of the lake?'

'Again, no. I'm afraid Jacob was found floating on the surface. Face down.'

Claude was now very surprised.

They walked slowly back to the car with Claude lost in his own thoughts. He was intrigued by the Jacob Unsworth murder and had already started to speculate about events. However, he knew that things were not entirely straightforward.

'Whilst we're very flattered to be asked to help, Lord Unsworth, there is one obvious difficulty with all of this,' he said.

'Oh lord, is there?' asked Marjorie, disappointed.

Claude carried on addressing Lord Unsworth.

'Marjorie and I are just ordinary citizens and we have no access whatsoever to police records. I really don't see how we can go off interviewing however many suspects there were.'

'I'm afraid Jacob made enemies wherever he went. It would be easier to make a list of people who weren't suspects,' said Lord Unsworth, unhelpfully.

'Well, you see the difficulty.' Claude pondered for a moment. 'Having said that, there is one thing we can do straight away. The law says that if there's an autopsy then the next of kin is entitled to see the autopsy report. Will you ask for it, please?'

'Certainly. I'll give the Chief Constable a ring.'

Claude and Marjorie both looked at him, surprised.

'Sorry, you know Peter Selby?' asked Claude.

Lord Unsworth laughed out loud.

'I've had the feeling we've been at slight cross purposes all morning,' he said. 'It was Chief Constable Selby who recommended you both.'

'We had no idea,' said Claude.

'Yes, he obviously holds you in the highest regard Mr Simmons, from your days together in the Met I assume. And he was very complimentary about you Mrs Watson. At least, I think it was a compliment.'

'What did he say?' asked Marjorie, intrigued.

Lord Unsworth recounted for them the Chief Constable's theory about lengthy murder enquiries getting stuck in a rut and everybody starting to think in the same way.

'What were his exact words?' he said, scratching

his head. 'Oh yes, "When groupthink sets in you need someone like Marjorie Watson. She'll barge over a couple of beehives for you straight away".'

Claude started the car and they headed back towards the gates. The gatekeeper appeared and Marjorie gave him a regal wave as they drove past. She sat thinking about the Chief Constable's words.

'Beehive barger. I quite like it,' she said, eventually.

'Well, it's another slogan to add to the list, isn't it?' said Claude.

Two days later, Claude drove back to Beckwith Hall to collect the autopsy report which had been duly delivered by Chief Constable Selby. It was in a sealed envelope and Lord Unsworth had not read it. Afterwards, he drove to Fern Lea to collect Marjorie.

They had agreed that she would come and stay with him at his flat again while the new murder investigation was underway. Claude was looking forward to having his eccentric companion back. He bumped into Mrs Woodbine as he came in through the front door.

'Emily, good morning,' he said.

'Good morning, Claude,' she replied. 'Marjorie is all packed and ready. I think she's waiting in the lounge.'

They walked along the corridor together.

'By the way, happy birthday,' she said. 'Were you

going to tell us at any point?'

Claude laughed. 'Oh, thank you,' he said. 'It's not exactly something you broadcast when you're my age.'

Mrs Woodbine opened the door to the lounge and stepped back to let Claude enter first. He walked in and found the room thronging with residents, all wearing party hats. Marjorie, the ringleader as usual, immediately led everyone in a rousing chorus of "Happy Birthday To You", accompanied by Margaret on piano. Once he'd recovered from the surprise, Claude looked pleased.

After the song had finished, Marjorie stepped forward and lit the single candle on the birthday cake which sat on the coffee table.

'Happy birthday, Claude,' she said. 'We wanted to have all eighty one candles alight on the cake but unfortunately the Fire Brigade wouldn't allow it.'

She seemed oblivious to the fact that, firstly, this was a very old joke and, secondly, was at the expense of not just Claude but of pretty much everyone in the room, including herself.

'Very funny, Marjorie' said Claude, politely.

'We've all clubbed together to buy you a present,' Marjorie continued. 'You'll never guess what it is.'

From behind her back she produced what was very obviously a walking stick, tightly wrapped in brightly coloured paper. Everybody clapped enthusiastically.

Back at Claude's flat that evening, he sat admiring the new walking stick. Actually, it wasn't new. It was an antique and he was really rather pleased with it. Eventually he put it down and picked up the autopsy report. He thumbed through it quickly, re-acquainting himself with the format and the technical language. Then he settled down to read the whole thing in detail.

Marjorie was desperate to hear the contents of the report and impatience set in quite quickly. She stared at Claude intently, trying to find meaning in his every facial expression. She huffed and puffed. She got up and went to the kitchen to refill her gin and tonic. When she returned, she sat drumming her fingers on the arm of the sofa.

Claude seemed oblivious. He particularly took his time over the last two pages of the report. He rotated the folder to get a better view of one of the photos. Marjorie started to convince herself that he was punishing her for something.

Eventually, he dropped the autopsy report back on the coffee table. 'Shame,' he said.

'What's a shame?' asked Marjorie.

'No, sorry. The murderer didn't just want to kill Jacob Unsworth. He wanted to shame him as well.'

'How do you mean?'

Claude hesitated for a moment. 'How can I put it?' he asked. 'Umm, he'd had a couple of body parts cut off.'

He should have known better. Trying to spare Marjorie's blushes was an entirely futile exercise.

She furrowed her brow. 'Oh!' she said, realisation dawning. 'You mean he'd had his balls cut off?'

CHAPTER TWO

C hief Constable Selby was distracted. He gazed out of his office window, tapping his pencil absent-mindedly on the desk. He had recently made a decision about allowing Claude Simmons and Marjorie Watson to help out with a cold case, but the truth was he remained in two minds about it. Now they were on their way to see him, doubtless keen for an explanation.

His problem wasn't that they weren't good at what they did. Claude and Marjorie had solved the murder of their friend Audrey Patterson in the Fern Lea residential home and in doing so had run rings round his own investigation team. Then, in pursuit of a second murderer, they'd uncovered a web of police corruption that had resulted in three officers, including his one-time colleague Chief Inspector Charlie Wainwright, ending up behind bars.

They were certainly effective. The problem was that they were also downright dangerous. With a combined age of about one hundred and sixty years they seemed to have developed a scant regard for life and limb, particularly their own. In the Audrey Patterson case, Claude had tried to goad the murderer into making a mistake and had nearly ended up being suffocated himself. In pursuit of Charlie Wainwright, Marjorie had managed to get herself kidnapped and Claude had wilfully put himself in harm's way yet again.

Now he was about to help them with a new assignment. It suited him because it enabled him to offer at least a small ray of hope to Lord Richard and Lady Camilla Unsworth about the unsolved murder of Richard's brother, Jacob. In truth, the case had been stubbornly intractable for years and he saw little chance of Claude and Marjorie making any significant difference to it.

Nonetheless, he had the distinct sensation of being drawn, moth-like, to the flame.

They arrived and Marjorie, as ever, went straight on the offensive.

'It would have helped if you'd mentioned you were recommending us to the Unsworths,' she said, still in the process of sitting down.

The Chief Constable decided that the best policy with Marjorie might be to fight fire with fire.

'I'm sorry, it was Sergeant Deacon's idea and I was a bit luke-warm about it when he suggested it,' he replied. 'Well, I say luke-warm, the prospect of you two coming to work for us actually terrified me. So I thought I'd play for time and let you meet the Unsworths, to see if you actually got on.'

'We got on perfectly well – they'd like us to take on the case,' Marjorie persisted.

'I know, so my bluff has been well and truly

called,' he said, ruefully.

Claude decided to interrupt this little sparring match with a practical question.

'But why do you need us, Peter?' he asked. 'What on earth's happened to the investigation?'

The Chief Constable was forced to admit that the Jacob Unsworth case was now fifteen years old and that there had been no progress for as long as he could remember. He had been giving the illusion of keeping the investigation open because it was so high profile but now with the latest round of budget cuts he was struggling just to keep enough officers on the streets.

'I have no choice but to designate it a cold case,' he said.

'That's ironic because Claude and I are nearly cold as well,' said Marjorie, attempting irony yet again. She grinned. No-one else did.

Claude pressed on.

'So what are you thinking, Peter?' he asked. 'If we're going to try and help, then realistically we're going to have to be given something like Special Adviser status.'

'That's exactly what I was thinking,' he replied. 'In fact, I've already organised it.'

Marjorie looked a little confused.

Claude explained to her that the Chief Constable had the power to bring in any experts he chose, to help with a case. Special Adviser status was normally reserved for forensic scientists and pathologists but it could work just as well for Claude and

Marjorie, particularly given Claude's background. It meant they could be given complete access to all the police records in the Jacob Unsworth case.

Marjorie beamed. In her head, she was already referring to herself as Special Agent Watson. She felt another new business card coming on.

The Chief Constable got up, signalling that the meeting was coming to a close.

'Excellent,' he said. 'Sergeant Deacon's going to be in charge of you since it was his bright idea. Please try not to compromise him too much.'

Sergeant Deacon was duly summoned and took the new Special Advisers off to have their ID cards made up. Marjorie was delighted with hers and clutched it tightly. He led them along a warren of corridors to a disused office in the basement. He opened the door and switched on the light.

'We've set you up with your own investigation room here,' he said.

It was windowless and contained the bare minimum of furniture. There were two chairs, a table which housed a single computer and next to it a white board complete with coloured marker pens. On the floor were fifteen boxes of records, each with a lid. Claude surveyed the scene.

'Presumably all the records have to remain here?' he asked.

'They do, I'm afraid,' replied the Sergeant. 'And the Chief Constable is at pains to point out that, according to the strict letter of the law, the Unsworths are still suspects. None of this evidence is to be shared with them, please.'

Claude nodded.

Sergeant Deacon left them to it and headed back to his own office. Claude and Marjorie sat down, sizing up their new empire. Claude reached forward and removed the lid of one of the cardboard boxes. It was crammed full with papers.

'What is it they say?' he mused. 'Oh, yes. Be careful what you wish for.'

The next morning they arrived bright and early and made a start on the mountain of records. They hunted through the boxes and found a photograph of Jacob Unsworth. Claude fixed it to the top of the white board and wrote his details underneath. Marjorie had brought a pad of Post It notes with her, with a view to drawing a quick sketch of each of the other suspects if need be. Mindful of the Chief Constable's words, they began with Richard and Camilla Unsworth. They retrieved their written statements and settled down to read them.

Claude frowned as he studied Richard's statement and read what it said about the true extent of his possible motive. Aside from the small matter of inheriting Beckwith Hall upon his brother's death, there were also numerous stories of big brother bullying little brother. Some of them, like Jacob trapping five year old Richard in the family's mausoleum for three hours, bordered on the downright sadistic.

There certainly seemed to be no love lost between the two boys.

'Crikey!' said Marjorie, who was reading from Camilla's statement. 'They were about to be evicted.'

'Who were?' asked Claude.

'Camilla and Richard. From their cottage. Jacob was divorcing his first wife, Lady Elizabeth, and he was going to give the cottage to her. They were about to be out on their ear.'

Claude and Marjorie sat and debated this new information while Marjorie began her first Post It note sketches. The Unsworths had asked them to re-open the case and yet the evidence against them was worse than they'd let on. What did that mean?

Marjorie put down her magic marker and handed the sketches to Claude. She had put her drawing skills to good use in the Audrey Patterson case and had now cleverly caricatured Camilla and Richard. He stuck them on the board, underneath Jacob.

They rooted back through the boxes and found Lady Elizabeth Unsworth's statement. Claude read through it while Marjorie sketched. Unsurprisingly, it listed further incidents of bullying by Jacob, some of them bordering on domestic abuse, but contained one other significant fact: Elizabeth had moved out of Beckwith Hall and rented a house in Provence just before Jacob's murder. A note had been made on her statement declaring that the French police had confirmed her alibi.

By ten the next morning, they'd added another five suspects to the board. All of them were business associates of Jacob Unsworth and all of them had fallen foul of him in some way or other.

'Bloody hell, what a sense of entitlement!' exclaimed Marjorie, reading aloud from another folder. 'Never paying bills, reneging on debts, bankrupting old friends . . .'

' . . . and then using his nasty solicitor to sue the very people he owed the money to,' said Claude, reading from some court documents. 'Basically, he was trying to tie everyone up in litigation. In my old squad, we used to call that bullying people with the law.'

Half an hour later, Claude had moved on to another pile of papers. He stopped reading and laughed out loud.

'Well, I suppose that was inevitable,' he said.

'What?' asked Marjorie.

'Jacob, suing his solicitor.'

By the afternoon of the third day, the desk was piled high with paper and the floor was strewn with cardboard box lids. The white board was crammed with suspects except for a space in the bottom right hand corner. Claude picked up a magic marker pen and wrote in the space:

HI_ A__ND_NT L_ES

Underneath it he added:

HIS ABUNDANT LIES

He added in a large question mark, straddling both lines. He returned to his seat next to Marjorie. They sat in silence, studying the board for some time. Claude was troubled.

'Fourteen suspects in all,' said Marjorie, eventually. 'Does anyone take your fancy?'

'I'm afraid not,' said Claude. Even he was struggling to make sense of it all. 'Shall we go and have a coffee and let it all sink in?'

They wandered off to the police canteen and joined the queue at the counter. Ahead of them was a uniformed policewoman. She turned round to discover two eighty year olds behind her, each with a lanyard and an ID card.

'Oh, hello,' she said, surprised.

'Hello. Special Agent Marjorie Watson. Pleased to meet you,' said Marjorie, confidently.

The policewoman now looked perplexed.

'It's Special Adviser,' hissed Claude.

'Same thing,' said Marjorie.

They found an empty table and sat down with their drinks. Claude stared into his coffee, stirring it distractedly. If he was being honest, he felt he knew less now than he did when he'd read the autopsy report. He tried to outline the problem to Marjorie.

'Too many suspects?' she asked.

'Too many suspects being made to fit one theory,' he answered. 'I'm afraid I'm not buying it.'

Claude tried to elaborate. He was convinced that the investigation team had talked themselves into the fact that Jacob's murder was a classic revenge killing. They saw it almost as a mob-style execution, with the dismemberment in the gazebo being thrown in as a macho warning to others. They seemed to have seen everything through that single lens.

Marjorie was doing her best to follow along but was confused.

'But the Unsworths were the prime suspects and they don't really fit that profile, do they?' she asked.

'They've been made to fit that profile. That's my point,' said Claude. 'The way I read the notes, the team seems to have convinced themselves that Richard and Camilla killed Jacob and tried to make it look like a revenge killing to cover their tracks. There was even some suggestion that they might have used a professional for exactly that reason. I think that's what Peter must have meant when he said group-think had started to set in.'

Given all of that, Marjorie asked how they should be considering the message in Jacob's mouth.

'His abundant lies? I think we should regard it as far too convenient, like everything else.'

'It's a very odd phrase anyway, isn't it? Sounds as if it's been badly translated from a foreign language.'

Claude looked at Marjorie and raised his eyebrows. 'Perhaps it is a foreign language,' he mused.

He drove them both back to the flat. On the way, Marjorie continued with her relentless questioning.

'Sorry Claude, I'm still struggling with this. Surely the murderer must have had some sort of revenge in mind? What's the point of the murder otherwise?'

The truth was, Claude's instincts has been shouting very loudly to him as he had worked his way through the evidence and his mind had already set off in a very specific direction. But he was struggling to explain it to Marjorie, probably because he hadn't had a great deal of practice explaining anything to anyone for the last twenty years.

He tried again.

'Of course there had to be an element of revenge. But, in my opinion, this was a revenge that had been festering away with the murderer for some time, probably years. And it had become warped and twisted with the need to humiliate Jacob Unsworth. As I said before, it's the shaming that makes this so unusual.'

He pulled up outside the flat and looked over at Marjorie. He clearly wasn't convincing her.

Later that evening, Claude settled into his armchair. He had poured himself a single malt and he'd brought a gin and tonic for Marjorie. He decided to give the explanation one final shot. Perhaps he'd been pussy-footing around the subject a bit too much.

'Let me try it this way,' he said. 'The police believe this was a murder carried out for public consumption. To let the whole world see that a score had been settled. But that means when Jacob was castrated, his testicles would almost certainly have been placed . . .'

'In his mouth!' said Marjorie, triumphantly. She'd seen a couple of Mafia films in her time and the penny had finally dropped.

Claude rounded off the argument.

'On the contrary, this was actually a murder carried out for the private benefit of one man,' he said. 'He was telling his own private story with his own private ritual and symbolism. I doubt he gave a damn whether anyone else knew or not.'

CHAPTER THREE

It was dark in Claude's lounge apart from a small sliver of light breaking through the curtains from the street lights below. Someone navigated their way carefully through the furniture and reached down to switch on a table lamp. It was Claude himself.

He was dressed in pyjamas and dressing gown and carried his mobile phone. He picked up the autopsy report from the coffee table and sat himself down on the sofa. He removed the photograph of the message fragment from the folder and studied it closely under the light. After a while, he tapped a search into his mobile phone and waited. The results appeared and he read them carefully. He tapped in a second search.

He reached forward and picked up a pad and pencil from the table. The new results appeared on his phone and he started to make notes on the pad. He continued searching and scribbling for some time. He swung his legs round and put his feet on the sofa, making himself comfortable. He stared at the pad while he puzzled over the findings.

Four hours later, he woke with a start. Marjorie

was standing over him, fully dressed.

'Heavens, Claude!' she said. 'What's happened?'

'Oh, sorry,' he said, groggily. 'I only meant to get up for ten minutes. Must have dozed off.'

Marjorie drew the curtains and went off to the kitchen to make them both a cup of tea.

'I couldn't sleep last night thinking about that message in Jacob Unsworth's mouth,' Claude called out to her. 'Got it into my head that it might be some sort of Latin phrase.'

'And was it?' she called back.

'I'll show you. Could you bring that little blackboard and some chalk when you come, please?'

Marjorie reappeared carrying a tray with two cups of tea and one of those small blackboards that people use for to-do lists. Several pieces of white chalk rolled around on the tray. Claude took the blackboard which currently had "milk", "tea bags" and "car service" written on it. He wiped it clean with the sleeve of his dressing gown and picked up a piece of chalk. He wrote down the message:

HI_ A__ND_NT L_ES

'I mean, it's about sixty five years since I read Caesar's Gallic Wars,' he said, 'so I had to use the internet quite a bit. But the forensic team made a big mistake with the last word – there are three letters missing, not one. It should actually be . . .'

He rubbed out the last word and wrote in a new one:

LEONES

'Leones?' queried Marjorie.

'Yes, lions,' said Claude.

He moved on to the middle word, explaining that this was the only one of the three that had actually been correct. He filled in:

ABUNDANT

He worked his way forward to the first word and added a C instead of an S at the end.

'Leaving just the Latin word for "here".' he said.

He wrote in:

HIC

Marjorie peered at the new sentence. It read:

HIC ABUNDANT LEONES

'But what does it mean?' she asked.

'Here, lions abound,' said Claude, pleased with his handiwork.

Marjorie frowned for a moment. 'Oh, sort of like a school motto or something, you mean?'

'That's what I was thinking,' said Claude. 'But I'm afraid I fell asleep at that point. Do you want to work the oracle with your iPad and see if you can find out anything more?'

He went off to shower and shave and get himself dressed for the day. He was in his bedroom, knotting his tie expertly in the mirror, when he heard a very loud 'Bugger me!' from the lounge.

He came out to find Marjorie peering intently at her iPad. He sat down next to her. She had once been a computer illiterate but she was now quite fluent at it. She retraced her steps for Claude's benefit.

'I thought I'd go straight to Jacob Unsworth's Wikipedia page,' she said, stabbing a mildly arthritic finger at the touch screen.

The page duly appeared and she pressed the link to "Early years". Up came the details of Jacob's education, including a further link to Bellingfort school. She pressed it and the school's home page loaded, complete with pictures of gothic facades, quadrangles and vaulted ceilings. She read out the relevant details from the page.

'Here we are . . . Bellingfort school . . . educating young men for leadership in the modern world . . .' She looked at Claude. 'Motto: Hic abundant leones.'

She clapped him on the back, slightly too hard.

'Genius, Claude!' she said.

Later that morning, Chief Constable Selby appeared at Sergeant Deacon's desk. The Sergeant sat up, startled.

'Sorry sir,' he said. He hadn't done anything wrong but thought it best to apologise anyway.

'As you were,' said the Chief Constable. 'I just wanted to check on Claude and Marjorie, see how they're getting on.'

'Oh, I think they're fine, sir. Haven't heard a peep out of them. But then they've got an awful lot of case files to get through. Could be at it for weeks.'

'Perhaps we should drop by and say hello? See how their spirits are holding up?'

Sergeant Deacon got up from his desk and led the Chief Constable to the basement. He opened the door to the investigation room and turned on the light. The room was empty.

The cardboard boxes had been neatly stacked up. The table had been tidied. The white board was crammed full of information. But no Claude and Marjorie. The Chief Constable looked at Sergeant Deacon, questioningly.

At precisely that moment, Claude's car was cruising along in the middle lane of the M3 motorway.

'Continue on the current road,' said the satnav.

Marjorie gazed out of the window, lost in thought. Eventually, she turned to Claude.

'I'm not daft you know,' she said.

'I never thought you were,' he replied.

'Ever since Audrey's murder, you've been telling us all – me, Tom Deacon, everybody – that we're far too obsessed with serial killers.'

'I have.'

'And apart from the fact that they're the subject of every other TV drama, you keep saying they're actually very rare.'

'They are.'

'But Jacob Unsworth's murder – symbolism, ritual, shaming. Don't you think it's possibly a serial killing?'

'Oh, I think it almost definitely is.'

Marjorie was shocked. She demanded to know why he hadn't told her earlier.

He tried to explain that he hadn't wanted to say anything until he was absolutely certain, particularly with serial killings being such a high octane subject.

'Why aren't you certain?' she persisted.

'Well, in case you haven't noticed Marjorie,' he said, 'we've only got one body after fifteen years. Bit of a drawback when you're chasing a serial killer, isn't it?'

They turned off the motorway and followed the satnav's instructions as it took them to the outskirts of a rural town. They found their destination and pulled off the road onto a long, meandering drive. They passed a sign which read: "Bellingfort School. Established 1824. Headmaster: Dr R J Phillips". There was a coat of arms with "Hic abundant leones" written underneath on a scroll.

They managed to find their way to the office of the school secretary, Mrs Everett. They were unannounced and she was surprised to see them, particularly when they presented their ID cards. They outlined the reason for their visit and she reluctantly agreed it was something the headmaster should deal with himself. She led them into his study.

'Dr Phillips, this is Claude Simmons and Marjorie Watson,' she said. 'They're from . . . erm, the police.'

The headmaster stood up from behind his desk, an imposing figure dressed in black gown. He looked confused as Claude and Marjorie entered the room.

'I know what you're thinking, Dr Phillips,' said Marjorie. 'Police officers are looking younger and younger these days, aren't they?'

She grinned. The headmaster now looked baffled.

Claude stepped forwards and showed his ID card. He explained that he and Marjorie were Special Advisers to the police and had been attached to a cold case from fifteen years ago.

'It's the murder of one of your old pupils, Lord Jacob Unsworth,' he said.

The headmaster seemed surprised. 'And why should that concern us?' he asked. He gestured them towards the two seats in front of his desk.

'Well, a new piece of evidence has come to light which directly involves Bellingfort school,' said Claude, sitting down.

'Really?' The headmaster narrowed his eyes.

'I wonder if you could tell us about Jacob's time here, please?'

'Apart from the obvious things like him being Head Boy and captain of rugby, I'm afraid I can't really help,' he replied, after a pause. 'I believe Jacob left the school in the late seventies. I joined the mathematics department here in 1988.'

'So you're not aware of any incidents or unusual circumstances regarding his time here?' asked Claude.

The headmaster paused again, this time for longer.

'I'm afraid I'm not,' he said.

Claude asked about access to the school's records. He received a short lecture in return about the seriousness with which the school took the privacy of its pupils.

'And that privacy extends to a murder enquiry?'

asked Marjorie, chiming in.

The headmaster had had enough. He got up from his desk and walked towards the door.

'Mrs Watson, you are two complete strangers who have turned up out of the blue today with credentials which I can only describe as flimsy,' he said. He opened the door and held it ajar. 'Forgive me for not immediately handing our records over to you and then possibly finding our good name ruined in the newspapers tomorrow.'

Duly dismissed, Claude and Marjorie headed back to the car park.

'Flimsy credentials? Pompous bastard!' said Marjorie loudly, before they'd got in the car.

For once, Claude would have gone slightly further. His instincts told him that the headmaster was probably lying, at least by omission, and was almost certainly trying to cover something up. Fortunately, he'd had an idea. There was an obvious way to find the information they needed and simply bypass Bellingfort. He asked Marjorie to programme a new destination into the satnav on her phone. He started the engine.

Twenty minutes later, they were being ushered into Beckwith Hall's study by the butler. He took their coats and Marjorie took the liberty of ordering a gin and tonic.

They thanked Lord Unsworth for seeing them at short notice and they all sat down. He was clearly hoping for some major news about the case and was surprised to be asked instead about Bellingfort.

'Was your brother involved in any trouble there?' asked Claude. 'Fights? Bullying?'

'Oh yes, both. You have to remember that Jacob made an art form out of bullying.'

Claude asked about particular examples.

'Well, the obvious one was the boating lake incident,' said Lord Unsworth.

Claude looked at Marjorie. Another lake?

Lord Unsworth sat back and painted a grim picture for them. Jacob had been in the fifth form at the time. He was out on the lake in a rowing boat with one of his cronies – Marcus Taylor. A first former had taken a boat out without permission and managed to crash into Jacob. The accident had happened at about one mile an hour and caused no damage whatsoever. Nonetheless, Jacob was not prepared to let it pass. He reached over and grabbed the side of the other boat and tipped it up, ejecting the first former into the water. He and Marcus Taylor rowed off, apparently finding the whole thing very funny.

'Presumably the boy could swim?' asked Marjorie, anxiously.

'No, he certainly couldn't. In the end, a fourth former called Sebastian Greening had to jump in and save him.'

'And then?' asked Claude.

The butler returned with Marjorie's gin and tonic. She thanked him. Claude shook his head.

Lord Unsworth continued. Evidently, Sebastian Greening was a strong lad who had himself rowed stroke for one of the school's eights. He had waited for Jacob to moor his boat, walked up to him and punched him full in the face. This had produced a cheer from quite a lot of onlookers. The unfortunate thing was that Jacob's housemaster, Mr Fairfax, had arrived at precisely that moment, having heard the initial commotion. He chose to regard it as an un-provoked attack and reported it to the headmaster. There was a brief enquiry and Sebastian Greening was expelled.

'No! How can that be?' exclaimed Marjorie, out-raged.

'Oh, quite easily. Particularly when you consider the Unsworths were the school's major benefactors and my father was chairman of the board of gover-nors at the time.'

Claude asked about the boy who nearly drowned.

'Hugo something?' said Lord Unsworth. 'I'm afraid I was in the junior school at the time so my memory is a bit hazy. I don't remember seeing him after that so I suppose his parents must have moved him. You would, wouldn't you?'

'And Sebastian Greening?'

Lord Unsworth looked down at his shoes. He paused for a moment.

'I'm afraid he killed himself five years later. Just after his twentieth birthday.'

Back at the police station, the Chief Constable had appeared at Sergeant Deacon's desk again, not in the best of moods.

'Sergeant,' he said, 'do you happen to know any-thing about Bellingfort school?'

'Well, until five minutes ago, no sir,' the Sergeant replied.

'What does that mean?'

'Mrs Watson just rang me. She said they need a search warrant for Bellingfort school's records.'

The Chief Constable closed his eyes for a second in exasperation. He himself had just received an irate call from Bellingfort's headmaster who had wanted to know if the two old people who had visited him today were legitimate or whether they were each trying to impersonate a police officer.

He turned and started to walk back to his own office.

'While you're here sir there is one more piece of , umm . . . news,' said the Sergeant. He looked a little nervous.

'Well spit it out man,' said the Chief Constable.

'They now think Jacob Unsworth's murder was a serial killing.'

CHAPTER FOUR

Claude and Marjorie had had to ask for a second white board for their investigation room. Claude was busily filling it up with Post It note portraits, drawn by Marjorie. She had begun with a good likeness of Jacob Unsworth and imagined the others in something of a Beano school kids style. There were pictures of Marcus Taylor, Sebastian Greening and Hugo, the first former who had nearly drowned. Marjorie handed the last caricature to Claude. It was of Jacob's housemaster, Mr Fairfax, and she had caricatured him wearing a gown and a mortar board. He stuck it on the white board and wrote in the details. Across the bottom of the board, he wrote:

HIC ABUNDANT LEONES

Claude stepped back to study the new configuration. Almost immediately the door opened and Chief Constable Selby and Sergeant Deacon walked in. The Chief Constable seemed to be in a testy mood. He demanded an update on the case and sat himself down in Claude's chair, without waiting to be invited. The Sergeant perched himself on the edge of the desk.

'Why don't we start with Bellingfort school since the headmaster's just been bending my ear?' he asked, bluntly.

If the Chief Constable's whirlwind entrance had been intended to impress Claude then he hadn't succeeded. After all, the murder investigation had been mired in confusion and mistakes for fifteen years. Now Claude was certain they were starting to get somewhere and he wasn't going to be thrown off track. He began by describing the breakthrough they'd had with the message fragment in Jacob's mouth and how it had turned out to be Bellingfort's motto. He used his walking stick to point to the two different messages on the two white boards.

'It wasn't about "lies" at all,' he said. 'It was about "leones".'

The Chief Constable frowned.

'Here, lions abound,' said Sergeant Deacon, reading from the second board.

Everybody looked at him.

'Sorry. A-level Latin.'

'You should have been on the investigation team, Tom,' said Marjorie. 'They could certainly have done with you.'

Claude picked up his thread again quickly before the Chief Constable had a chance to respond to this. He described his trip with Marjorie to the school and their abortive meeting with the headmaster, Dr Phillips.

'I don't think we should be fooled by his bluster, Peter,' he said. 'He's being aggressive because he's trying to cover something up.'

'And you know this how?'

'Because we went straight to see another of Bellingfort school's old pupils – Lord Richard Unsworth.'

The surprises kept coming for the Chief Constable. He looked at Sergeant Deacon, not altogether warmly.

Claude pressed on. He recounted Richard Unsworth's story about the boating lake incident - the attempted drowning of the first former by Jacob Unsworth, the heroics of Sebastian Greening and the subsequent incident involving the housemaster.

'Brace yourselves, it gets worse,' he said. 'The school ended up exonerating Jacob Unsworth and expelling Sebastian Greening.'

'It gets much worse,' said Marjorie, joining in. 'Five years after being expelled, Sebastian Greening killed himself.'

'Seriously?' said the Chief Constable.

He got up from his seat and went to study the two white boards in detail. Any reservations he'd had about Claude and Marjorie's exploits were rapidly evaporating.

'So, you're presumably suggesting some sort of connection between the incident in the Bellingfort lake and the drowning of Jacob Unsworth in the Beckwith Hall lake?' he asked.

'We certainly are,' said Claude.

The Chief Constable sat down again, still pondering. He had studied under Claude and his mind now worked in a very similar way.

'But there's only one body, isn't there? Why a serial killing?' he asked.

Claude leant on his walking stick, forced to deliver some bad news.

'I'm sorry to be critical, Peter, but the likelihood of this being a serial killing was evident from a simple read of the autopsy report. Nobody seems to have picked it up.'

'Even though the testicles were missing!' said Marjorie, trying to be helpful.

'There will be other bodies,' said Claude. 'It's just that everyone's been looking in the wrong place.'

They drove back down the M3 the next day in Sergeant Deacon's car. Marjorie sat in the front, being uppity as usual. She accused the Sergeant of mollycoddling her and Claude. He was accompanying them to Bellingfort school to present the headmaster with a search warrant. Marjorie insisted they could just as well have done it themselves.

'Sorry Mrs Watson but there's no way round it,' he responded. 'It's an official police document so I'm afraid I have to present it.'

Claude leaned forward from the back seat.

'We're Special Advisers, Marjorie,' he said. 'So while we're part of the team, we can't go around giving orders.'

'More's the pity,' she said.

They arrived at Bellingfort. Sergeant Deacon had followed Claude's advice and given the school no advance notice of their visit. It was unlikely that the school would attempt to tamper with the records but it was best to be cautious.

They found Mrs Everett and she led them anxiously into the headmaster's study. The headmaster stood up, astonished to see Claude and Marjorie again. He eyed up Sergeant Deacon suspiciously.

The Sergeant stepped forward, displaying his ID.

'Good morning Dr Phillips, I'm Sergeant Tom Deacon,' he said. 'I have a warrant to search the school's records with regard to a former pupil, Jacob Unsworth.'

The headmaster took a moment to collect himself.

'This is highly irregular,' he said, affecting the same indignation he had displayed during Claude and Marjorie's last visit. 'As I've already made clear, our pupils' records are confidential – I'm afraid I am unable to simply hand them over. I'm sure the school's solicitors can clarify the matter for you.'

Sergeant Deacon removed the search warrant from the envelope he was carrying. He unfolded it painstakingly and handed it to the headmaster.

'Unfortunately, this is not a request, sir. This is a formal police instruction, signed by a magistrate. Respectfully, you can either provide us with the documents now or we can return with a number of uniformed officers – we'll probably need five or six – and we can take all of your records away. It's up to you.'

Marjorie looked at Claude. She was thoroughly impressed by Sergeant Deacon's show of authority.

'I've changed my mind,' she said. 'I rather like being mollycoddled.'

Half an hour later, Claude, Marjorie and Sergeant Deacon were sat in an empty classroom, each with a stack of folders in front of them. They were searching for the Board of Governors' records and Marjorie eventually found them at the bottom of her pile. She thumbed through the folder and pulled out a one page document. She started to read it out loud. It was headed: "Minutes of an extraordinary meeting to discuss a serious breach of school rules at Bellingfort boating lake on June 2nd 1974."

They'd hardly got started but, hearing the date, Claude immediately got up from his seat and walked over to the window. He stared out.

'Well that means . . .' he said.

'That means what?' asked Marjorie. She hadn't even read out the minutes yet.

'Nothing,' he said and sat back down.

Marjorie looked at him, confused. She returned to the minutes which were short and to the point. They recorded that the chairman had thanked the headmaster for his thorough investigation. After that, the board had voted unanimously to accept the headmaster's proposals, including the immediate expulsion of Sebastian Greening. It was signed, "Edward Unsworth, Chairman of the Board".

Claude listened carefully to Marjorie. He started

to root around for the folder that contained the headmaster's own report on the incident. He found it eventually and started to read. It began by dealing with the first former, whose full name was Hugo Foster.

'I'm paraphrasing here,' said Claude, reading and speaking at the same time, 'but the headmaster chose not to believe a word that Hugo Foster said . . . found the claim that Jacob Unsworth had tipped him out of the boat absolutely preposterous . . . actually gave Foster a detention for taking the boat out without permission.'

Marjorie was taking notes. She asked if there was anything about Jacob's henchman, Marcus Taylor. Claude flipped through the pages and found the relevant piece. He read it out loud, not quite believing what it said.

'Quote: "Several classmates came forward to verify the incident, notably Sam Middleton and Harry Russell. And the fact that Marcus Taylor and Jacob Unsworth's stories completely tallied must be regarded as extremely significant".'

Unfortunately, there was more. Claude turned the page. The headmaster's report went on to praise Mr Fairfax for his prompt arrival at the scene, allowing him to witness Sebastian Greening's assault.

' . . ."thereby putting the matter beyond all reasonable doubt",' said Claude, reading the final sentence. 'Good grief.'

He sat back in his chair and threw the folder onto the desk. He reflected for a moment.

'Sergeant,' he said. 'After all this fiction, I think we could do with a few facts. I'd like a copy of the police report on the death of Sebastian Greening. And while you're at it, I'd like a copy of the autopsy report as well, please.'

Sergeant Deacon made a note in his notebook. He had been struggling for some time to find the correct way to address Claude, now that he'd got to know him a bit more. Should it simply be "Claude"? Or "Mr Simmons"? Or "Chief Superintendent"? Having watched him in close proximity for a while, he made a decision.

'Certainly, Chief Superintendent,' he said.

They set off back to Mrs Everett's office. Sergeant Deacon thanked her for the help she'd given and requested that they be sent a copy of all the documents they had just reviewed.

'Of course,' she said. 'And can I just apologise for the . . . . umm, misunderstanding earlier. The headmaster wasn't trying to mislead but he's inherited an impossible situation. He knows – we all know – that the Jacob Unsworth incident was a major black mark against the school.'

They had all formed the opinion that the headmaster was actually an oaf, but it was good of her to apologise nonetheless. They headed for the door but Claude stopped at the threshold.

'Oh, one more thing Mrs Everett,' he said. 'Do you have an old pupil organisation? You know, an alumni sort of thing?'

'Of course.'

'And who administers it?'

'I do. Keeping tabs on all the boys is my favourite hobby.'

Five minutes later, Claude, Marjorie and Sergeant Deacon were seated in Mrs Everett's office on a row of chairs normally reserved for pupils nervously waiting to see the headmaster. Marjorie had her notebook open and was asking questions. Mrs Everett was trying find the answers on her computer. She had already retrieved the details of Sam Middleton and Harry Russell. Evidently, they were both keen alumni and attenders of reunions. As far as she knew, Sam was in publishing and Harry was in insurance.

Marjorie asked about Marcus Taylor and Mrs Everett delved into her computer again. She read from the screen. It said his parents were South African and they had owned a big vineyard in Stellenbosch. Apparently, the Taylor Estate's cabernet sauvignon was much sought after. Marcus had eventually returned to South Africa to help run the business.

'He kept in touch for a while,' she said, still reading, 'attended one reunion . . . not heard from since. It happens.'

Next on Marjorie's list was Hugo Foster. Mrs Everett turned away from her computer and faced her guests. She looked a little embarrassed. She confessed she had no records for Hugo because his parents had moved him immediately after the boating lake incident. Indeed, they had sued the school for a refund of the whole year's fees.

'But I've tried to follow his fortunes nonetheless,' she said. 'I'm glad to say he's done very well. Now a professor of something-or-other at Cambridge. Anthropology, I think.'

They finished off with the details of the two teachers involved. The headmaster, Mr Hetherington, had died of cancer in 1996. Mrs Everett reported, not without further embarrassment, that the housemaster, Mr Fairfax, had been promoted to deputy headmaster two months after the boating lake incident. He was now retired and living just outside of Cheltenham.

They thanked Mrs Everett again and walked back to the car. Sergeant Deacon started the engine and they set off for Claude's flat.

Marjorie was in the passenger seat, studying her notes closely. Eventually, she turned round to address Sergeant Deacon and Claude.

'So, by my reckoning the Unsworths are no longer prime suspects and we now have two new front runners,' she said. 'One is a Cambridge Professor and the other one committed suicide twenty five years before Jacob Unsworth was murdered.'

Sergeant Deacon raised his eyebrows.

'Good summary, Marjorie,' said Claude.

CHAPTER FIVE

Early the next morning, Claude and Marjorie boarded a train from King's Cross to Cambridge. They had each booked a window seat and they settled down to enjoy the journey. Claude opened his copy of the Daily Telegraph and Marjorie gazed at the suburbs rolling by.

Back at the police station, Sergeant Deacon was standing in front of the Chief Constable's desk, recounting the events of the previous day. The Chief Constable had taken to tapping his pencil distractedly and staring out of the window as he listened. What the Sergeant had outlined presented him with a real dilemma. There was now enough evidence to appoint a whole new investigation team. Truth be told, police protocols probably demanded he do just that. Yet it would have meant immediately side-lining Claude and Marjorie. He may have been slightly reluctant about their appointment at the outset but the fact was they had made more progress in what seemed like fifteen minutes than the previous murder team had made in fifteen years. Why on earth would he want to stand them down now?

On the train, the breakfast trolley arrived. Claude

sized up the only remaining bacon baguette. Plainly, the British Rail breakfast wasn't what it used to be. Mind you, British Rail wasn't what it used to be. He decided to risk it and took the baguette and a cup of tea. It was a little early for a gin and tonic so Marjorie settled for a tea and a packet of shortbread biscuits.

The Chief Constable had made a decision. 'Right Sergeant, I'm officially going to start thinking about appointing a new murder investigation team and I want you to make a note of that in the case records, please,' he said, dropping as many heavy hints as he could. 'Unfortunately, it's going to be a long, slow process what with budgets and bureaucracy and meetings and schedules. Am I making myself clear?'

'You certainly are, sir.'

'That means we're going to have to rely on Claude and Marjorie for a little bit longer. I'm assigning a new uniformed officer to work with you in the short term and between you I want you to give them all the help you can. And make sure you dot all the i's and cross all the t's.'

'Yes, sir.'

Claude and Marjorie arrived at Cambridge station. They picked up a taxi from the rank and made the short journey to Professor Foster's college. They showed their ID cards to the porter at the lodge and made their way across the college's front court and up a narrow flight of creaking stairs. They found the Professor's room at the end of a corridor and knocked on the door. For once, they had made an appointment and he greeted them warmly.

He cut a slightly eccentric figure in a tweed suit, peering at them over a pair of half moon glasses. His study bordered on the chaotic. The bookshelves were crammed full and books had spilled over into piles on the floor. Various masks and headdresses hung from the walls and there was a glass cabinet crammed full of knives, bows, arrows and spears. The Professor cleared away the papers and books that had wandered onto the chairs and they all sat down. Claude began by reiterating the reason for their visit.

'Jacob Unsworth,' responded the Professor. 'That's a name I was hoping not to have to speak again.'

'I can imagine,' said Claude. 'So you were aware that he was murdered in 2004?'

'Oh yes. Drowned in his own lake, didn't he? I think that's what we call the sense of humour of the gods.'

Claude asked him about his recollections of the boating incident itself. The Professor's memory seemed to be fragmented, perhaps because he was only twelve years old at the time or perhaps because it was still painful to bring to mind. Certainly he could remember the panic of drowning, he said. Then there was the strange sensation of being dragged to the surface by his hair. His strongest memory seemed to be the braying laughter of Jacob Unsworth and his sidekick.

Marjorie looked up from her notebook. She asked about him being taken out of school. He set off on a long ramble about the fact that boarding school had been his father's idea and had been something his mother had never approved of. She had never been able to get the hang of sending her only child away to live somewhere else and had seen the boating lake incident as the perfect opportunity to have him back. She went to war with the school and the whole thing nearly ended up in the High Court. He ended up at the local day school, ten minutes down the road. He described it as the best thing that possibly could have happened to him.

The Professor was less pleased to talk about Sebastian Greening. Evidently, he had never had the chance to thank him for saving his life. There was a big age gap between them and it had been impossible to keep in touch after they'd both left Bellingfort. There was no internet back then and he didn't try and track him down until he went to university. Sadly, by that time Sebastian was already dead.

The Professor stood up, as if trying to shrug off the bad memories. He started to pace around the study.

'Let's get to the point, shall we?' he said, after a moment. 'I've seen a few episodes of Grantchester so I know you're going to ask me if I have an alibi for the time of Jacob Unsworth's murder. Let's be honest, I have an excellent motive, don't I?'

He smiled.

Claude was slightly taken aback by the Professor's directness. He reiterated that he and Marjorie were only Special Advisers and that a police officer would have to take his formal statement later.

'Let's do it now, shall we?' the Professor insisted.

He walked to one of the bookshelves and ran his hand along a long line of books with identical spines. He explained that his mother had insisted he keep a diary while he was at Bellingfort, so she could share the experience with him. It was a habit he'd never broken. He asked Marjorie for the exact date.

She consulted her notebook. 'June second, 2004,' she said.

He took down the relevant book and thumbed through it until he found the right page. He read it out loud.

'Here we are . . . . "Filmed some of the craft of arrow making this morning. They are endlessly painstaking in their methods and the tipping of the arrows with the poison itself is nothing short of tribal science".'

He looked pleased with himself.

'Sorry, what does that mean?' asked Marjorie, completely lost.

'It means I was in the Orinoco river basin at the time, carrying out fieldwork. A six month trip – the Anthropology Department will confirm the details to your police officer.'

Claude looked at Marjorie.

'Just one more question, Professor,' Claude asked. 'What was the poison you were filming?'

'Curare, of course.'

They thanked the Professor and said their goodbyes. Outside of the college they decided to walk for a while, collecting their thoughts. Marjorie eventually broke the silence.

'If I remember correctly, Claude, you described the drug the murderer used to immobilise Jacob Unsworth as "a bit like curare".'

'I did.'

'So, what do you make of what we just heard?'

Claude stopped and leant on his walking stick for a moment, dramatically framed by King's College Chapel.

'Well, it's either an extremely big coincidence, or the Professor is taunting us.'

Marjorie had finished sketching all of the new leads that had emerged from their last trip to Bellingfort. Claude took them and began to stick them to the second white board. He arranged everyone in two opposing groups. Basically, it was Jacob Unsworth, Marcus Taylor, Sam Middleton, Harry Russell, Mr Hetherington the headmaster and Mr Fairfax the housemaster on one team. And Sebastian Greening and Hugo Foster on the other.

'Not the fairest of fights, was it?' said Marjorie.

The door opened and Sergeant Deacon came in, followed by a uniformed policewoman. He introduced her as Constable Curtis and explained she would be working closely with him. Everybody exchanged a greeting.

Sergeant Deacon had brought with him the police

files and the autopsy report for the death of Sebastian Greening. He handed them to Claude.

'Thank you,' said Claude, 'That reminds me, can we find out the details of Greening's next of kin, please?'

'Already done,' replied the Sergeant, gesturing to Constable Curtis. She read from her notebook.

'Both parents deceased . . . one sister, Sophie . . . living quite near Beckwith Hall. I'll let you have the address.'

The two police officers turned to leave. Constable Deacon stopped at the door.

'One more thing,' he said. 'We're struggling to track down Marcus Taylor at the moment. There seems to be some confusion with the records in South Africa. Just to let you know, I'm going to contact the Taylor wine estate directly.'

Claude and Marjorie finished up at the police station and headed for the car. Back at the flat, Marjorie cooked them both mince and potatoes, Claude's favourite, and they sat down and enjoyed it with a glass of red wine and a gin and tonic.

Afterwards, Claude sat in his armchair studying the new documents he'd been given by Sergeant Deacon. Marjorie couldn't help being impressed. He was reading the police file and the autopsy report simultaneously, with one balanced on each knee. She couldn't help being impatient either. She huffed and puffed and squirmed and fidgeted. After fifteen minutes, Claude thought he'd probably tortured her enough.

'That's unusual,' he said.

'What is?'

'Well, Sebastian Greening committed suicide by driving his car very fast into a brick wall.'

'Why is that unusual?'

'Sorry to be blunt Marjorie, but if you drive your car into a brick wall, no matter how fast, there's no guarantee of death is there? Just a guarantee of serious injury.'

'But he did die, didn't he?' countered Marjorie.

This was already getting complicated. He had indeed died, but only because the car had burst into flames. Claude decided to leave it for a moment and returned to reading the reports.

Marjorie was only able to sit quietly for a further thirty seconds.

'Did the police suspect foul play?' she asked.

'Quite the reverse,' he said.

In the end, the police had decided not to even open a formal investigation. There had been a long and detailed suicide note which a handwriting expert had analysed and pronounced authentic. Claude took it from the folder and showed it to Marjorie. Then there was the fact that the car that had been driven into the wall was Sebastian's father's Jaguar. Tellingly, some of Sebastian's engraved wristwatch had managed to survive the blaze.

Marjorie's questions kept coming. She asked about the autopsy.

'Well, they did their best but the body was very

badly burned,' said Claude, leafing back through the report. 'They managed to retrieve some teeth fragments but not enough to identify him.'

Marjorie paused. 'Presumably you can still recover DNA from a burned body, though?' she asked. 'Couldn't they identify him that way?'

'Ordinarily you could,' said Claude. 'But this was 1979 and forensic DNA testing didn't start until 1983.'

Claude found two other significant points in the autopsy report. The pathologists had attempted a basic toxicology screen and found evidence of alcohol in the bloodstream. They had also found evidence of smoke inhalation in the lungs and trachea. He tried to explain this to Marjorie.

She frowned. 'So you're saying he was still alive when the fire started?'

'Exactly the point I was trying to make earlier,' he said. 'The crash itself didn't kill him.'

Claude and Marjorie set off for the house of Sebastian Greening's sister, Sophie Tyler. Marjorie was attempting to engage in a serious conversation. She was trying to explain to Claude how odd she found it that two boys could each suffer major traumas and yet react so differently. In this particular case, Hugo Foster had gone on to become a Cambridge Professor and Sebastian Greening had gone completely off the rails. Claude thought about this for a while, not least because it was an extremely difficult question. His best guess was that Hugo's close relationship with his mother would have played a significant part for him. He was curious to find out how Sebastian's parents had reacted to the drama.

They arrived at the house and Sophie Tyler greeted them. She was probably in her early sixties and didn't appear to be in the best of health. She leant on an NHS walking stick and walked stiffly. Nonetheless, she insisted on making them a cup of tea and they eventually settled down in the lounge. They began by talking about the boating lake incident at Bellingfort. The expulsion of her brother was clearly still fresh in her mind, even after forty odd years.

'Well, our father was what you might call old school,' she said. 'He'd sent Sebastian to Bellingfort to learn the do's and don'ts of this world and he was horrified by the expulsion.'

'What? Sided with the school, you mean?' asked Claude, frowning.

'Absolutely – no sympathy for Sebastian whatsoever. Refused to pay another penny for his education.'

Claude asked about their mother. Sophie gave a shrug of resignation.

'Oh, she loved Sebastian and she tried to be sympathetic. But the truth is she was . . . well, very highly strung. The whole thing pretty much tipped her over the edge.'

'You do realise that Sebastian was the hero in this

story, not the villain, don't you?' interrupted Marjorie, her sense of natural justice in danger of becoming outraged again.

'I do, yes. I had a lovely conversation with Hugo Foster, the boy he saved. But unfortunately it was . . .
'

She trailed off, a little upset. She got up, leaning heavily on her walking stick. She went over to the mantelpiece and picked up a framed photo of Sebastian, taken on a family holiday when he was in his early teens. She handed it to Claude and Marjorie. It was the first time they'd seen a picture of him. He was tall and blond and suntanned.

She sat back down, having regained her poise. Claude asked her about Sebastian's time after Bellingfort. She shrugged again. She described how he'd gone off to the local secondary school and arrived as the new boy from the toff's school. Not the easiest of starts. Having said that, he had apparently done quite well to begin with. He was very bright, she said, and for a while there was a hope that he might aim for engineering at university. Then came the sixth form. By that time, he had started to withdraw into himself and in the upper sixth he had become completely solitary. His A-levels were a disaster.

'Do you think he was slowly internalising all the problems?' asked Claude, struggling to build up a psychological profile of Sebastian.

'Who knows?' she said. 'He was a lovely boy with a strong sense of right and wrong. And then he was severely punished for saving another boy's life. Not just by his school but by his father as well.'

Claude and Marjorie said their goodbyes and drove back to the flat. Claude was mulling over what they'd just heard and Marjorie appeared to be totting things up in her notebook again.

'By my count, we now have three suspects,' she said. 'One was dead at the time of the murder, one was up the Orinoco and the third is a lady who apparently now has MS. I'm not sure we've cracked it yet, Claude.'

'I have to agree, Marjorie,' he said.

CHAPTER SIX

C laude and Marjorie were up early. They had finished breakfast and were readying themselves to leave. Marjorie's phone rang.

'Hello, Special Agent Marjorie Watson,' she said into the phone.

Claude gently shook his head.

'Oh yes Tom, good morning,' she continued. 'Really? . . . well, we're just on our way in so we'll be there shortly . . . indeed, see you then.'

'That was Tom Deacon,' she said to Claude. 'We've been summoned to a meeting in the Chief Constable's office.'

Claude drove them along the now familiar route to the police station. Twenty minutes later they arrived at the office and found Sergeant Deacon and Constable Curtis already there. The Chief Constable emerged from behind his desk and sat down with Claude and Marjorie. The Sergeant and the Constable remained standing.

The Chief Constable looked troubled.

'Sergeant Deacon and I were slow walking our way towards a new murder enquiry in order to give you two some more time,' he confessed to Claude and Marjorie. 'But I'm afraid events have now over-taken us.'

'What's happened?' asked Marjorie, half expecting to be told off.

'We've finally tracked down Jacob Unsworth's friend Marcus Taylor,' he continued. 'It turns out he was murdered in South Africa in 1989.'

'Heavens, thirty years ago?' said Claude, looking from the Chief Constable to Sergeant Deacon. 'How did that slip through the net?'

The Sergeant opened his notebook and attempted to explain. It transpired that Marcus had married a South African girl, Jessica Houghton, five years earlier. In keeping with the latest trend, they'd agreed to take each other's surnames, so they became the Houghton-Taylors. When the local police records were computerised some years after his murder, it seems he had simply been listed as Marcus Houghton.

'And how was he murdered?' asked Claude.

'That's what we're about to find out,' said the Chief Constable, getting up. 'The Cape Town police are digging out the records as we speak.'

Everyone followed him to a room furnished with a very large TV screen. A camera hung from the top of the screen, pointing back at a row of chairs. They all sat down.

The Sergeant fiddled with the remote control and the TV sprung into life. After several seconds, a man appeared on the screen and announced himself as Inspector Jesse De Villiers. The Chief Constable introduced everybody else. The Inspector was evidently being filmed by his own laptop, with the hustle and bustle of a busy police station in the background. He was clearly a little perplexed by the information request he'd received.

'I'm afraid all this was before my time,' he said, kicking things off. 'But the fact is we've already had someone serving a life sentence for this murder – the victim's business partner, Eddie Van Vuuren.'

The Chief Constable sat forward in his chair.

'Then we may possibly have some bad news for you,' he said.

Inspector De Villiers tried to stick to his guns. He referred to the case notes in front of him. Marcus and Van Vuuren had had a violent argument two days before the murder, he said. Three witnesses had heard Van Vuuren make death threats. The trial had been very short and the verdict had been unanimous.

'Sorry Inspector, this is not a competition to prove you wrong,' said Claude, intervening. 'But we strongly suspect this may be the first of a number of serial killings.'

The Inspector looked back from the screen, blinking.

'How can you possibly know that?' he asked. 'I haven't even told you anything about the murder itself yet.'

'No indeed,' said Claude. He couldn't help the fact that he was about to embarrass the Inspector. 'Can I ask, did your victim drown?'

'Well, yes. Face down in his own swimming pool. But I thought that was public knowledge.'

'And was there a muscle relaxant found in his bloodstream?'

The Inspector referred to his notes. He looked up again, surprised.

'Yes. Something called Pancuronium.'

'And had the victim had a body part removed? A body part that was never found?'

Marjorie had been well behaved for slightly too long. She leant across to Chief Constable Selby.

'I'm guessing penis,' she whispered.

Oblivious to Marjorie, the Inspector read directly from the autopsy report. He shook his head.

'It says here, "the victim's tongue had been removed. Ante mortem". Damn.'

Claude sat back in his chair, deliberating.

'Of course,' he said, addressing the group in the teleconference room. 'The boy who lied to protect Jacob Unsworth has his tongue removed.'

Claude reflected for a moment. He had one final question.

'Sorry for the inquisition, Inspector,' he said. 'But was there a piece of paper found in Marcus's mouth, with some sort of message on it?'

The Inspector thumbed through his notes one more time.

'Yes, but damaged by the blood and the chlorine in the pool. Two words still legible – abundant leones. Abundant lions in Latin, apparently. The team could find no significance for it.'

He looked up, now slightly shell-shocked.

The meeting broke up and the Chief Constable headed back to his office. The others made their way towards Claude and Marjorie's investigation room. Marjorie was feeling slightly sorry for the Cape Town police. She was trying to make the point that there actually was an abundance of lions in South Africa so it must have been very confusing for them.

Claude, not listening at all, stopped abruptly.

'Sergeant Deacon, what was the exact date of Marcus Taylor's murder?' he asked.

The Sergeant consulted his notebook quickly.

'June 2nd, 1989.'

'Oh, good grief.'

Claude set off rapidly down the corridor, with everyone else trying to keep up. He arrived at the investigation room and rushed inside. He immediately set about clearing the original white board and unceremoniously threw each of the portraits of the fourteen suspects on the floor. He picked up a magic marker pen. On the left hand side of the board he wrote:

BOATING LAKE INCIDENT JUNE 2nd 1974

He moved to the right and wrote:

MARCUS TAYLOR MURDERED JUNE 2nd1989

'Fifteen years after the boating lake incident, to the day,' he said, talking as he wrote.

He moved to the right and wrote:

JACOB UNSWORTH MURDERED JUNE 2nd 2004

'Another fifteen years later, to the day,' he said.

He paused for a moment. He wrote down the next

date in the sequence, fifteen years on:

JUNE 2nd 2019

'And what's today's date?' he asked, turning round to face everyone else.

'June 2nd 2019,' said Marjorie.

Everybody stared at the board, wide-eyed. Claude grabbed the portraits of Sam Middleton, Harry Russell and Mr Fairfax from the other white board.

'All of which puts these three in considerable jeopardy,' he said, sticking the portraits above the final date. 'Sergeant Deacon, we need to act very quickly.'

After a brief debate, Claude and Marjorie set off for Mr Fairfax's house, driven in a police car by Constable Curtis. They hadn't got very far when Marjorie's phone rang. It was Sergeant Deacon letting them know that Sam Middleton and Harry Russell had both been contacted and were both safe. They were to be interviewed later that afternoon.

However, there was no reply yet from Mr Fairfax. Claude frowned. He leaned forward from the back seat.

'I think we'll have to get a move on please, Constable,' he said.

She turned on the siren and the blue lights and put her foot down. Even so, it felt like an age before they eventually arrived at Mr Fairfax's house. They got out of the car and walked up the garden path. The house itself was a small, detached cottage and Claude hammered repeatedly on the front door. There was no response. Marjorie peered through the bay window. She could see nothing. Constable Curtis circled round to the back of the house and returned, shaking her head.

'Right Constable,' said Claude. 'Look the other way.'

Using his elbow, he struck the glass panel in the front door and it shattered. He continued to use his elbow to remove the remaining fragments of glass before putting his arm through and releasing the lock. He entered the house, crunching over the broken glass. He was followed by Constable Curtis and then by an over-awed Marjorie.

'Mr Fairfax, it's the police!' called out Constable Curtis, loudly.

There was no answer. They walked from the hall to the lounge to the dining room to the kitchen. Nothing. They climbed the stairs and the Constable called out again. Still no answer.

They reached the top and Claude used the sleeve of his jacket to carefully open the first bedroom door. He walked inside. Constable Curtis remained on the landing with Marjorie, wondering if she should perhaps have been taking the lead. The trouble was, Claude had automatically reverted to being Chief Superintendent Simmons as soon as he had arrived at the potential crime scene. There wasn't much she could have done about it. There really wasn't much anyone could have done about it.

He emerged from the bedroom, shaking his head. He tried the remaining two bedrooms and found them empty as well. This left one door, presumably to the bathroom. Claude opened the door carefully and walked inside. He stood and surveyed the scene, obstructing the view of Marjorie and Constable Curtis. Eventually, he bent forward to touch something and afforded them a brief glimpse of what appeared to be a pair of legs sticking up in the air from one end of the bath. If it wasn't macabre it would have been comical. Claude turned and walked back out.

'You need a full forensic team here, Constable,' he said. 'By my guess he's been dead for some time. Face down in his own bath.'

Constable Curtis guarded the crime scene while they waited and eventually the forensic team began to arrive. They each donned their protective clothing and made their way inside.

With yet more time to wait, Claude and Marjorie wandered off in search of civilisation. They hadn't eaten anything since breakfast and eventually found a small café. Claude wasn't in any way squeamish but his appetite felt slightly diminished after what he'd just witnessed. He studied the menu and settled for a plain omelette. Marjorie, entirely unperturbed, ordered a rump steak, rare, with chips and peas.

'Typical isn't it?' she said, tucking into the steak.

'What is?' asked Claude.

'Well, you wait ages for a murder and then two come along at once.'

She reached over for the ketchup and squeezed a large dollop onto her chips.

They finished their meal and went to the counter

to pay. They bought a cheese roll for Constable Curtis, just in case, and wandered back. Shortly after they arrived, the front door opened and a zipped up body bag was wheeled out and lifted into the back of an unmarked black van. It was followed out by the pathologist, in the process of removing his face mask and the hood of his protective suit. He had heard about the body being discovered by an unconventional investigation team and he wandered over to speak to Claude and Marjorie. Claude stepped forward and introduced himself and Marjorie as Special Advisers. He asked about the cause of death.

'We'll obviously find out more back at the lab, but it looks like drowning to me,' said the pathologist.

'Anything unusual about the body?' asked Claude, fishing for details.

'Sorry, how do you mean exactly?'

'Did he have any bits cut off?' asked Marjorie, bluntly.

The Pathologist looked surprised.

'Well yes, actually. He'd had his eyeballs removed. While he was still alive, I'd say.'

'Hmm, the man who chose not to see the truth about Jacob Unsworth,' said Claude, largely to himself.

The pathologist wandered off, slightly confused. He wondered if perhaps he'd given the information away to the wrong people.

Next morning, Claude was putting the final touches to the investigation board, updating it with the new information about Mr Fairfax. He was being watched by Marjorie, Sergeant Deacon and Constable Curtis. He stepped back and they all surveyed the montage of victims and suspects. Sergeant Deacon took the opportunity to point out that a new and more comprehensive board was now being set up in the main investigation room and suggested that perhaps they should all be using it.

'No thank you,' said Marjorie, firmly. 'We much prefer ours.'

Claude appeared to be lost in his own thoughts. He asked if Professor Foster's alibi had checked out. Constable Curtis flipped open her notebook.

'The university confirms the Professor was definitely in Venezuela at the time of Jacob Unsworth's murder,' she said. 'I've also checked his movements on the day of Mr Fairfax's murder. He gave a lecture and held two seminars in Cambridge, followed by a Fellows' dinner at his college.'

Claude listened to this, not particularly surprised. He was rapidly coming to a conclusion.

'There's only one thing for it,' he said. 'I'm afraid we're going to have to interview Sebastian Greening's sister again.'

Everybody looked at him. Marjorie pointed out the blindingly obvious, that Sophie Tyler was seriously ill with MS and couldn't possibly have murdered Mr Fairfax.

'I know, that's why we need to pay her another

visit immediately,' said Claude. He turned to Sergeant Deacon.

'And I suspect we're going to need Constable Curtis again, if that's okay.'

'Of course, Chief Superintendent,' said the Sergeant, baffled.

An hour later, Claude and Marjorie were seated on the sofa next to an anxious looking Sophie Tyler. She hadn't expected to see them again, certainly not accompanied by a uniformed police officer. Claude tried to reassure her that she wasn't a suspect herself. He told her they were just trying to eliminate certain possibilities and certain lines of enquiry. This was almost the truth.

'Have you kept anything that belonged to Sebastian – perhaps from when he was a baby or a toddler?' he asked, pressing on.

'I only kept photographs myself,' she said, thinking about it. 'But mother used to hoard stuff like that. She was very sentimental.'

'Do you still have it?'

She frowned for a moment.

'I haven't seen it for years but I suspect it's probably somewhere in the loft.' She paused and patted her walking stick. 'I'm afraid I don't go up there much these days.'

Claude looked at Constable Curtis and she gave a resigned shrug. Here was the reason she'd been invited to tag along. She rummaged around and eventually found a step ladder in the garden shed. She struggled it up the stairs and set it up on the landing, underneath the loft. With some difficulty she clambered in and switched on her torch.

The beam picked up the dust she had disturbed and revealed a space crammed with objects, most of them probably long forgotten. There was a large steamer trunk, various suitcases and cardboard boxes in all shapes and sizes. There were rolled-up rugs and even a set of four dining chairs, upholstered in Draylon. She pulled the first cardboard box forward. She rolled up her sleeves and started to sort through it.

Back in the lounge, Marjorie was not entirely following what was going on. Claude appeared to be going through one of those phases whereby his thinking suddenly leapt ahead and she was forced to try and catch up. He continued to fire off questions.

'Can I ask,' he said, addressing Sophie, 'what did your father do for a living?'

'Oh, he was an anaesthetist. A consultant anaesthetist,' she replied.

Claude raised his eyebrows. 'I don't suppose he ever brought a medical bag home with him, did he?'

'You ask the strangest questions, Mr Simmons. But yes, he did. He had a beautiful old leather Gladstone bag.'

He asked if she still had it.

'There's the thing – it was stolen one day. Someone smashed a window at the back of the house and broke in. Highly embarrassing for father with the police and the hospital.'

Claude gave Marjorie a knowing look. This wasn't

much use to her since she was thoroughly confused. He pressed on.

'This next question is definitely a bit strange, I apologise,' he said. 'Did any pets go missing in the area around the same time? Cats? Dogs?'

'Well, yes,' she said, very surprised. 'Our Retriever vanished into thin air one day. We hunted high and low for him and put up posters everywhere but never found him. I was heartbroken. How on earth did you know that?'

Constable Curtis had worked her way through most of the stuff in the loft. Several cardboard boxes remained at the back and she pulled one forward. She shone her torch inside. The light found a tiny pair of blue baby shoes.

She called down from the loft opening. Claude appeared in the hall and climbed the stairs. She managed to lower the box down to him and then clambered back down herself. She spent some time on the landing, trying to remove the dust from her uniform.

Downstairs, Claude placed the box on the table. He reached in and produced the baby shoes. He put them down in front of Sophie and she looked at them, ruefully. Marjorie reached in and found a piece of card that had a tiny hand print on it in red paint. She looked at Claude.

'It would help if we knew what we were looking for,' she said, still a bit lost and now a bit grumpy.

'Sorry,' said Claude. 'Perhaps a baby's hairbrush? Or a comb?'

He picked out a pretty lace shawl and placed it on the table.

'Nope,' he said.

Marjorie delved in one more time. She found what appeared to be a small jewellery box. She shook it and the contents rattled. She took the lid off and everybody peered inside.

'Perfect,' said Claude. 'Baby teeth.'

CHAPTER SEVEN

Claude closed the front door of the flat and locked it. They were on their way to the police station, to see the Chief Constable again. They set off along the corridor.

'The problem is, I just don't have a dank and murky mind like you, Claude,' Marjorie said.

This was an unusual conversation starter and Claude was struggling to take it as a compliment. They started to walk down the stairs.

'You know what I mean though,' she continued. 'I like to pride myself on a straightforward sense of natural justice. If someone crosses you, you kick them straight in the goolies.'

They went out through the front door and found the car. Claude couldn't get a word in edgeways.

'But with a serial killer, everything festers away until it's upside down, inside out and back to front.'

They got into the car and Claude started the engine. Marjorie hadn't finished.

'Take our current serial killer, if I might call him that. I mean, why is he only killing someone every fifteen years?'

Finally, a question. Claude mulled it over.

'As I keep saying, I'm no expert on the subject,' he said. 'But what was Sebastian Greening's age at the time of the boating lake incident?'

Marjorie consulted her notebook. She looked up. 'Bugger! Fifteen.'

'So here's my attempt at serial killer logic,' Claude went on. 'If Sebastian Greening's life was effectively over at fifteen, why shouldn't someone else lose their life every fifteen years to make up for it?'

'Bugger!'

Claude and Marjorie arrived at the Chief Constable's office. Initially, he was pleased to see them. The case was now making real progress, so much so that he'd been able to ring Lord and Lady Unsworth and tell them they were no longer suspects. However, his mood changed quite quickly when he heard the reason for their visit.

'You want to exhume Sebastian Greening's body?' he asked, in disbelief. 'For heaven's sake, is there anything even left of it?'

'We're hoping there is, Peter,' said Claude, standing his ground.

The Chief Constable stopped and thought about it for a second.

'So you're suggesting what? He faked his own death? At the ripe old age of twenty?'

'It's not likely I know, but we've ruled out everything else so it's what we're left with.'

Sergeant Deacon was standing by the door as usual, notebook in hand. The Chief Constable put him on the spot and asked him what he thought. He was forced to agree with Claude.

'Particularly given the new evidence about the anaesthetist's bag,' he added.

The Chief Constable frowned - he was in the dark again and he didn't like being in the dark. Claude tried to explain. He recounted Sebastian Greening's sister's story about her father's anaesthetist's bag being stolen from their home and how it certainly would have contained, amongst other things, Pancuronium.

'I mean, the burglary could have been carried out by the local drug addict but I'm not sure how many addicts are into muscle relaxants, are you?' he said. 'So my money's on an inside job, carried out by Dr Greening's clever son, Sebastian.'

The Chief Constable stared out of the window, tapping his pencil on the desk.

Two days later, Claude and Marjorie had left the flat and gone for a walk to the shops. They were waiting for news and Marjorie's patience was already being sorely tested. She was towing her shopping basket on wheels and zig-zagging it distractedly.

The exhumation had taken place the day before and had been a particularly grim affair, witnessed by Sergeant Deacon and Constable Curtis. The body had been in the ground for almost forty years and parts of the coffin itself had started to decompose. It was laborious and unpleasant work for the pathology team.

The remains were now in the charge of Professor Ross. Claude and Marjorie had come across him before when he had carried out the autopsy on their friend Audrey Patterson and they were pleased he'd been assigned to the case. He was an undoubted expert, if a little prone to eccentricity.

'So we're entirely relying on teeth for DNA?' asked Marjorie as they strolled along.

'Well, it ought to be possible in theory,' said Claude. 'Extracting DNA from the baby teeth should be comparatively straightforward. It's the body that's the real problem. There were teeth fragments when it was buried forty years ago. Who knows if they're still viable?'

They turned away from the hustle and bustle of the main road into an alleyway that eventually led back to the flat. It was suddenly narrow and quiet.

'The trouble with disinterring a body is it's so upsetting for the family,' said Claude as they sauntered on.

'There's only Sebastian's sister left,' said Marjorie. 'And she might be pleased to know her brother's still alive.'

'Only to find he's a serial killer?' queried Claude.

Marjorie pondered on this for a second.

'Well, you can't have everything, can you?'

Claude and Marjorie were eventually summoned to the police station to hear the autopsy report. They were seated in the teleconference room, next to Sergeant Deacon and Constable Curtis. Everyone was a little anxious. The screen suddenly flickered into life and Professor Ross appeared, wearing scrubs and a white apron. He was being filmed by his own laptop and a lab assistant was visible in the background, working at a large stainless steel sink.

'Good morning Professor!' said Claude.

'Good Morning Chief Superintendent! Good morning everyone!' said the Professor, cheerily. 'It's a bit like Eurovision isn't it? I am pleased to announce the results of . . . the tests on the body we exhumed four days ago!'

He peered out from the screen, grinning. Unfortunately, no-one else seemed to find it funny. Even Marjorie regarded it as being in slightly poor taste. The Professor gave up and consulted his notes instead.

He began by reminding everyone that the original burial had taken place in 1979 and that the body itself had been very badly burned. It was, he said, now in an extremely advanced state of decomposition. Notwithstanding that, he picked up a small plastic specimen bag and waved it in front of the camera, almost triumphantly. The audience at the police station were straining to see what the bag actually contained.

'However, these three fragments of teeth remain,' he said. 'I'm glad to say that, after a somewhat lengthy and complicated procedure, we have been able to extract DNA from them.'

Claude sat forward in his chair. The Professor

consulted his notes and brandished a second specimen bag.

'We have compared this to the DNA we extracted from the baby teeth we believe belonged to Sebastian Greening.'

He took a moment to point out they had also swabbed Sophie Tyler, Sebastian's sister, to rule out the fact that the baby teeth could have belonged to her.

The audience were willing him to get on with it, craning forwards to hear the verdict.

'All of which means, I can tell you the body is categorically . . .'

The professor paused to turn over the page again.

' . . . not that of Sebastian Greening.'

The relief was palpable in the teleconference room. Marjorie clapped Claude on the back, slightly too hard again.

'Thank you, Professor,' said Sergeant Deacon, trying to stay focused. 'Since this is now another murder, is there any other match for the victim on the database?'

'I'm afraid not, Sergeant. The DNA database didn't even start until four years after the victim's death, so . . . '

The Professor shrugged his shoulders in resignation.

Claude and Marjorie made their way home. What they had just learned was probably not cause for celebration but they felt they had earned a drink nonetheless. Claude poured himself a single malt whisky and Marjorie had her usual gin and tonic. They settled down to discuss the events of the day. Marjorie got the ball rolling.

'Claude, I've been enjoying your master classes on serial killers but I'm confused again. I feel I need a new one on how to fake your own death, if you don't mind.'

'You mean you want me to guess how Sebastian Greening did it?' he asked.

'Yes please,' she said, settling back on the sofa as if it was time for an episode of "Listen with Mother".

Claude collected his thoughts for a second. Yes, he probably could have a stab at describing how most of it was done. In his time, he'd seen any number of murders made to look like fatal car crashes. Plus there were several big clues in what they'd already learned about Sebastian Greening.

He began by reminding Marjorie of the theft of the anaesthetist's bag from the Greening house. Assuming that Sebastian was the guilty party, that meant he'd had immediate possession of syringes and muscle relaxant drugs. After that, a process of experimentation would almost certainly have begun – first on any wildlife he could capture and ultimately on the Greening family's unfortunate Retriever. Marjorie looked wide-eyed as the penny dropped about the dog's disappearance.

Next, Sebastian would probably have begun touring local parks and open spaces at night. Eventually, he would have found what he was looking for – a rough sleeper stretched out on a bench, more or less his own age and build. Given that the autopsy had found alcohol in the victim's bloodstream, he'd obviously struck lucky with someone who was already partially immobilised.

He would have injected him there and then with a muscle relaxant like Pancuronium, something that was never likely to show up on a standard tox screen. After that, there was a great deal of man-handling of the inert body to deal with. Firstly, dragging him to the car and heaving him inside. Then, having driven him to the intended crash site, heaving him back out again and completely re-dressing him in a set of his own clothes. The final touch would have been strapping his personally engraved watch to the victim's wrist.

Then came a few modifications to the car. Claude asked Marjorie if she remembered Sophie Tyler's remark about Sebastian possibly reading engineering at university. The modifications in question were hardly advanced but they would have required a bit of mechanical ingenuity, nonetheless. The most important task would have been to find a way to temporarily hold down the clutch pedal. He'd seen it done once before with a cut down scaffold pole, one end jammed on the depressed clutch pedal and the other jammed against the car's roof interior. The device would have needed to have had a rope attached to it and trailed back out through the open driver's window. He would also have needed a mechanical gizmo to lock the steering wheel and make sure it drove straight at the wall. He would have painstakingly researched all of this.

Once he'd heaved the victim into the driver's seat he would then have been able to turn on the ignition and jam down the accelerator, most likely with a house brick. He would have put the car into gear – probably second gear, to reduce the risk of stalling and guarantee a good top speed – and finally closed the driver's door.

Claude looked across at Marjorie to see if she was following things. She was no longer sitting comfortably but was now perched instead on the edge of the sofa. She was clearly keen for him to carry on with the story.

Claude explained that, according to the police report, Sebastian had initially parked the car on what was a large piece of wasteland, aimed squarely at a brick wall some distance away. The wall apparently bordered the property of an old, disused sanatorium. So, with the engine screaming and the car in second gear, it would have only remained for him to yank the rope attached to the scaffold pole-type device, thereby releasing the clutch and setting the car in motion. The car would have trundled along over the wasteland, gathering speed, with the victim lolling around inside. It would have struck the wall head on at probably something in excess of fifty miles an hour.

Sebastian would have known that the impact would probably not have proved fatal and that he would need to further conceal the victim's true identity anyway. He would almost certainly have had several jerry cans of petrol with him.

Having removed the improvised devices and the house brick from the car, he would then have doused the car thoroughly in the petrol and set light to it. Bearing in mind this was officially his graduation as a clinical psychopath, he would almost certainly have stood and watched it blaze.

Claude broke off to enjoy a sip of single malt. Marjorie, who'd finished her gin and tonic, was completely taken aback. She didn't know whether to be more amazed by the labyrinthine nature of Sebastian Greening's plot or by the brilliance of Claude's forensic reconstruction of it.

'The whole thing's like a weirdly perverted case of identity theft, isn't it?' asked Marjorie, still trying to get her brain round the murder, and serial killings in general.

'I suppose you could say that,' Claude mused. 'The poor old rough sleeper is going to end up re-buried in an unmarked grave. Meantime, Sebastian Greening is now an entirely new person.'

CHAPTER EIGHT

Much of the case was now solved, apart from the tricky business of actually finding Sebastian Greening himself. The police had hired a photo-fit artist to create a picture of how he might now look but, after forty years, it was very much a shot in the dark. Everybody knew the plain truth – Greening could not only be anywhere, he could also be anyone.

Claude and Marjorie had embarked on a slow stroll to the shops. They needed to stock up on a few things, particularly gin. Claude walked along lost in thought, twirling his walking stick occasionally. Marjorie, however, seemed to have something on her mind.

'Now I don't want you to be cross, Claude,' she said.

Claude looked immediately nervous.

'The thing is, I feel I haven't been pulling my weight in the detective agency,' she went on. 'What with all this bizarre serial killing business and people faking their own deaths, I've been feeling a bit out of my depth.'

'Really? And?' he asked, now distinctly suspicious.

'And I might have been a bit, well . . . impetuous.'

She explained that she'd gone into town a couple of days beforehand and had happened to walk past the offices of the local newspaper, The Examiner. An idea had occurred to her and she'd gone in to discuss the possibility of putting a missing persons ad in the paper. Just on the off chance that it might jog someone's memory about Sebastian Greening, she said.

Claude looked positively relieved. A missing person's ad? What harm could that possibly do?

'I spoke to a very nice young man for about half an hour,' Marjorie went on. 'He seemed very interested and very keen to help. He even made me a cup of tea.'

They walked on for a while, chatting. They rounded a corner and approached the local newsagent's shop. Marjorie stopped.

'Buggeration!' she said, loudly.

Ahead of them was one of those newsstands which held newspapers and have a poster on the front advertising the day's headline. The poster read:

"PRIVATE EYE PENSIONER SEEKS MISSING
MURDERER"

Claude picked up a copy of the paper and studied it. The article dominated the front page and included both a picture of the young Sebastian and the new police photo-fit reconstruction. Somehow or other, it also included an up-to-date picture of Marjorie.

'Good work, Marjorie,' said Claude, trying hard to put a positive spin on things. 'I think that counts as another beehive barged over.'

At more or less the same time, Sergeant Deacon walked urgently into Chief Constable Selby's office.

'I think you should see this, sir,' he said, placing a copy of The Examiner on the desk.

The Chief Constable jumped up out of his chair, carrying the newspaper with him.

'Private eye pensioner seeks missing murderer? Special Agent Marjorie Watson?' he spluttered, reading aloud from the front page. 'What's going on, Sergeant?'

Sergeant Deacon had read the whole article and it was even worse than it appeared. Irresponsibly, the journalist had also managed to reveal the location of Claude's flat.

'Good grief!' exclaimed the Chief Constable. 'You need to round Claude and Marjorie up right away – this is potentially disastrous. And when you do, you need to assign them a permanent protection officer. Well get on with it!'

He slumped back in his chair.

Meanwhile, Claude and Marjorie had set off back to the flat. They had turned off the main road and were walking down the quiet alleyway.

Claude was trying to reassure Marjorie. He was trying to convince her that the worst thing she'd have to endure would be the wrath of Peter Selby.

'Oh, I always know I'm doing something right when the Chief Constable gets grumpy,' she said, with just a trace of hubris.

The alleyway started to narrow slightly as they almost reached the end. Suddenly, a man appeared in front of them, blocking their exit. He was in his late fifties or early sixties and wore the uniform of a security guard. He bore a passing resemblance to the photo-fit reconstruction even though he now shaved his head. Claude and Marjorie were in no doubt they were looking at Sebastian Greening.

He held a huge Alsatian dog on a short leash. The dog barked furiously and leapt and lunged at Claude and Marjorie. They were trapped. There was no-one around to help and they couldn't have outrun the Alsatian even if they were in their twenties, let alone their eighties.

Greening used the dog expertly to herd them out of the alleyway towards a large white van. On the side, it bore the name:

"SECURE TWENTY FOUR"

He opened the back doors and pulled down a single, retractable step. He held out his hand for their mobile phones and gestured for them to climb inside the van. With further loud encouragement from the Alsatian they had no choice but to comply and sat themselves down awkwardly on a narrow bench that ran along the right hand side of the van. They were separated from the driver's compartment by a metal grille. They watched as Greening allowed the dog to jump in first and then climbed in himself. He put the mobile phones in the glove compartment and started the engine. He drove off, with the dog glaring back at Claude and Marjorie.

Claude's mind was racing. He was anxious about Marjorie and silently mouthed 'are you okay?' to her. As ever, he needn't have bothered.

'Oh, I'm better than okay, Claude,' she said, loudly. 'In fact, I'm finally about to make a proper contribution to the case.'

Marjorie leaned forward to speak through the grille.

'It's good to meet you at last, Sebastian,' she said.

There was no reply from Greening but she could see his eyes watching her in the rear view mirror. The dog started barking again.

'I do hope it's okay to call you Sebastian,' she continued. 'Claude and I have been following your exploits for some time and we feel like we already know you quite well.'

He continued to watch her in the mirror. The dog continued to bark. Marjorie leaned further forward and banged the grille with the flat of her hand.

'Shut up! I wasn't talking to you!' she shouted at the dog.

The dog fell silent.

Claude looked at Marjorie, shocked and fascinated at one and the same time. Taunting a serial killer and attacking his Alsatian dog were not strategies he'd come across before. But what did he know?

They drove on for some time and eventually turned onto an unmade road. They bumped along through the potholes for a while and arrived at what appeared to be a large, disused factory. It was surrounded by a chain-link fence and the van pulled up in front of a large pair of gates. Claude and Marjorie were straining to see from the back. A sign on the gates read:

"Protected by SECURE TWENTY FOUR"

Greening got out and unlocked the chains that were intertwined between the gates. He threw the gates open and drove the van into the front yard of the factory. Everywhere was scruffy and overgrown with weeds. Pieces of old, disused machinery were littered around in the yard. To one side, several large metal hoppers lay sideways on the ground, rusting.

Claude and Marjorie were coerced out of the van by the dog and forced into the factory itself. They walked past yet more rusting machinery and through an avenue of huge metal chains that hung down from the ceiling. Greening led them down some stairs to the basement and they eventually arrived at a room with one outside window high up in the wall. The original function of the room was unclear. All of the old machinery had been removed and all that remained were several metal rings embedded in the concrete floor, rather like quayside mooring rings. Incongruously, an old sofa had been moved into the room and now stood against the wall opposite the window. There was also some rubbish left lying about – old newspapers and polystyrene cups. Perhaps it was somewhere Greening slept on occasion.

Five minutes later, following guidance from the

Alsatian, Claude and Marjorie found themselves seated on the sofa. Greening was in the process of binding their wrists in front of them with plastic zip-tie handcuffs. The dog had sat himself down in the doorway and glared back at Claude and Marjorie, encouraging compliance. Despite all this, Marjorie was feeling as unconstrained as ever.

'Well, it's been lovely to have this little chat, Sebastian,' she said, now resorting to full-blown sarcasm. 'Particularly good to have the chance to catch up on your news after all these years.'

Greening glanced at her for a moment, quizzically. He produced a further long length of plastic strip and zip-tied it to Marjorie's handcuffs. He threaded it through one of the metal rings embedded in the floor near the sofa and zip-tied the other end to Claude's handcuffs. They were now handcuffed, tied together and loosely anchored to the floor. Completely trussed up, in other words.

Another twenty minutes and Greening was gone, still without uttering a single word. The dog had followed him faithfully back up the stairs. He had left Claude and Marjorie with a metal beaker of water each. He had put Marjorie's handbag and Claude's walking stick out of reach on the windowsill opposite the sofa. Finally, he had spent some time fixing a CCTV camera to the wall and its red light now blinked slowly at Claude and Marjorie. Sebastian Greening might not have been very chatty, but he was certainly very efficient.

Back at Claude's flat, a police car was parked half

up on the kerb. Sergeant Deacon was pacing around anxiously on the pavement, speaking to Chief Constable Selby on his mobile phone.

'They appear to have disappeared into thin air, sir,' he said. 'Yes, I know, sir . . . well no, a neighbour saw them leave an hour ago and there's been no sign of them since . . . both phones switched off I'm afraid . . . we will, sir, of course, sir.'

A second police car arrived and the driver got out. He looked at the Sergeant and shook his head.

Meanwhile, Claude and Marjorie were trying to get used to their surroundings. The factory was now completely silent but for a slow and relentless drip of water from somewhere nearby. Marjorie reached for her beaker which was on the floor in front of her. She hadn't accounted for the fact that she was now zip-tied to Claude via the metal ring in the floor and as she leaned forward she dragged him sideways with her.

'Sorry, Claude,' she said.

He seemed mildly amused and encouraged her to try again. This time when she leaned forward, he swayed in towards her and it worked perfectly. They returned to pondering their fate. Marjorie eventually broke the silence.

'What I don't understand is, why hasn't he already bumped us off?' she said, bluntly.

Claude had been asking himself the same question. 'I know what you mean,' he said. 'But we don't fit the profile of his normal victims, do we? Now that he's got us, I think he's genuinely confused about what to do with us. He's particularly baffled by you, Marjorie.'

She asked him what he meant.

'I mean he's used to terrifying people almost to death with ritual amputation while they're still conscious. He clearly enjoys it. I don't think he can cope with the fact that you're an eighty year old woman and you're not even vaguely frightened of him.'

'Ah yes, the pensioner's superpower,' she said, proudly. 'It never disappoints.'

Claude was forced to bring Marjorie back down to earth. He was convinced that Greening would be back fairly soon, most likely with some dreadful new ritual, designed especially for the both of them. In Claude's opinion, he was almost certainly keeping them alive with water while he worked out the details of their demise.

In other words, they needed to quickly work out a plan. The trouble was, there wasn't a great deal to work with – polystyrene cups, old newspapers and not much else. Eventually, Claude's gaze settled on his walking stick, standing on the windowsill, leaning against the window frame. An idea slowly formed in his head. It was, quite literally, a long shot but he explained it to Marjorie nonetheless. Actually, it was probably their only shot.

'And remember, he'll be checking the video feed regularly so we'll have to work quickly,' said Claude.

'Ready when you are,' Marjorie replied, trying to sound confident.

Claude reached forward to pick up one of the

beakers and, with perfect synchronisation, Marjorie leaned in towards him. He sat back up and took aim with it several times, trying to get used to the fact that, thanks to the handcuffs, he was going to have to throw two-handed. He launched the beaker towards the walking stick but badly misjudged the distance. It fell short and hit the wall below the window, clattering noisily onto the floor.

'Hopeless!' he said.

With Marjorie still leaning in, he grabbed the second beaker. He took aim again and launched it more aggressively. It was a better distance but sailed off to the right and only succeeded in smashing one of the panes of glass in the window. The beaker disappeared outside with most of the broken glass.

'Better!' said Marjorie.

'Not much,' said Claude. 'Shoe please, Marjorie.'

With further teamwork, Claude leaned in towards Marjorie, allowing her to reach down and take off her shoe. She handed it to Claude. He weighed it up, took aim and launched it. This time, it struck the walking stick head on. Tantalisingly, the walking stick danced for a moment on the windowsill before falling forwards onto the floor.

'Bullseye!' said Marjorie

'Right, let's work quickly,' said Claude. 'Belts off!'

They struggled to take off their belts given their encumbrances but eventually succeeded. Marjorie buckled them together to make one long belt and handed it to Claude. She leaned in again and Claude reached forward as far as he could. He threw one end of the belt towards the walking stick whilst holding on to the other, as if he was casting a fishing line. It landed short by two inches. He tried again, with the same result.

'Bugger!' said Marjorie, still leaning in. 'Shoe please, Claude!'

He reached forward, untied one of his brogues and took it off. He handed it to Marjorie and she threaded the laces through the belt's last punched hole, tying it with a rather fancy looking knot.

'Girl Guides, 1949,' she said, handing the contraption back to him, now four or five inches longer.

Claude reached forward and cast again. Tantalisingly, the shoe landed just on the other side of the walking stick's handle. He tried to drag it back in slowly but it failed to get any purchase and the shoe simply bumped over the handle. He took aim a second time.

Sebastian Greening, meanwhile, was gazing thoughtfully into the middle distance. He had parked in a lay-by, next to a van which served hot drinks and fast food. He had balanced a cup of coffee on his dashboard and was enjoying a hot dog.

He decided to check on the camera he'd set up. He continued to eat with one hand and pulled out his mobile phone with the other. He scrolled through and found the link to the CCTV video. He pressed it and was dumbfounded by the image that appeared on the screen. One of his prisoners appeared to be throwing a shoe, attached to something that looked like a leather belt, across the room. The other one sat permanently at an odd angle as if she was a motor-bike and sidecar passenger, leaning in on a fast corner. He tipped the remains of his coffee out of the window and threw what was left of the hot dog to the Alsatian. He started the engine and set off for the factory.

Claude tried again with the contraption. He threw it and the shoe landed just on the other side of the walking stick. He reeled it back in slowly and this time the heel of the shoe caught against the walking stick's handle. He dragged it backwards inch by inch and eventually managed to grab it, cheered on by Marjorie. Claude gripped the body of the walking stick in one hand, held the handle in the other and pulled them apart. A blade appeared. It was a sword stick.

'Be honest, that's the most thoughtful present you've ever been given,' said Marjorie.

Claude could only agree and set about applying the sword stick's sharp edge to Marjorie's plastic handcuffs. He ran it backwards and forwards repeatedly and eventually they broke. Marjorie was free. They reversed their roles and Marjorie brandished the sword stick. There was a lot of huffing and puffing and considerable amounts of swearing but, miraculously, she managed to cut Claude free. And without actually stabbing him in the process.

'Right, shoes on. Let's go,' said Claude, urgently.

They picked up their shoes, untangled their belts and quickly re-dressed. Claude set off through the door and headed for the stairs. Marjorie paused for a moment to offer a defiant V-sign to the CCTV camera. She hurried after Claude.

They rushed across the main hall of the factory, back past the rusting machinery and the hanging chains and found themselves outside in the yard. Claude stopped for a moment and surveyed the scene. There was no sign of Greening yet but the front gates had been chained and padlocked again. With a high fence surrounding the rest of the factory there were very few options. Claude spotted the abandoned metal silos lying among the weeds and they hurried over and took refuge behind them.

Everything seemed to be happening at a furious pace and Marjorie seemed to be struggling to regain her breath. Eventually, she managed to ask Claude what the plan was. He paused for a moment. The short answer was, he didn't have a plan.

Five minutes later, though, his hand was forced. Greening's van arrived. He threw the gates open and drove the van in, screeching to a halt in the yard. He rushed in to the factory, followed quickly by the Alsatian, barking furiously.

Marjorie looked at Claude. He had drawn the sword from its wooden sheath again.

'Are we attempting a cavalry charge?' she asked.

He ignored the question. 'Follow me!' he hissed.

He set off for the van as fast as he could and clambered into the driver's seat. Marjorie still seemed to be struggling and by the time she had climbed into the passenger seat and closed the door, Claude had already used his sword stick to jemmy open the fascia below the steering wheel. He pulled out a handful of coloured wires and studied them briefly. He used the sword stick to cut one of them, followed by another.

'Boy Scouts, 1948,' he said.

He forced two different coloured wires together and produced a strong spark but, unfortunately, no ignition. At that moment, the Alsatian came charging back out from inside the factory, followed behind by Sebastian Greening. The dog raced towards the van and hurled itself against Marjorie's door, leaving a trail of drool across the window.

Claude forced the two wires together again and held them for longer, with the dog still barking and snarling at the window. Suddenly, the engine burst into life. He put the van into gear and accelerated away as fast as he could, leaving Sebastian Greening vainly flailing his arms. The dog pursued the van gamely for a moment longer, still barking, but sat down at the gate as Claude turned off onto the unmade road. They had escaped.

Claude drove on with his foot flat to the floor, not taking any chances. He tried to negotiate the potholes as he went, careering this way and that across the road. At the same time, he kept one eye on the rear view mirror, just in case. He tried to collect his thoughts. The next course of action was obvious and Marjorie would ordinarily have been underway with it. But she seemed to be sitting quietly and he had to prompt her.

'Marjorie, try the glove compartment for the

phones, please,' he said, still concentrating on the road ahead. 'Call Sergeant Deacon and let him know we need a full search team. Including dogs.'

They drove on for a while longer. Claude became aware that the uncharacteristic silence was continuing. He took his eyes off the potholes for a moment and looked across at Marjorie. She was slumped to one side, eyes closed.

'Marjorie! Marjorie!' he called out, panicking.

He stopped the van and leant across to her.

She was unconscious.

CHAPTER NINE

Marjorie lay in the hospital bed, still unconscious. She was hooked up to an impressive array of medical equipment that beeped and flashed and displayed a whole series of intricate wave patterns. Claude had been at her bedside for two days and was now waiting anxiously as the consultant examined her.

'The good news is there doesn't seem to have been any permanent damage,' he said, addressing Claude while still studying Marjorie's notes. 'Her heart rhythm is strong and there's no evidence of stroke. It's as if her system has just decided to shut down for a while, as some sort of defence mechanism. Rather like a trip switch has been triggered.'

Claude felt at least a small sense of relief.

'Has she suffered serious shock or stress lately?' asked the consultant.

'Well yes, both of those I'm afraid,' Claude replied, sheepishly.

Of course, he could have given a slightly fuller answer: that he and Marjorie had formed a detective agency while they were in their eighties, that they'd been hired to find a murderer who turned out to be a serial killer, that the serial killer had taken them captive and that they'd escaped using only an antique sword stick. But, on balance, he didn't want to risk himself being admitted to the hospital for a psychiatric evaluation.

After the doctor had left, Claude sat back down in the chair next to Marjorie's bed. He reflected on the case and the fact that, on this occasion, the pensioner's superpower seemed to have backfired badly. Having said that, he knew that Marjorie would completely disagree with him. He looked forward to her waking up, ridiculing him for his concerns and carrying on as if nothing had happened.

Chief Constable Selby and Sergeant Deacon came striding into the room. They looked anxiously at the unconscious Marjorie and the bank of medical equipment.

'How is she, Claude?' asked the Chief Constable.

Claude stood up. He outlined the details of the doctor's diagnosis and the good news about her underlying health.

'So we're just waiting for her to come round in her own good time,' he added.

The three of them congregated at the foot of the bed.

'That's very good news,' said the Chief Constable. 'Meanwhile, you might like to know we've caught Sebastian Greening. Sergeant Deacon's supervised his first manhunt.'

The Sergeant looked embarrassed to be put on the spot.

'Well, it turns out that he was better at pursuing people than he was at being pursued himself,' he said. 'Your idea was spot on Chief Superintendent – our dogs sniffed out Greening's Alsatian in no time at all. We found the pair of them in another disused building, five miles away from the factory.'

They all looked pleased although the Chief Constable still seemed to have some reservations. In truth, he couldn't help feeling remorseful about allowing Claude and Marjorie so far into harm's way. He instinctively turned away from the bed and started to lower his voice.

'I'm delighted with the arrest,' he said. 'But it's a high price to pay what with Marjorie and everything, isn't it?'

Claude and the Sergeant weighed this up.

'Oh bugger off Chief Constable,' said a loud voice.

They all turned around. Marjorie was awake.

'I'm absolutely fine and you've got four serial killings solved. What more do you bloody want?'

It was a beautiful early summer's day. Claude, Marjorie and Chief Constable Selby were strolling across the Beckwith Hall estate, following Lord and Lady Unsworth towards the gazebo. Marjorie seemed to have recovered from her spell in hospital although, for the time being at least, she too was using a walking stick.

Lord Unsworth was holding forth satirically

about the fact that he and his wife were suddenly Britain's most popular couple.

'How many dinner party invitations is it this week, Camilla?' he asked.

'Five at the last count,' she said.

'And will you be accepting any?' asked Claude.

'No, not a single one,' he said.

They had almost reached the gazebo. A large round table had been placed in its centre, covered with a crisp white linen tablecloth. It had been set for lunch with silver cutlery, bone china and a multitude of fine cut glass.

'And what about the army of trolls on social media?' asked Marjorie as they climbed the gazebo's steps.

'Oh, they seem to have got bored and wandered off,' said Camilla. 'The biggest controversy on our twitter page at the moment is whether the Rhododendron Garden should be open to the public at nine or nine thirty.'

They sat down to what was a beautiful but poignant setting – Pallant's gazebo with the Beckwith Hall lake shimmering in the background. There was a distinct sense that the Unsworths were putting something behind them.

Not that Marjorie had any intention of allowing herself to be over-awed by the splendour of Beckwith Hall again. The butler leaned in and offered to fill her champagne glass.

'The Dom Perignon 1996, madam?' he asked.

'Oh, not for me,' she said. 'Just a gin and tonic,

thank you.'

Lord Unsworth looked amused.

A second member of staff leaned in and proffered a silver platter of cold meats.

'It's not tongue is it?' asked Marjorie. 'I've gone right off tongue.'

Claude shook his head.

The main course was a whole poached salmon and was followed by a summer pudding, both equally delicious. Once the staff had cleared away, Lord Unsworth raised his glass.

'I'd like to propose a toast to you, Claude and Marjorie, for all you've done,' he said. 'Claude, thank you for being the one person to see the truth behind all this. And Marjorie, well, we were promised you'd barge over a few beehives . . .'

' . . . and in the end you kicked over a whole row of hornet's nests,' the Chief Constable finished off.

Everybody laughed at this. Marjorie felt a warm glow of pride. Lady Unsworth and the Chief Constable joined Lord Unsworth in raising their glasses.

'Claude and Marjorie!' they chorused.

Claude had driven Marjorie back to the Fern Lea residential home. They took a stroll around the beautiful gardens, each with their walking sticks. In truth, they were both feeling wistful about the Unsworth case finally coming to an end. Claude, trying to move things on, asked Marjorie if she had any new slogans for the detective agency.

'I think you may have been right all along,' she said. 'Perhaps some of the slogans were a bit trite. I've decided we need something a bit more substantial.'

'Like?'

'Like an insignia or a coat of arms. I thought we might have something like a pair of crossed walking sticks . . .' She crossed her two index fingers to illustrate the point. '. . . you know, like crossed spears or lances. And then a Latin motto underneath, to give us real authority.'

'Go on,' said Claude.

'I thought to myself, why don't we just go for: Hic abundant leones et leaenas.'

Claude furrowed his brow. He was slightly struggling with his Latin vocabulary.

'So,' he said. 'Here lions . . . and lionesses abound?'

'Exactly!'

Claude thought about this for a moment. As ever with Marjorie's ideas there was only one course of action and that was to embrace them enthusiastically.

'Why not Marjorie, I like it. Here's to the lions!'

He withdrew the blade from his walking stick and brandished it in the air.

Needless to say, Marjorie's walking stick was also a sword stick. She withdrew the blade and brandished it in the air.

'And here's to the lionesses!'

BOOKS IN THIS SERIES

The Dilapidated Detectives

The Dilapidated Detectives

The Dilapidated Detectives Down Under

Printed in Great Britain
by Amazon